"Emma Seckel's debut crackles with dark energy, conjuring a world where the skies are full of crows, ghosts walk the moors, and the islanders are haunted by loss. Seckel knows how to write heartache but these pages are also bursting with a fierce love for the living and the dead. *The Wild Hunt* is a wonder of a novel."

—BRENDAN MATHEWS, author of *The World of Tomorrow*

"*The Wild Hunt* is a thriller, and a family drama; a mystery, but also a romance; a war novel and a ghost story. It's a social commentary. It's a tear-jerker. I'm not sure how one novel can be all of these things, and also be gut-punchingly sad, beautifully written, and oddly hopeful, but it is. Evocative, haunting, and deeply compelling, *The Wild Hunt* weaves together the known and unknown worlds in pursuit of the answer to the most elusive of life's questions: how can life go on after devastating loss?"

—AMY BRILL, author of *The Movement of Stars*

"*The Wild Hunt* is a gorgeously written, entirely captivating debut novel set on an island off the coast of Scotland in the wake of World War II. Rich in atmosphere and historical detail, this novel and its exquisitely drawn characters will transport even the most reticent reader to a different time and place, and captivate them until its satisfying conclusion. A deeply engrossing read."

—CRISTINA ALGER, *New York Times* bestselling author of *Girls Like Us*

THE WILD HUNT

EMMA SECKEL

TIN HOUSE / Portland, Oregon

To my family

1.

On the first of October they arrived. They gathered in places they could see the whole island, the rolling hills and the farmland. Sitting in trees and on curbs, on barns and along low pasture walls. Across from the church and atop the green moss-glow of the epitaph in the shadows of the high street. In October the crows always came in threes.

Dawn was about to break, and on the beach Leigh Welles watched her father burn. It was a small funeral party. A girl, a man, the minister, a border collie sitting dutifully next to them. A few others scattered across the beach. If Leigh had asked, probably more people would have shown up, but when the minister appeared at her door the day after she'd arrived, she made it clear that she didn't want a lot of fuss.

The boat burned only with the help of a great deal of petrol, struggling against the incoming tide. A man waded into the water to attempt to push it back out to sea without displacing the shrouded figure nestled within. Leigh called to him to be careful, but the wind reclaimed her words into air.

This wind was indiscriminate in what it took and only fragments of the minister's committal reached Leigh's ears ("—the body of our brother, Graham—"), which had gone numb with the cold. The collie, Maisie, nudged her wet nose into Leigh's palm and the sky slowly lightened, through indigo to violet to purple to pale mauve. Leigh watched her father's body burn ("—dust to dust—") and wondered if he cared how many of the islanders showed up. Likely not. If Leigh did not like a lot of fuss, she had learnt how from him. Besides, it didn't matter how many people were there. Her brother, Sam, was not. The boat crested a wave and seemed finally to be on its way out, and the flames grew stronger, taller, brighter ("—in the sure and certain hope of resurrection—"), until they hurt Leigh's eyes to look at. Above her and behind, the stone circle towered on the bluff. Perched on one of the stones, three crows, inky punctuation.

The man (Tom) waded back in to shore. Drenched from the top of his head to the hems of his trousers. He trudged up the beach, shoes squelching, and rejoined the little funeral party, patted Maisie once on the head, scrubbed the water from his hair, and turned to face the sea.

That morning Leigh had woken to the unreality of it all and had tiptoed through the house like a thief. There were the two bedrooms upstairs with neatly made beds and hers with a tangle of sheets like a burrow. There were the pans in the sink, the herbs hanging above the counter, the tiny diamantine droplets of condensation on the windows. Leigh let Maisie out to run circles in the yard, flinging up clumps of dirt as she went. The autumn air was stiff, and everything shrouded in the mist rolling down from the moors, dripping and crystalline.

She looked up at the Ben. Once she had thought it a mountain, until she went to the mainland and discovered it was barely more than a hill. This place, she thought. There was the dog in the yard and the goats in the barn but really it was just her, just her and this island, nobody else. Her mother had been the first to leave, disappearing one night when Leigh was ten, gone to the mainland for a better life. Her brother had been the next to go, and then in time Leigh had followed. For Sam there was a fancy school and a fancy degree—a terrible interlude for the war, of which he never spoke—and now a clean bright office in Edinburgh, clients coming in and out all day. For Leigh there had been a job as a secretary, a flat with two girls from work who were nice enough but interested mostly in each other. Two years of never knowing what to say or what to do, what to wear or where to go. Then, this: getting sacked and falling behind on her rent, her flatmates kicking her out, a series of increasingly decrepit flats. A fight with Sam and then another, an end to the lunches they had once gotten every other week. A dream about her mother and a bitterness lingering in her chest for days. (This is what you left us for? This dark and dirty city. These shops and this noise instead of us.)

Sam had never set foot in her flat, but he had sent a cheque or two to keep her afloat. Neither of them wanted to worry their father. The last time Leigh turned up at Sam's office to ask him to get lunch, he'd been furious. ("Interrupting my work, Leigh. And dressed like that?") And then a telephone call from Tom McAllister: "Come home. Your father's been in an accident. We can't get hold of Sam."

And her last banknote spent on the ferry ride home, and everyone's eyes on her threadbare coat, and the whispers that swirled around her like a breeze when she walked through town. Yesterday Leigh had been trying to patch one of the dozen holes in the barn roof, and as she stood on the shingles she looked up at the hills and down at the grass and wondered whether it might be all right to fall.

The boat disappeared into the grey morning. There'd been a dream, Leigh realised as she watched it go, and that was what had woken her with cheeks cold and damp from tears she didn't remember crying. A dream she'd had before. The sea. A blurry, smudgy figure wading into the waves. Three crows perched on the rocky shore. Nothing but a series of discrete and half-formed images.

The minister dropped her off at home in the sleek green car that Leigh had always thought he looked too tall for. After the funeral Kate McClare had taken Leigh by the elbow and asked her to come for breakfast but Leigh shook her head, she wanted to be alone. When they arrived, the minister patted her hand kindly and said, "Come to church, Leigh, it'll be good for you," and then Leigh clambered into the cold air again, and Maisie leapt from the back, and the minister pulled away down the driveway, gravel crunching beneath the wheels.

Leigh watched the light dance on the glossy car as it departed. Her father had always eyed it jealously, curious hands itching to bury themselves in the engine, wrap themselves around the steering wheel. In the corner of the yard Graham's car sat rusting under canvas. Leigh couldn't bring herself to drive it. Graham had taught her how when she was fourteen ("I'll take you out where the only thing you could hurt are sheep. Just you and me. It'll be fun. Your brother was always a terrible driver. Don't tell him I said that"), by which time she had already been able to take apart the engine and reassemble it with her eyes closed. It wasn't the same car she had learnt on, not anymore. The year after she'd moved away, Graham had sold that first car and bought a new one, a terrible extravagance that he never managed to explain.

She went inside to make tea. The floorboards had always creaked, but now they sang discordantly. The corners had always been dark and shadowy, but now it seemed that something might be lurking in them. A thick dust coated the counter, broken by the jetsam of desiccated herbs that had fallen from the bunches hanging from the ceiling. This room did not look like a room that anyone lived in. This room looked abandoned, and dirty, and sad. And all of it hers now. Presumably. Leigh put out her hand to the wall to steady herself. Maisie circled around Leigh's feet, whining plaintively, big eyes looking up at her with reproach as though to say, Pull yourself together. Leigh placed a hand on the dog's head.

"You're right," she said to Maisie. "Let's go."

Moving was better. The pumping of her legs and the pedals, the whipping of the wind against her cheeks, the panting of Maisie's breath as she bounded beside the bicycle. Sea mist hung in the air, dusting Leigh's face and collecting in her eyelashes. Soon the grass and grazing sheep gave way to smoother pavement and a low stone wall, the church spire reaching towards the sky in the distance.

A row of three crows on the uneven stone wall along the road, jet black. Leigh squeezed the brakes hard, stuttering to a stop. Maisie stopped, too, and her tail dropped between her legs. Leigh got off her bicycle and walked past the crows, walked until they were safely behind her before swinging back onto her bicycle and riding off again.

She had forgotten what it felt like, seeing them for the first time. It had been years since she had been on-island in October and she'd forgotten what it felt like. Her heart fluttering. The press of every damp, chill particle of air against her skin. The wheels of her bicycle spun her towards town. It was the first of October, and the *sluagh* had arrived. The sluagh always came in threes.

Years ago at around this time a tourist came through town. She was tall and willowy and glamorous and entirely out of place, and the whole time she was here the only thing anyone talked about was why. She wasn't a naturalist, a bird-watcher come to gawk at the many species that still survived only on this island's craggy shores. She wasn't anyone's relative, not even a distant one. She wore a white coat with fur around the collar and her hair was the colour of hot chocolate. Leigh wondered at the time whether maybe she'd been a movie star, though Sam had scoffed at the idea. She'd stumbled across Leigh helping some of the McAllister boys hang bunting outside the pub. Across the street the MacEwans were setting up their stall. The festival was just days away.

"What's all this?" the woman asked in a slick and bright accent. ("American," Sam said knowingly when Leigh mentioned the woman's funny voice later.)

"We're decorating for the festival," Leigh said, teetering on her stool. Her shoelaces dangled dangerously towards the ground. She hadn't learnt to tie them yet and her mother had been busy as she'd raced out the door, so Sam had done them. Possibly he'd done them wrong on purpose.

"Hallowe'en?" the woman asked, and Leigh tilted her head, confused. She glanced back at the McAllister boys, but they looked just as confused as she felt.

"What's Hallowe'en?"

"It's Bonfire Night," the woman's companion said. His accent was more familiar but still wrong, clipped. ("English, you know English people," Sam snapped when Leigh mentioned the man's funny voice later.) The boys behind Leigh snickered.

"Nah," said the eldest McAllister, Liam. "It's not that either."

"What's your festival for?"

"To keep away the sluagh," Leigh said. The middle McAllister boy, Neill, swore and elbowed her in the ribs. "Don't say it."

Leigh rolled her eyes. "People say it all the time," she said. "That part's fake." She looked up at the woman and said, helpfully, "But you really shouldn't run. The sluagh like a chase. And don't go out alone after dark."

"The—sloo-ah?" the woman echoed back, and Leigh nodded approvingly.

"They come every October," she said. "They look like crows but they carry the dead's souls. My dad says they used to kill animals in the night, but they haven't in ages. If you leave your west windows open, they'll come and take you away to be one of them."

"They can show you things, too," Liam said. "Trick you into thinking that you're seeing ghosts or something, to try to lure you to your death."

The woman looked aghast, her eyes darting back and forth between Leigh and the McAllister boys, as if waiting for one of them to leap up and declare it all a great joke. "It's true," Neill said. "Our great-great-great-grandfather got taken. It hasn't happened in ages, but you can't be too careful."

They'd finished with their bunting. "Come on," Liam said, and Leigh hopped off her stool and tripped after the boys.

The only thing different about today, Leigh thought as she swung onto the high street, was that the tall and glamorous tourist was nowhere to be found. Mrs. McCafferty shooed her cats inside to safety. The youngest McAllister, Fraser, teetered on a stool with a soapy bucket in one hand and a sponge in the other, scrubbing the windows till they shone. He waved at Leigh as she passed. Maisie ran over to him for a pet before bounding to catch up with Leigh again.

It was alarming, actually, how little the village had changed since the last time she had seen it. The houses were crying out for new paint, their once brightly coloured doors drab and peeling. The street signs had not been returned to the corners, and though the hour had just changed, the church bells were silent. It was like stepping back in time. It was like the war had never ended at all. She glided round the corner as a woman flung open the shutters of an upstairs window and three crows took flight off the roof. The woman's voice carried down to the street as she scolded an unseen companion: "It's time to get up."

2.

It's time to get up.

Light streamed into the room. Iain pressed his face deeper into the pillow, the blankets pulled up over his head like the great stone slabs interring poets and princes at Westminster Abbey. Not that he was a poet or a prince. He had been a pilot once, but now he was just a man.

"It's time to get up," Mrs. Cavanagh said again, and she whipped away the sheets. "They've arrived, and I need you to do the windows." Her footsteps retreated towards the door, and he wondered if she was taking the blankets with her. Despite the light streaming in like summer, the room was October-chilled. "Five years," she said, her voice a sighing fall from somewhere near the door. "Five years, and it feels like it was yesterday. Doesn't it?"

Iain turned his head to the side to free his mouth. For a moment when he tried to speak he couldn't, only air coming out. At last: "Yes," he said. "Yesterday."

A sound like the catching of breath, and then she went.

He dreamt about flying.

After the initial shock wore off, almost all the eligible boys on the island enlisted. Alexander Brodie, Angus Gordon, the two Hendrix boys, Sam Welles. Nearly an entire generation off to fight for a country they'd barely thought of until now. Fewer of the men, because "this island can't just run itself, you know," and the men could not be spared.

The Hendrixes were fishermen, so the Hendrix boys joined the navy. Alex's and Angus's grandfathers had fought in France in the Great War, so Alex and Angus joined the army. Sam Welles wanted to join the army, too, but his father wouldn't hear of it, so Sam joined the medical corps, something of a compromise. And Iain had always dreamt of the sky, so Iain joined the RAF.

It had been four years since he had flown, but it was still everything. He dreamt about flying. Sometimes just of the silence and the peace of it, the endless blue and the patchwork land beneath him, those days before his war had really started. While he soared over the provinces of Canada, his counterparts across the Atlantic bombed the German fleet, dropped propaganda leaflets, flew and crashed and died. He joined them soon enough. Sometimes the dreams were fiercer, and over the roar of the engine he could hear the falling wail and then the explosion of a bomb. The screams of the people he crushed beneath the heel of his boot. He dreamt of flying but also of the landing, the empty bunks in the Nissen huts after each sortie, the dozens of boys left lying beneath the grey waves of the North Sea.

The Hendrix boys did not come back, except for their names on two identical telegrams. Alex Brodie came back but was a different man than he had been before, and three days after the sluagh appeared that first October he bought a one-way ticket for the mainland and disappeared. No word from him until two years later, when a telegram arrived informing his parents that their son had leapt in front of a train in the Underground at Clapham Common. Most of Angus came back, except for the leg he left in Italy, and he lasted a little longer: not quite one year back on-island, walking past the old memorial on the way to church every Sunday, sitting in Iain's front room during October, drinking Iain's whisky. Until Angus, too, had enough, and showed up on Iain's doorstep with all his things packed into a kit bag. "I've got a cousin in Canada," Angus said. A burst of fondness for the blue, the peace, the patchwork fields. "There's opportunity there. More than just fishing and farming, and none of those god-awful crows. You're welcome any time, pal."

The Hendrix boys, Alex Brodie, Angus Gordon. Sam Welles had not even tried to come back.

Others had also gone. Matthew McClare was the only other island boy to join the RAF right at the start, and his and Iain's wars had shared alarmingly parallel paths, until one day they hadn't. Many of the younger boys joined up late in the war, in time for the landings in France. No word from them since.

"All those boys," Caroline had said as they were sitting in a café in Kensington, one of Iain's few days of leave. This was maybe a year, eighteen months before it ended. Bomber Command wasn't trying to cripple Germany anymore so much as completely obliterate it. Caroline started to say something else but lost her words, and instead just sighed again, "All those boys."

All those boys, and only Iain MacTavish came back to stay.

Mrs. Cavanagh yanked away the top pillow. Iain rolled onto his back. "It's been days," she said. Caroline used to tease him about refusing to call her mother by her given name. Perhaps he would, he retorted, if her mother had been invited to the wedding, if Caroline hadn't dragged him into the register office on a whim. "Come on," Mrs. Cavanagh said. "We haven't all got all day to lie around." Iain thought she was being particularly mean to him. He did not particularly think he deserved it.

He stood. The floor was cold on his bare feet. He swayed a little as the blood rushed to his head; he'd been lying down for so long he thought maybe he was not made to stand anymore. "There," Mrs. Cavanagh said. "That wasn't so hard. Now, you're going to go take a bath, and if you aren't clean and dressed in half an hour, I swear to sweet Christ I will come in there and scrub you myself, and I'd bet good money that neither of us wants that for our Saturdays."

How the days ran together. Perhaps it would be better if he could find something to turn his mind to. His father had died mid-war and left Iain with more money than he cared to have. After Angus left, Iain decamped for London once more, rented a little flat but couldn't find a job to hold his attention. He went on a walking holiday in the Peak District but spent most of the time standing outside his bed and breakfast staring at the hills he was supposed to be climbing and smoking endlessly. He thought about travelling Europe but found he had little desire to return to the continent he had just spent four years dutifully attempting to obliterate. He considered returning to school but he did not particularly want to be a lawyer anymore, or a banker, or whatever it was he had been planning to do, before. His inheritance turned out to be a curse disguised as a blessing. Without the need to work for a living the rest of Iain's life spread out before him boundlessly.

He forced himself to walk towards the door on legs that felt mechanical, detached from his body. Mrs. Cavanagh put a hand on his cheek, bearded only out of inattentiveness, her palm soft and smelling of rose lotion. The same lotion that Caroline had used. "Oh, love," she said. "You go get washed up, and shave. Tomorrow, we're going to church."

3.

It was, apparently, quite a beautiful island. A postage stamp of grass and rock and heather floating in the middle of the sea. The seasons came rough and strong, rushing down the moors and leaving various calling cards in their wake. Wildflowers, flooding, frost. The skies turned from minty blue to charcoal grey in an instant, peeled back for the aurora in winter and cracked wide open for much of the summer. If one had asked Graham Welles, he would have said that this island had some of the most magnificent sea cliffs in the country, tumbling down from the farmland to the waves. It was a place made for arriving.

Which Hugo McClare wouldn't know, because he had never left. His only arrival here an unremembered February morning seventeen years earlier, come squalling into the world. One of the ferrymen had once told him that a person hadn't seen this island until he'd seen it from the sea. Coming over from the big island through the rocky waves, watching the cliffs appear as if by magic out of the fog. "Like something out of a fairy tale," the ferryman said. Hugo had turned around and considered the harbour and the village behind him. "Like stepping back in time." It didn't seem like anything out of a fairy tale, it just seemed like home.

He had thought about leaving often. At first more in passing, to know what it was like to arrive. Today he was ready to do it, as he sat in the room he shared with his brother George ("I'm not thrilled with the arrangement either," George had said the last time Hugo complained) and listened to George fighting with their sister, Kate, downstairs. The house was always full with the swelling and ebbing of some argument. Hugo placed a cigarette between his lips, lit up, did not inhale. He was new to smoking and didn't care for it much, but it felt like a grown-up thing to do. He'd been rummaging around in the attic a few months ago and found an old lighter, a nice one, heavy brass. He wasn't sure where it had come from, perhaps it had been his grandfather's. Now he carried it everywhere.

He flipped a page in his book. One ear open in case George should decide to come upstairs. There was another room down the hall, but neither George nor Hugo dared suggest the other's eviction. Once, Hugo had eased open the door while everyone else was at chores and tiptoed into the mausoleum quiet. The layer of dust was even and complete, proof that nothing had been disturbed since the room's occupant packed a rucksack and left on the ferry one fine November morning a decade prior. Hugo had sat on his eldest brother's bed and tried to remember the boy who'd once slept there. He found he barely could. He had been only seven when Matthew left for the war. He had lived with his brother's ghost longer than he'd lived with his brother himself.

Everyone else remembered. Hugo clattered downstairs one morning to find everyone sombre and silent, all day received nothing but tight-lipped disapproval from his mother, until Kate reminded him that it was Matthew's birthday. Hugo found some old comic books in the attic and lounged in the yard reading until George told him to put them away—Matthew had collected them. Hugo looked up from the wireless one golden evening to find his father staring at him, dazed. Apparently he was growing up to be the spitting image of his lost brother.

Sometimes it filled him like a tide. The unfairness of it. The senselessness, that it should fill him like a tide at all. Sometimes he stared at his face in the cracked mirror above the bathroom sink and looked for Matthew in his features. He saw only himself. Sometimes he listened to the aftershocks of George's bad humour and thought that the war had taken the wrong brother. Then went downstairs and faced George over dinner and hated himself for thinking it at all.

So home was a sore spot, and Hugo spent as little time inside it as he could. It wasn't hard to avoid. Hugo had cultivated a list of the best chores, the ones that kept him outside in the brisk air with the sheep and the sky as long as possible. He stayed out late with his friends, and his parents never asked where he'd been or when he was coming home. The boys would drink themselves silly in some unused field or barn and blunder home in the early morning light just in time for chores. On one of these whisky-drenched mornings Hugo thought he saw someone coming out the back door of the McClare house, walking through the mist over the fields. A man too young to be his father and the hour too early for it to be George. Hugo called out to the man he was certain was Matthew, but by the time he had vaulted clumsily over the fence, the man had disappeared. Hugo stumbled to bed, and when he woke still drunk an hour or two later, he was already convinced it was just the whisky.

When October came and brought the sluagh, thoughts of Matthew were everywhere, even more than normal. A day couldn't pass that his mother didn't try to hide her damp and splotchy cheeks, or his father didn't disappear into the barn for hours, or George didn't fall into even greater distemper than usual. Hugo watched the crows and thought of his brother in the air—and then the loss of flight, careening to earth in a burst of flames. It seemed unfair, he thought, that so much feeling should come from the absence of a person he hardly remembered at all. Or perhaps the unfairness was the feeling. The grief of things unknown.

Now the sounds of Kate and George's row were fading and a pair of heavy feet was lumbering up the stairs. Hugo slid his schoolbook under his pillow. By the time George appeared in the doorway, Hugo was the picture of indolence, head lolling off the edge of the bed, a dog-eared comic book (not one of Matthew's) crumpled into one hand. Hugo peered at George upside down. "What d'you want, then?" he asked.

Here was Hugo's secret: he loved school. His subjects, even the ones that gave him trouble (geography, maths), were mountains to be climbed, rivers to be forded, puzzles to be unscrambled. At the beginning of summer the headmaster, a papery old man named MacDonald, had asked if Hugo was considering university. The word said like a sacrament. Not that reverence made the question any less needless. It was miraculous that he was still in school at all; George's indifference to the farm suggested it would fall to Hugo to keep up. University was an impossible dream for an island boy, anyway. Hugo was not, he thought, the next Sam Welles. Two days later an application packet had turned up on Hugo's desk. Hugo folded it up and threw it in the wastepaper basket on his way out of class. As soon as he reached the front door, he turned and fished it out.

Here was Hugo's second secret: the dreams he harboured of leaving, of filling out the application packet now shoved under his mattress, of slipping out the door in the night and not turning back. Fanciful nonsense, really. But it was nice to dream.

"What're you reading?" George asked.

"Nothing," Hugo said. "What d'you want?"

George tapped his fist against the doorframe. "Leigh Welles is over there trying to do her windows," he said. "I don't reckon she knows what she's doing, do you?"

A fizz of indignation bubbled in Hugo's chest. The kind of protectiveness one might feel for a sister or a cousin. "Leigh Welles has always had a much better grasp on what she's doing than you," he said. When he had been just a snotty-nosed bairn and his siblings had wanted nothing to do with him, Leigh had always forced them to let Hugo join their games. As they cavorted about the island, any time Hugo fell behind, Leigh had hoisted him onto her back without a second thought, his sharp chin digging into her bony shoulder. He would never admit it but he had been more upset the day Leigh Welles sailed away for the mainland than the day the telegram came consigning Matthew to oblivion.

"No," George said, "I mean with how it is now. She's doing it the old way."

This was a different matter entirely. "Oh," Hugo replied, sitting up. "No one's told her."

"This is what I'm saying," George said. "I'm going over there now to give her a hand. Coming?"

He supposed he was. He threw his unsmoked cigarette into the wastepaper basket dispassionately and followed his brother down.

The windows were a problem. What to do with them. In the autumns of Leigh's childhood they had simply closed their shutters and tied them down with bits of red braid. A festive effect when one walked through town. Then there'd been an incident in '41 and everyone began to nail the windows shut instead.

As she considered the problematic windows with a hammer in one hand and a slimy old board in another, one of the goats ventured out of the barn, the black one named Rufus by a much younger Leigh. The white one, Matilda, dared not venture into the soggy afternoon, but Rufus started to munch his way through the grass towards the house. They'd been a gift, the pair of them, for Leigh's ninth birthday, a glorious May morning when the war was still just a spectre looming, when they were still a family of father, mother, daughter, son. They'd breakfasted out in the garden, and Leigh and Sam had bickered about what to name the goats until their mother had intervened and said, firmly, "Leigh can name her goats whatever she likes."

This was what had characterised her childhood— good-natured (mostly) bickering between headstrong Leigh and domineering Sam, eight years Leigh's senior, which Áine always managed to snuff out just before the moment of ignition. Áine had been swept away by Graham Welles at the same age Leigh was now. Seduced by the stories he told of a place where life was sweet and simple, where the sun never set in summer and the winter skies danced with lights. She'd been from a well-to-do Edinburgh family who, Leigh pieced together in the way children often did, were less than thrilled with the match. (Years later Leigh would walk through Morningside and think about all the family she might have hidden away in one of these houses, one of these other worlds.)

They moved into the green farmhouse that Graham had recently inherited. A large, temperamental house, aching for Áine's attention. She gave it dutifully, chose new wallpaper and arranged old furniture, set things working like a clock. The garden was perhaps the best of the farm; a tall, leafy tree sheltered the earth from the worst of the weather so that something could grow other than heather. Sam arrived, a first-anniversary present, and spent many hours lying in a hamper under that tree. A long interlude, then Leigh showed up, almost an afterthought. Any hopes of Sam helping with the baby were dashed when Áine came upon him dragging Leigh's basket out his open upstairs window. "I like sitting on the roof!" he cried as Áine hauled him back inside and gave him a smack. "I thought she'd like sitting on the roof!" Áine decided it was best to leave Leigh in the garden, where she could see her through the kitchen window, to be watched over by the dog, a lumbering creature named Bo who had been purchased to help Graham with the sheep but, it turned out, was much better with babies.

Now there was hardly any garden to speak of. Not much of a farm either. Graham had always been more interested in his books and his research than farming, and now it showed. The sheep sold off and the land left to waste. The fence wilting towards the ground, the grass nearly as tall as Leigh. What would Sam say if he saw it? Something awful, surely.

"Having some trouble there?"

Leigh jumped and nearly dropped her hammer on her foot. Maisie leapt up from her spot in the grass, barking, as George and Hugo McClare strolled down the gravel walk. "You're a wee bit late," Leigh muttered to the dog. "What sort of a watchdog are you, anyway?"

"A good one," Hugo said, crouching down to pet Maisie. Leigh felt a little burst of affection for him. A memory of his tiny hand clutched in hers as they played some game in the woods. Years ago now. Another lifetime. It was almost hard to believe that the young man in front of her was the same boy. Maisie sat in his lap and offered her ears up for more scratches.

"You'll need fresh boards," George said. "We've extra over at ours." He had a way of speaking as if he were picking up a conversation they'd just left off. It had been four years since they'd seen each other, at least two since they'd so much as exchanged letters. Leigh barely recognised him, standing there in work clothes that were old and well worn but neat, his coat and scarf hanging open, no hat on his head. The faint shadow of a beard around his jaw. He looked like he was engaged in a constant battle with the land but one that, so far, he seemed to be winning. Callused and weathered and wearing it well. Leigh looked a little less victorious than he did, looked something worse than scruffy. She felt her face grow warm.

"Thanks," she said. "Do you want some—some tea, or something?"

"Nah, thanks, we had lunch," George said. "We saw you over here and thought we'd come help. Haven't really spoken since you got back."

"We haven't," Leigh agreed. She clutched her hammer between her hands tightly to keep herself from fidgeting. "How have you been?"

"Oh, you know me," George said, though Leigh wasn't sure that she did anymore. How much she had changed in the past four years. It was hard to imagine anybody else staying the same.

Hugo was still sitting in the dirt with Maisie in his lap. "We just came over to see if you have the charms," he said. Leigh looked at him blankly. "Guess they were going to let you figure it out yourself." Hugo freed himself from the dog, reached deep into his coat pocket, and pulled out a clutch of little iron charms strung onto red ribbons. "For the doors," he said. "Put them on the handles. The barn too. And keep one in your pocket in case."

He handed her one of the charms to look at. It wasn't shaped like much at all, just a long, thin piece of iron that lay cold and heavy against her palm. "What are they for, though?" she asked.

"The sluagh," Hugo said. "They've been a little . . . feisty, the past few years." He rolled the charms around his hand like dice. Glanced between George and Leigh. "I'll go put them on for you." And he strode away, Maisie following excitedly at his heels, leaving George and Leigh to continue staring at each other.

"Are you going down tonight?" George asked. "For the ritual and everything?"

"Oh," Leigh said. "I suppose I ought to."

George's mouth twisted ruefully. Leigh had not been to the ritual in years, not since before she left. Even then her attendance had been spotty at best. When she was small her parents had often gone just the two of them. During the war Graham had often gone alone.

"Well," George said. "I don't reckon it's the kind of thing you'd want to go to alone. Not today, of all days. D'you want to come with me? Us, I mean."

Her eighteen-year-old self would be giddy with it, this invitation. George standing in her driveway. He had kissed her once, only once, on VE Day under a midnight sun. The intervening years stretched between them like physical distance, but there was this invitation, a bridge.

Leigh shrugged and said, "All right, then."

George smiled at her again, a wide smile, as Hugo and Maisie came bounding around the side of the house in such a frenzy that it was hard to tell who was chasing whom. "Excellent," George said. "I'll swing by here, back of six?" Maisie abandoned Hugo and sprinted over to George, and he crouched down to pet her before tipping his forgotten hat to Leigh, saying, "Come on, Hugo," and heading off down the gravel driveway again.

Hugo lingered for a moment, an inscrutable sort of look on his face. "See you tonight, then," he said. Leigh nodded and Hugo took a few steps down the path before pausing, turning halfway to her. "Leigh?" he said. "I'm glad you're back."

Leigh didn't know what to say. She thought of all the letters that had sailed the ocean between here and the mainland the four years she'd been away. Letters from Kate and George and her father—and Hugo. How she'd let the side down after two, stopped writing back to everyone but her father, and eventually everyone but her father had stopped writing too.

Except Hugo. She'd gotten a letter from Hugo every month or two, the whole time she was away, long after she had stopped writing back. His letters never implored her for a response directly. Often they were short. Little vignettes about island life, a joke he had found funny, his thoughts on the latest book he had read.

Sometimes they were different. Sometimes they felt like more than letters. Like shouts across the water, a hand pressed to a windowpane. Sometimes she was so close to writing back, but she didn't know what to say.

"Thanks, Hugo," she said at last, and Hugo nodded once and turned after George.

4.

Some hours later Leigh stood in front of her mother's closet, shivering, the bathwater still draining away. When she was small, she would sit on the tiny stool in the corner and watch as her mother dressed. The elegant way she flicked through the hangers, how she swept her selected dress free with a flourish. "What do you think?" she would ask, and Leigh would give her approval or else send Áine to make a different selection. Sometimes Áine would let Leigh play dress-up in the closet, and Leigh would come out bedecked in her mother's jewellery, a hat slipping down over her eyes and the sleeves of a dress waterfalling over her hands, the skirt trailing behind her like a gown.

Leigh reached out to touch a dress. She liked to think she could still catch the delicate scent of Áine's perfume hanging about, but of course it was impossible, after all this time. A simple desire to feel pretty. To put on a pretty dress and a pretty face and pretend for a moment that there was nothing in her head but pretty thoughts.

She chose a dress. It fit now, no waterfalling sleeves or long trailing skirt, though somehow Leigh felt no different from the six-year-old playing dress-up. After her hair had dried she caught sight of herself in the mirror and she looked so much like Áine that she took a breath. She had let her mother's memory sit as a bitterness in the back of her throat, but bitterness, left to steep, turned quickly to anger. Leigh turned away from the glass, then back again. Tried to find the bits of her face that looked like her father, but today she was all Áine, in the curve of her mouth and the line of her nose and the set of her brow. The way her hair fell golden to her shoulders. Leigh looked like her mother had the last time Leigh saw her, a memory twelve years old but fresh like a raw wound.

"Enough," she told her reflection firmly, and she went downstairs.

A knock on the door at six heralded George's arrival. He had parked his truck in the driveway and himself on the porch beneath the unlit lamp. He blinked twice when she opened the door, as if he had something caught in his eye. "Evening," he said, finally. "You look nice."

The slightest bit of a thrill, stepping into an October evening. A feeling like a breath on the back of one's neck. There were still three quarters of an hour until sunset but already the light was slanting and low, the promise of darkness in the air.

"Where are the others?" Leigh asked as she followed George to the truck.

"Oh," he said, "they've all been out and about all afternoon. Kate and the parents had some errands, and who knows where Hugo goes off to. They'll meet us there."

The inside of the McClares' truck smelled like cut grass and earth but showed no evidence of either, the seats clean and the floor clear of debris. George drove smoothly, fluidly, like the truck was an extension of his body. He skilfully manoeuvred around a pothole that Leigh could not see in the blinding golden light but knew from experience was particularly treacherous. The road was bad up here, worse the farther from the village one went. Up north near the abandoned Bruce farm, the house and pastures left empty since the family departed after the first war, it was barely a road at all but viciously cratered and pockmarked by time. The only other things that far north were trees and fields and the ruins of an ancient cathedral perched on the cliffside. No other signs of the long-forgotten people who must have built it. A mystery so old that it had lost its allure, mostly.

"I'm sorry I didn't come to the funeral," George said, as they came up on the untilled field that tonight held several cars and trucks, the other islanders on their way to the ritual. Leigh looked over at him, but his attention was trained on the road ahead.

"It's all right," she said. "I don't think he would have minded."

"Did you?"

Leigh shrugged. She could still smell the petrol that Tom had poured over her father's shrouded body this morning.

"Bad business," George said. He parked the truck expertly between two others. "My dad hasn't been himself since—well, you know."

She did know. Mr. McClare (John) had met her off the ferry, two days after her father's body had been fished out of the sea. The McClares had been looking after Maisie and Mr. McClare had gone to the doctor's to check Graham's body for any family heirlooms Leigh or Sam might want. He handed Leigh her father's wedding ring but wouldn't let her look at him. "Let me spare you this," Mr. McClare had said to her outside Dr. Delaune's, broad hands on her shoulders as though she were going to try to make a break for it. "It doesn't even look like him anymore, lass."

This was what death did to a person, she supposed as she slipped out of the truck and followed George off along the bluff. Turned one from a "him" to an "it."

Heat pressed against Iain's face and for a moment he thought he could smell the faint scent of burning hair, melting rubber, flesh. He blinked and saw a hand pulling back a curtain, a series of pins on a map. Cologne, Munich, Braunschweig, Dresden.

He blinked again and returned to himself, to the bonfire before him, roaring up into the air. He wasn't sure what had possessed him to come tonight, other than that his moods came and went quickly these days, like riptides. One moment all he wanted was to return to his bed and sleep off the past week, month, decade, and the next he could not spend another moment in the house. Maybe it was the day's work, out in the yard nailing the westward windows shut, where there was too much world, too much light and breeze and clean fresh air, where he could hear the distant lull of the North Sea lapping against the island's edges just a few hundred yards from the house. That watery graveyard.

Whatever it was he was here, waiting for the ritual to begin as the islanders arrived in fits and starts and settled into wide circles around the fire. He always felt like an anthropologist at island events, especially October ones. As soon as he'd finished primary school, he'd been tucked away on some moss-green campus, morning dew in his eyes, no magic but the quiet of a library or the cracked spine of a book.

"Captain!"

Hugo McClare came bounding up to him, October energy dripping off him. Hugo McClare was the only person who called him "captain," and most of the time Iain wished he wouldn't. Especially times like now, when the half-light of the evening and the fire danced off his features and painted him into a slightly different vintage of McClare boy. If it had been up to Iain, he thought probably he would go out of his way to avoid Matthew McClare's youngest brother.

But it wasn't up to him. Every time Iain set foot beyond his front gate, Hugo somehow managed to find him. He had complained, in passing, to Mrs. Cavanagh, something about already having a shadow and not needing a second. "He probably just wants to know about his brother," Mrs. Cavanagh had said. "And you knew him better than anybody." He'd stopped complaining.

Truthfully he found he liked Hugo. If Mrs. Cavanagh was right about the boy's motives, he did a good job hiding it. It seemed they talked about everything except Matthew. School and the island and Iain's year at Cambridge, rugby, occasionally politics if Hugo caught Iain with a newspaper in hand. Lately Hugo had taken to showing up unannounced on Iain's front step and spending hours methodically combing through the books in the study. Sometimes the light caught the boy's face so and it was like stepping back in time, some half-term in a past life and Iain and Matthew gallivanting around the island before Iain returned to school. Moments that Iain dreaded and craved in equal measure.

"You don't have to call me captain," Iain told Hugo for the hundredth time. Actually it was a demotion. Not that it mattered.

"As long as you're still dressed like one," Hugo said. Iain buried his hands deeper in the pockets of his flight jacket. The leather soft with creases around the elbows and the shoulders, a long gouge in the right sleeve from a bit of flak that had narrowly missed him. A topographical map of his body and the sky.

Hugo retrieved cigarettes and a lighter from his pocket. A heavy brass thing, probably it was an antique. His fingers were clumsy as he tried to light up until Iain said, "Here, let me," and did not think about what Caroline would have said, something about bad influences and corrupting youth. He leaned in to take the lighter and caught the smell of Hugo's breath. It wasn't October energy dripping off the boy at all, it was whisky. "I see you got your night started early," Iain said. He lit one of his own cigarettes with Hugo's lighter—he'd forgotten his own at home—and handed it back.

Hugo took a deep drag on his cigarette and coughed the smoke out. "Can you blame me, if I'm expected to make it through this fucking nightmare of a night?" He gestured vaguely with his cigarette at the air above. The crows lurking on the low stone wall by the road, clustered on top of the cars and tractors in the neighbouring field, lined up neatly on top of the standing stones encircling the bonfire. "I honestly don't know why we don't just take a shotgun and have at them. Once and for all."

The bravado of youth. Iain wasn't sure how much of the island's legend he believed, but he thought it unlikely that nobody would have tried to do away with the crows before.

"Somehow I'm not sure a gun would do the trick," Iain said.

"It doesn't have to be a gun," Hugo said. He tried another puff on the cigarette, almost managed to suppress the subsequent cough this time. "I'd quite like to get my hands on one, wouldn't you?"

Iain's hands were already dirty enough. He tapped the ash out of his cigarette and changed the subject. "The rest of your family coming?"

"They're here," Hugo said, nodding towards the other side of the field. "George is over there with Leigh Welles, d'you see?"

Iain looked where Hugo pointed, across the field where a girl wearing a sombre face stood in the outermost circle, a young man hovering at her shoulder. Leigh Welles. Sam's little sister. A crisp memory of the docks at Aberdeen at the end, Sam grabbing Iain by the arm and crumpling a letter into his hand. ("I don't think I'm coming back.") Iain had resented being asked—or told, as it were—and had tried to get the errand over with as quickly as possible. He had never thought of Sam as much of a friend. There had been one or two raucous nights out when they were both on leave in London, but when they met up again that final summer it became clear that all they'd ever had in common was the war.

Leigh'd grown up a lot since he'd last seen her. He remembered the straight line of her eyebrows pulled across serious eyes, her mouth drawn small with disappointment. They looked alike, the two Welles children. Very alike. Fragments of gossip came to him unbidden, things he knew about her but shouldn't. (The Welles girl moved away to the mainland. I hear she couldn't keep her job. Living on her own and I hate to think of where she gets the money for that.)

"He was soft on her, before the war," Hugo said.

"George? On Leigh?" Despite spending all his gallivanting with Matthew, he had paid little attention to the comings and goings of the rest of the McClare brood.

"Aye," Hugo said. There was a look on his face like he had smelled something bad, like he wasn't too keen on the idea of George being soft on Leigh. "Maybe he'll be better natured now she's back."

Iain thought of the things he'd heard about George these days. "Is that likely?"

"No," Hugo said, "but one can hope."

The rest of the McClares stood a few yards away from George and Leigh. Iain looked away before he accidentally caught their eye. He wasn't sure who had started it. Whether he had avoided them when he first stepped off the ferry with Sam Welles's letter in his pocket, or if they had avoided him. Either way it was habit now, the lurch in his stomach, the instinctive turning of his head. A few months ago when Hugo was ensconced in his study, Iain had asked whether Hugo's parents knew where he was spending all his time. "I certainly haven't told them," Hugo had said, turning a page. Iain had not asked again. Probably it was best for everyone involved if they kept their distance.

"You coming to church tomorrow?" Hugo asked.

"Mrs. C says I am."

"Well, and her word's as good as law."

"Seems like it."

Hugo grinned, and then it faded off his face. "After church tomorrow," Hugo said. "There's something I want to talk to you about."

"Oh?" Iain said, absentmindedly. He was still watching Leigh Welles. "What's the matter?"

"Nothing," Hugo said. "Just something I want to tell you. Now's not the time. It's starting." He threw his cigarette into the damp grass and ground it out. Across the bonfire Leigh Welles's thin face danced in the flames.

When Leigh had first stepped out of the truck she'd been momentarily stunned by it. The sheer size of the bonfire, a great pillar of flame and smoke and spark. The fires before the war had never been so grand, and during it they'd been scarcely more than a handful of sticks, the islanders' bodies nestled around it to shield it from the sky. There were no air-raid sirens on this little island; if some rogue aeroplane still carrying its bomb-load saw their fire and thought it had found a target, there would be no advance warning.

But now. Now the bonfire was an immense thing, roaring, raging, and the islanders in concentric rings around it. All the people in the innermost ring wore billowing white robes and a great birdlike mask over their faces—awful carved things, sharp curving beaks and wide gaping eyes. The October thrill zipped down Leigh's spine. It was not that she couldn't tell who everyone was—they were the town council, Mr. Harrower and Young Mr. Morrison, the MacEwan grandmother, Mr. Gordon—it was everything else. These people she had known her whole life, swallowed by the robes, the masks, the night. The smoke curling into the clear, darkening sky, curtaining off the little pinprick stars. The whole world on this island, the whole universe in this fire.

It was half six, and it was beginning. Like the striking of a church bell, everybody said,

An doras a 'fosgladh.

(The door opens.)

The Gaelic began as a low hum, a single voice rising out of all their chests in unison. Leigh felt her lungs tighten, her ribs weld shut. Something pressing against the inner walls of her heart, trying to get out. George nudged her in the side and whispered, "Join in." She did. It had been four years since Leigh had spoken Gaelic. Her eyes stung and she told herself it was from the smoke, but it wasn't. It felt as though she had not been on this island for a hundred years, it felt like she had been here only yesterday.

One by one the white-robed islanders stepped forwards to the edge of the fire and tossed a handful of earth onto the flames. From the north. From the south. The east. The west. The mountain and the valley. *An doras a 'fosgladh.* A memory, many years old, of her father telling her how the border between this world and the next grew thin each autumn. A doorway opening,

38

easy to fall through accidentally if one wasn't careful. ("Wouldn't want anybody slipping away, would we?")

It didn't take long, perhaps a quarter hour. The town elders in the white robes finished their offerings of earth. The firelight threw the carvings of their masks into sharp relief, burrowing through the wood, sliding down the curved beaks. As though following some ancient choreography the onlooking crows took sudden flight from their perches on the standing stones and swept down through the sky. Leigh squeezed her eyes shut as the air stirred with their feathers, squeezed them shut as she had each year she had come, half expecting to feel the creatures' talons scrape across her scalp like nails against a blackboard.

Someone screamed and Leigh's eyes snapped open again. A boy silhouetted against the fire with something clenched in his fists, his hands raised triumphantly in the air.

Hugo McClare. Hugo McClare with a crow clenched between his palms.

"Hugo!" Kate shouted. "What the hell are you doing?" He had snatched one of the birds as it swooped down from its perch, a feat of athleticism and youth. The creature looked wrong clenched between Hugo's pale fingers, a thing that wasn't supposed to happen. It writhed and twisted, but Hugo's grip was tight. Two other birds circled Hugo's head in a frenzy, but he hardly seemed to notice them. He fell to his knees and pinned the crow to the dirt, his free hand scrabbling in the grass until he found what he was looking for, raised his fist into the air clenching a stone. He brought the rock down onto the bird and it cried, a long, tortured wail. Kate was crying for him to stop but there was something wild in his face, in the firelight dancing on it. He beat the bird with the rock, over and over until it glistened with something black and thick. The sluagh screamed and it sounded almost human in its anguish. The rest of the birds had taken to the air and cried out in unison as Hugo attacked, circled madly in the air like a great dark tornado.

Finally someone managed to wrestle Hugo away from his prey, Leigh couldn't tell who in the smoke and feathers, and Hugo shouted, "All right!" as the bloodied stone fell from his hand. Hugo shook himself out of the man's grip and strode away into the falling evening, and for a long moment nothing moved at all. The body of the creature lay there in the grass, barely recognisable anymore. Leigh stared at it, stunned. The smoke stung her eyes and she thought perhaps she could see something leaking from the creature's body, something thin and ephemeral like sea mist. When she blinked, it was just the mangled body of a crow.

She hadn't thought it possible to kill the sluagh. Couldn't quite wrap her head around it. Two other birds were hovering around the corpse, and then a third joined them. She found something in her heart had begun to ache. The sluagh weren't the enemy, or so her father had always said. Especially during the war. "They're lost souls, *mo ghràdh*," he told her on the nights they could hear them wailing on the moors, worrying at the boards on the windows. "Just lost souls trying to find the next world." She felt, now, surprisingly close to tears. The cruelty of killing a thing that was already dead.

One of the council stepped towards the murdered crow. Mhairi Taylor, given away by the bright red curls tumbling out of her mask. She removed the mask and placed it in the grass, shook her arms out of her robe. Wrapped the corpse up in the white cloth like swaddling a baby. She knew what she was doing. When her husband died in the war she had taken over as the island's butcher, and there was some muttering about it until suddenly there wasn't.

With the creature out of sight its spell seemed to be broken, and the air began to vibrate with the islanders' voices. The gossip machine churning to life. It was just the normal chatter but somehow to Leigh it sounded still like the droning hum of the Gaelic, humming on in her ears like the persistent low song of electricity she had never gotten used to on the mainland.

A hand at her back: George. "Are you all right?" he said.

Leigh wiped at her face. "I'm fine," she said, and thankfully her voice was close to sounding it. "I just—I want to go home."

George nodded. "I suppose everyone will be going home now. We can get a head start on the rush for the cars. I'll take you."

"Shouldn't you go after Hugo?"

"He needs to blow off steam," George said. "I won't be much help with that." His hand slid across her back again, turned her away from Mhairi Taylor and her terrible bundle. Leigh sidestepped him and his hand fell away.

"Really," she said, when they were far enough from the bonfire that the air had cleared, mostly, of the smoke, that she could breathe again. "I'm fine. You don't have to come with me."

"Don't be silly," he said, and Leigh bristled. He reached out and grabbed her wrist. "Besides, it's barely half six."

"It's been a long day," she said, trying to yank her hand free. "I'm going to eat something and go to bed."

"Come on," George said. He dropped her wrist and reached for her waist. "You were fun, once."

Panic fluttered between her ribs. She tried to step away but he had a good hold on her now. When she pushed with both hands on his chest he hardly moved, stood as steady as one of the stones they had left behind. "George," she said. "I don't know where you've gotten this idea."

"Don't be like that," he said. "No one has to know, you needn't pretend."

"I'm not pretending," Leigh said. "I'm being serious, George. Let me go."

His fingers dug tighter into her sides. "You think I'm not good enough for you anymore?" he demanded. "Only mainland boys for the illustrious Leigh Welles? I was good enough for you before."

"Don't be daft. 'Good enough' has nothing to do with anything."

"Oh, come off it," he said. "Everyone knows what you got up to over there. All alone in the big city. No proper work, living on your own. How'd you pay your rent, Leigh?"

She slapped him as hard as she could across the face. He released her and she stumbled backwards. "Suit yourself," George said, but Leigh had already turned and started to run.

The uneven ground was treacherous and she caught her foot on a rock and fell, hard, onto her knees. Her hands sinking into the damp earth. She got up and kept running even though George was not following her, had turned back to the bonfire. At last the makeshift car park loomed into view, the familiar cars and trucks, and she stopped. Her lungs screaming for air and her eyes burning with fury.

At this time last week Leigh had been in her flat eating a sad dinner of sardines and toast. She had opened the window to try to air out the perpetual mustiness of the room and now sat before it, feeling the last bit of September warmth on her face. She'd found new work at a department store and wanted more than anything to quit. She looked out across the street at the city she had come to hate. It seemed now like another world entirely.

Here was the truth of it: Leigh had wanted to come home the very moment she left, and the telephone call summoning her back had been a black sort of blessing. She took a great gasping breath and it caught in her throat, a plaintive, choked sound.

"Hey, you all right?"

A man's voice. Leigh spun around, her hands pressed to her chest. Iain MacTavish appeared out of the twilight.

Here were some of the things people whispered about Iain MacTavish: He never spoke more than three words at a time. He walked the high street alone at night in his flight jacket, humming tunelessly. He didn't fear the sluagh the way the rest of them did, and he didn't need to. He had lost his soul somewhere over Germany.

Here were some of the things Leigh remembered about Iain MacTavish: The day he came home looking oh, so much the war hero in his flight jacket, kit bag thrown haphazardly over one shoulder. The other young men standing next to him—Angus Gordon with his missing leg, and Alex Brodie with his eyes darting all over the place, as though the enemy were about to appear from behind the fishing tackle. She remembered standing at the docks with her father and watching the ferry come in, and looking for Sam on board, and Iain MacTavish coming over to them instead with a letter in his hand. ("Mr. Welles? Sam asked me to give you this.")

Here was the only thing that really mattered about Iain MacTavish: a week ago, he was the one who had fished Graham Welles's body out of the sea.

He stood a few feet from her now, the flaming torch in his hand throwing a ring of light around them. In the flickering firelight his face looked almost as chiselled as those horrible masks the council wore. "What's happened to you?"

Leigh felt about to cry but she refused to. "Oh," she said, and she could hear it in her voice, "nothing, I—I was just upset. By what happened with Hugo and that poor bird. So I was going home, but I fell on my way back. I'm fine, really."

"You don't sound fine," Iain said. "Did you walk here?"

Leigh shook her head. "George drove me. McClare."

Iain nodded slowly. "Ah," he said. "I see."

Along with strangers, progress, and a great number of crops, this island was inhospitable to privacy. How she hated the way he said that. I see. Of course he saw. Everyone saw everything, heard everything, knew everything. The only way to keep something secret on this island was to tell no one. Not a friend, not the minister, not the wind.

"I can take you back," Iain said. "If you'd like. I was trying to find Hugo, but he's gone off somewhere."

She didn't want to think about Hugo. The look on his face. The blood on his hands. She said, "I can go by myself."

"I don't think that's such a good idea." Iain looked over his shoulder at the bonfire on the bluff, reached into his pocket and retrieved a packet of cigarettes, paused, put the box back in his pocket. "I've got my dad's old car," he said. "Come on."

They bumped out of the field in silence. Leigh wished she were driving herself, but her hands were still shaking, every muscle in her legs trembling like she had been running laps of the ring road. She folded her fingers together in her lap and tried to breathe slowly, but with every blink and every sharp inhale, all she could think of was Hugo, and the look on his face, and the blood on his hands. The faintly twirling mist rising from the sluagh's body, curling into the air, disappearing forever.

Iain glanced over at her and appeared to read her mind. "They seem to have that effect on people," he said.

"They didn't use to."

"Things are different now, I suppose," he said.

"Different how?"

Iain didn't answer for a long time. At last, he said, "I'm not the person to ask. I don't know what it was like before."

What was it like before? A month of birds flocking about the island, flying and swarming in strange formations in the sky. On their lunch break from school they would find a spot to sit and watch them, great black clouds of feathers forming and dissolving like a complicated ballet. A thrill in the evenings when the wind whistled down the street or through the trees because of all the old stories, the lore the McAllister boys had so gleefully recounted to that tourist. Festivals and treats and benign frights.

Then the war. Things were different during the war. And then Leigh left.

"Sorry about your old man," Iain said, abruptly.

"Oh," Leigh said. Another image jumping ahead in the queue of today's horrors: a gently burning boat. "Thank you."

They fell back into silence. Iain clenched and unclenched his fists around the steering wheel. He seemed oddly uncomfortable in a car. Leigh would have thought that manoeuvring a car around a pothole would be simple work for someone trained to heave a thousand-tonne bird of oil and steel into improbable flight. Perhaps that was the problem, perhaps it was too easy.

"Don't pay him any mind," Iain said. "George. He's a twat. Everyone thinks so."

It was awfully easy for him to say. Iain MacTavish. Pilot, war hero, protector of virtue. She looked away out the window and Iain said, "I mean it. I don't think you're the first girl he's tried to get the better of." This didn't, she thought, make it any better.

The drive home seemed much shorter than the drive to town and they were already back, crunching down the gravel driveway. The green house loomed out of the trees, little more than a shadow, unlit. A tightening of her heart as she looked at it for a moment, sinking into the leather seat. Iain stared at the house too, hands clenched on the steering wheel. The world around them still.

"Well," Leigh said eventually. "Thanks for the lift."

"Yes," Iain said, "of course."

"I suppose I'll see you in town."

She stepped out of the car and into the yellow beam of the headlights. The crunch of the gravel once more as Iain pulled away, and then darkness. The door swung shut behind her with a soft click. She slid her coat off her arms as she climbed into the darkness. Dropped it over the banister to clean up in the morning. Twisted her arms behind her back to unfasten the ruined dress as she turned down the hall towards her parents' bedroom.

She stepped into the musty closeness of her mother's closet and let the dress fall around her ankles. A sudden desire to burrow herself into the memory of those dress-up games at six, live in it forever, that time before the war and all this sadness. The air smelled of dust and of Áine. These things you left us to, she thought. These places where you left us alone.

5.

When Iain returned, only the Blakes were left in the field, trying to wrangle their many children into the cart hitched to
their tractor. The wind picking up over the sea, bringing in the
haar. Iain left the keys in the ignition and stepped out of his
father's old car. Eager to be free of it. He had only driven at all
because Mrs. Cavanagh had forced him. ("What's the use in
having it if you never drive? Besides, it looks like there's going
to be weather.") Between the look Leigh had worn as she stared
up at her dark house and the alarming intimacy of driving the
car—was it the first time he'd driven it since his father died? He
thought it might be—his head was buzzing like a swarm of bees
had flown in through his ear. The hollowness in Leigh's face had
been a look like a feeling he had endured himself. A memory:
Sam Welles's letter in his pocket, Angus Gordon's hand gripping his shoulder, steering him onto a boat.

He took a great breath of the cold air. He'd come back to see if he could find Hugo, but the boy was nowhere to be found. It had been Iain who had finally managed to wrestle Hugo away from the bird, drag him out of the bloodied grass, Iain who had strode after Hugo in the dark. "I'm fine," Hugo had shouted at him when he realised Iain was following. "Leave me alone, Iain!"

And so Iain had turned away and found Leigh Welles, instead.

"Excuse me," he called to Mr. Blake as the man intercepted one of the younger children, who was trying to make a break for it, "did Hugo McClare come back here?"

"Aye," Mr. Blake replied, flinging the child haphazardly up into the cart. "He showed up again. Don't know what he was playing at. Can you believe it?"

He would not get sucked into the gossip. Though the gossip had a way of sucking one in anyway, whether one liked it or not. "Where's he now, then?"

"He left a few minutes ago, you just missed him," Mr. Blake said, climbing up into the tractor. "Told him we'd give him a lift, but he said he'd walk." He glanced off towards the ring road, already wreathed in shadow. "Well, it's only the first. All those young lads know what they're about these days."

"I suppose so."

Headlights flared and Iain threw a hand up over his eyes. "Go on, then," Mr. Blake said, calling to be heard over the growling engine. "Best be getting out of the dark yourself."

The Blakes pulled away, leaving Iain standing in the empty field.

The next morning (a cold one, bright and brilliant, the kind of morning they usually didn't get until the end of winter) Iain sat on a low stone wall around the corner from the church. He lit a cigarette and gazed out over the road at the moss-green stone that stood as memorial to the first war. These days he came here often; sometimes he stayed for hours. His brain seemed to go quiet as his eyes passed over the names, which he'd long since memorised, though he didn't recognise most of them. About eight months ago he'd gone to a council meeting and asked if they'd be putting up a memorial for the second war. He had felt duty-bound to ask.

The head of the council, a Mr. Harrower, wouldn't meet his eye. His son had been one of the few younger boys who had joined the RAF instead of the army or the navy, sometime after Iain had come home on leave one Christmas. The last time Iain had seen his father. He supposed the boys had thought it all looked glamorous. ("You've got the sky in your eyes, lad," his father had told him. Iain often looked for it later.) He wondered if Mr. Harrower blamed him, that his own son never made it home.

We'll take it under advisement, the council had told him, and there'd been no talk of a second memorial since.

The war had not come as much of a surprise for the MacTavishes, not as it did for the rest of the island. They spent their summers on the mainland, usually, on Iain's aunt and uncle's estate near Inverness. They were Iain's mother's relations. His mother had died of a flu when he was very young and he hardly remembered her at all, but still they spent six long weeks in the Highlands. Days of conkers and sardines when Iain and his cousins (there were five of them: Claire, Grace, and Lily presided over by Franny and often terrorised by the eldest and only boy, Jock) were children; of croquet and occasionally cricket when they grew older.

The summer had been different that year—harder to hide from the reality of the world when everyone got their newspapers moments after they'd been printed, when everyone had a wireless and a telephone or two. There had been long arguments over dinner. Iain's father argued passionately for appeasement while Jock, a few years out of Cambridge and beginning to rise through the Home Office, was sure that war was inevitable. "You would have us lie down and give Herr Hitler everything he wants," Jock argued over pudding near the end of July. "Why not take down the flag at the palace and let him move in?" It had been sweltering and Iain was looking forward to pudding being cleared so he could release himself onto the (marginally cooler) verandah. The younger cousins had already escaped but Franny was similarly trapped, slouching in her chair across from Iain. She looked at him and pulled a face. This had been an argument in many parts, spanning many days. Iain had stopped paying attention. They rarely asked his opinion, and even when they did, he had to admit that he wasn't sure what his opinion was, and it was so hot that he couldn't think, and when his aunt cut Jock off mid-polemic to call for a ceasefire, Iain had been relieved.

In eighteen months, Jock would be dead, his number up, like so many were, in the Blitz. "All those boys," Caroline sighed some years later, but really that wasn't the half of it.

The McClares' truck rumbled down the high street and the McClares tumbled out, joining the trickle of people towards the church. All the McClares but Hugo. Iain didn't come to church often enough to know if it was odd, Hugo's absence, but he thought probably it wasn't. Especially today. He couldn't imagine Hugo sitting through as much as the call to worship today, with the island's eyes on him, scrutinising him for a trace of the blood on his hands, a glimpse of penitence. Mr. McClare passed him, and Iain ducked his head away. He could feel the man's eyes boring into the top of his skull. He did not look up until the McClares were safely in church.

"Have you had a nice visit?"

Mrs. Cavanagh perched on the wall beside him. Her hat pinned carefully atop her head, her thin hands gloved and folded in her lap. "Do you not get exhausted, lad," she asked, quietly, like a secret, "spending all your time with ghosts?"

He wondered who else she imagined him spending his time with. The Lewises passed Iain and Mrs. Cavanagh, and Mary Lewis stared fervently at Iain until she realised that he was staring back. Her eyes flicked up and down the jacket and then away, and she hurried her man and her youngest son towards the church. "For an island so haunted," Iain said, "our people don't seem to be very good at grieving."

Mrs. Cavanagh patted his knee. "Perhaps the haunting is why," she said. She stood, walked up to the monument, placed her hand flat on its mossy surface, her fingers splaying out across the names. "All those boys," Caroline had sighed, and Iain could hear her sighing it now.

Mrs. Cavanagh turned to him. Surely saw the way his brow had furrowed. "Come along, dear," she said. "Time for church."

6.

It was the third of October and Leigh Welles stood on East Sands at dawn. She stared into the sea grey and crashing, at the place she had last seen her father. His body disappearing amongst waves and weak flames. Down the beach Maisie had found a piece of driftwood nearly three times her size and was determinedly attempting to drag it across the sand. A few yards away three crows perched on a washed-up log.

She wasn't sure what she was watching for. Her father to emerge from the sea? Her father, or her mother. How very many people had disappeared across or beneath these rocky waves.

"How can you possibly be gone?" she said, to Áine, to Graham, to no one, and the wind whipped her words away.

The sun was still newborn but the town was already awake by the time Leigh trudged off the beach path and back onto the high street, clumps of sand falling from her shoes and clinging like thistles to Maisie's long fur. The fishermen small dots on the grey horizon, the farmers and the shopkeepers down at the dock waiting for the first ferry of the day to arrive, the smell of baking bread drifting lazily from the MacEwans' bakery. Leigh paused for a moment on the corner by the McCaffertys' book-store. There was still blackout paper in one of the windows, torn and crumbling in the corners, peeling away from the glass. Across the street the post office was still plastered with the propaganda posters that had come at the beginning, when England was caught in the Blitz. Like nothing about the island had changed. Like she had been gone only an hour.

She reached into her pocket. Her numb fingers found the little iron charm Hugo had slipped into her palm the other day. Cold and heavy and smooth. When she looked up, six crows had appeared as if out of the clouds, perched on the post office's windowsills. One of the birds cawed loudly and she hurried away, Maisie at her heels.

At the end of the high street where it widened into the square, she tripped over Tom McAllister, hunched over the pavement in front of his pub with a bucket of soapy water, scrubbing some-thing away from the paving stones. "Watch it!" he snapped as she nearly kicked over his bucket, and she jumped away with an apology. "What are you doing down there?" she asked, and then she looked again.

Blood. It was blood that he was scrubbing off the pavement, a huge, terrible smear of it. It trickled down the gentle slope of the street in ruddy rivulets. The suds in the bucket were tinged with pink.

"Bastards left a little present for Jennie to find this morning," Tom said. "One of the Brodies' pigs. Must have dragged it down in the night, the buggers."

Leigh watched Tom scrub the blood away, bewildered. He couldn't possibly mean that the sluagh had done this. They'd done it once or twice, dragged some creature all the way down to the village—but that was years ago, and it had been because of the war, and even if the street signs were not up yet and the blackout paper had not been taken down and the doors needed painting, the war was over. She knew that it was over. She had celebrated its ending, here, in this square.

"Tom," Leigh said. "What isn't everyone saying? About the sluagh?"

Tom did not look up. "I wouldn't know what you're talking about," he said. "The sluagh are just the sluagh, same as always."

"Not the same as always."

Tom sat back on his heels, wiped his hands on his trousers. He sighed, a weight-of-the-world kind of sigh. "You remember what it was like," he said. "You know. During."

It would be hard to forget. She remembered when the sluagh had grown so numerous that their once-elegant ballets in the air had blacked out the sky. Great unnatural clouds. She remembered coming across one of the island ponies that usually roamed free, set upon by so many birds that it had been torn to pieces. She remembered hearing them peck at the westward shutters, remembered them almost prying those shutters open, remembered the day her father nailed the windows shut for the first time as the birds sat in the trees and watched. Before the war it had been easy to think that was all they were. Birds. Just crows, until they weren't. Even still she wondered sometimes. Tucked away on the mainland, she'd found it easy to rub the sharp edges off and chalk it all up to superstition.

She said, "It didn't go back to normal."

Tom shrugged. "I suppose this is normal now," he said. "We have to cope, best we can."

The bloody water was still running into the gutter, barely an inch from Leigh's shoes. She watched it swirl away. "Does it work?" The way the crows had behaved in the war had been shocking in some ways but unsurprising in others. Under the midnight sun on VE Day she had supposed that everything would return to normal, to the slow and simple pace of the pre-war years, that impossible endless summer. As she sailed away one fine autumn morning, she was sure that the next time she saw the island it would be like the war had never happened at all. Not that such a thing was possible. Leigh had heard the reports on the wireless and read the newspapers when they came and was fairly convinced that nothing would ever be the same again. She suspected that nobody still left on this island really deserved the blissful ignorance that was prerequisite to that slow and simple life anymore.

It seemed the sluagh agreed with her. Tom scooped his bucket off the pavement, bloody water slopping over the rim. "There've been bad years before," he said brusquely. "We were too lucky for too long. It was never going to last."

For a moment they surveyed the street silently. The clouds seemed to be hanging low today, the air swelling with dampness. "Just add it to the list," Leigh said, "of things the war ruined."

Tom stiffened beside her, did not speak for a long time. When he did, his voice had softened somehow. "You know, lass," he said. "I know you don't mean any harm by it. But I wouldn't go talking about the war with anyone else."

"Why not?"

Tom grunted once, disapprovingly. "Nobody much wants to dwell on it, do they? There's no changing what's done. Best to just carry on. They'll be gone soon enough."

"Carrying on" didn't look how she thought it should. She opened her mouth to argue but was interrupted by the roar of an engine, a truck swinging round the corner and jolting to a halt in the square. The sluagh took flight in a great rush, a huge cloud streaming up to the sky, as Kate McClare leapt from the cab. (Here at least was something that had changed: when Leigh had left four years ago, Kate didn't know how to drive and had no interest in learning.)

"Tom!" Kate called, out of breath like she'd run all the way down from the farm. "Have you seen Mr. Harrower?" There was something wrong about her face, something tight and tense. She appeared to be making a great effort not to look at Leigh. Perhaps, Leigh thought, that offer of breakfast on the morning of her father's funeral had been her only chance to put it right between them. Her only chance, and she had missed it.

"Saw him heading towards the bakery a while ago," Tom said. "Not seen him since."

Kate nodded. "Right," she said. "The bakery, thanks."

"Kate," Leigh said. Kate paused mid-step but barely turned to look at Leigh at all, and Leigh's heart squeezed. There were so many things she ought to say but instead she asked, "What's wrong?"

Kate took a breath that seemed intended to be fortifying but came out staccato and stuttering. She turned but when she spoke, she looked only at Tom.

"It's Hugo," Kate said. "He's gone."

7.

This was not an island from which people disappeared regularly. This was an island where keys were left in ignitions and front doors sat swinging in the breeze. This was an island where everybody knew everybody, and where they were and where they'd been and where they were going. This was an island where secrets died loud and public deaths.

It had happened only twice in living memory. That a person had been there one moment and gone the next, as though they'd evaporated like sea mist, without a note or a war to explain their absence. Lucy McCafferty. On a mid-October evening she had walked herself down to the telephone box on the corner. Her older sister, Nancy, was training to join the First Aid Nursing Yeomanry. It was Lucy's first telephone call and at the start she yelled into the receiver as though nothing but the power of her lungs would carry her small voice across the miles. Nancy listened to her sister's voice coming down the weakly connected line and was so happy that she forgot momentarily why it was that she had been so far from home for so long, why her sister had cause to make her first telephone call at all. At the end of the call Lucy stepped out of the telephone box, and vanished.

Of course, Lucy reappeared. They found her body the next morning, strewn in an unused field, already returning to earth. A shock of sluagh gathered around her like mourners.

The tragedy rocked the island like an earthquake. So many children gone already, flung across a world that had grown too large. There was no protecting the ones who had gone and, as it turned out, no protecting the ones who had stayed.

The search exploded over the island, flinging the villagers across it in groups of twos and threes like a bomb flinging shrapnel. While Kate McClare sat in McAllister's with Mr. Harrower, telling him over and over and over the last time anybody had seen Hugo, whether he might've had any plans to leave the island, whether this could all be a big mistake, the other islanders clambered over the moors and combed through the untilled fields, knocked on doors and called into darkened barns. The fishermen were called in from the sea and the boats counted, the cargo checked. The first ferry of the day was searched and searched again, the ferrymen's protests that their whole day would be thrown by the delay ignored, before it was permitted to sail into the fog.

As far as any of the McClares knew, nobody had seen Hugo since the night of the ritual. He had not gone home with his family. Everyone had agreed he needed time to cool off before squeezing into the back of a truck with his brother and sister, and so they had left him in the field with a few of his friends. There were conflicting reports as to when Hugo had returned home, whether he'd slept in his bed that night at all. George had stayed up late, alone in the sitting room, and had assumed when he slipped into bed in the wee hours that his brother was already asleep in the other bed. He had not turned on a light, he hadn't wanted to wake anyone.

In the morning Hugo hadn't been at home, but this was not unusual; he often was up and out with the sheep before anybody else awoke. He didn't turn up for church, which was less usual but not unheard of. He didn't turn up for dinner, and Kate grew concerned.

Why hadn't the search begun then? One night's less delay, Mr. Harrower muttered to Tom at the bar, might make all the difference. But the search had not begun then because none of this was unprecedented behaviour from Hugo. He was so rarely at home these days, was always out with some friend or another, who knew what those boys got up to. The McClares were thinking of other things. The anniversary of another McClare boy's disappearance was approaching.

So there were two nights' delay, and the search was undertaken grimly. Tom left Kate and Mr. Harrower in the pub and dragged his youngest son, the only one left, into the street. "Go check all the lads' places," he ordered, "aye? All Hugo's friends." Fraser McAllister would not meet his father's eye. "You know where he is?" Tom asked, but Fraser shook his head and ran off on his mission.

It had taken only hours to find Lucy McCafferty's body in '41, and already nearly two days had passed since Hugo was last seen. It was less a rescue than a recovery. With each mile they covered the islanders grew less and less certain that anybody would ever speak to Hugo McClare again.

There was one other time in living memory that someone had disappeared. An end-of-summer morning, August 1937. The day that Áine Welles had stolen Jack Calloway's brand-new, bright red boat, named *Siobhan* for his mother, and sailed away into a different world. Sam had turned eighteen a few days earlier. There were still remnants of the cake Áine had made sitting under a tea towel in the kitchen.

Leigh had known something was wrong from the moment she opened her eyes. Graham sat on the end of her bed, and he passed her a cup of hot chocolate even though it was summer and not a special occasion of any sort. His face looked thinner than it had the day before, and older, and grimmer.

"Mum's gone away," he said, "and I don't think she's coming back."

So while everybody else was thinking of Hugo and Lucy, Leigh was thinking of Áine. It was Leigh who went down to the harbour and rang the bell to call the fishermen in from the sea. It was Leigh who counted all the boats left ashore, and then counted each one as it came in to harbour. "Everyone's accounted for," Ben Hendrix said as he hauled his boat back in to dock. "The boats too." Maisie leapt into the Hendrix boat to sniff around at its cargo anyway.

"There weren't any special sailings yesterday?"

"It was Sunday." Mr. Hendrix shooed Maisie back onto the pier. "Nobody sails on Sundays. If that lad got off the island, he did it on his own steam."

Leigh called Maisie away from Mr. Hendrix's boat, and turned from the sea.

Leigh plodded up the hill away from town. She was not dressed for clambering over the moors and she thought she would go home and change before setting out into the dew-soaked grass to help with the search.

She paused at the place where the path split, one arm curving up inland towards the Welleses and the McClares, the other continuing for a few hundred yards along the cliffside before it was mostly devoured by grass and heather and thistle, became a thin track wide enough for one pair of feet. For many years it hadn't been overcome entirely only because of Graham Welles.

Leigh stepped off the path. Imagined for a moment her footsteps falling into his, one last distant touch. Maisie bounded off into the heather ahead. Perhaps thinking that Leigh was about to take up Graham's mantle, finally give Maisie a proper adventure. Of course, Maisie had gone everywhere with Graham. And now she went everywhere with Leigh.

The wind whipped her hair from its pins. She turned into it, letting the salt air beat her face. Was this where it had happened, where Graham had ventured too close to the cliff, had lost his balance, tipped over the edge? She took a step closer to the drop, and then another. The ground was uneven and the drop sudden. If the wind shifted, if the dog got underfoot, if it had rained and the ground was soft. Leigh took one more step forwards. She was close enough now that she could peer over the precipice, see down to the ocean below. Tide was high this morning and there was little beach to speak of, just water crashing against rock, slowly wearing the island down. Leigh stepped away from the cliff.

She turned back towards the path. A man was approaching, wading through the grass, Maisie leaping at his heels excitedly. "Oh, Miss Welles," he called. "I think your dog is trying to steal me." And, for the second time, Leigh found herself face to face with Iain MacTavish.

"She probably thought you were my father," Leigh said. Iain crouched down to give Maisie a good scratch around the ears. "And you needn't call me 'Miss Welles,' Mr. MacTavish. I'm only Leigh."

"Well, and I'm not 'Mr. MacTavish,'" he said. "I'm only Iain."

"Do you come up here often?" Leigh asked. "Only you never see anyone else round here." What she was really asking was whether this was the place that Iain had spotted something in the water, had gone down to the shore to find Graham Welles's bloated body wedged between two rocks, the tide going out. Iain gave Maisie a final pat and stood again, looked out at the sea. The expression on his face was inscrutable though his face itself seemed determined to tell a story. A thin pale scar through an eyebrow, a little crooked bump in his nose.

"Often enough," he replied. "It's nice to get some time alone." Which was an odd thing for him to say because, if the gossip was to be believed, Iain MacTavish spent all his time alone. She supposed there was Mrs. Cavanagh, his mother-in-law (was someone still a mother-in-law once one's spouse had died?), who had moved to the island months after Iain returned, after Leigh was gone. She thought of how she felt in her own house sometimes, early in the morning or late at night when she woke from some dream, lay in the dark with only the sound of her own breath and the wind outside. Sometimes it didn't feel like being alone at all.

"Have you—recovered," he said, "from the other night?"

Leigh felt her cheeks flush. "Oh, aye," she said, fishing some of her pins out of the tangle of her hair, an excuse not to look at him, something to do with her hands. "It's like you said, it's only George. No good getting upset over it."

But thoughts of George led to thoughts of Hugo. In the distance three tiny figures appeared over the hill, one of the search parties. Iain must have seen something change in her face because he turned to look over his shoulder. "Everyone's rather far-flung today, aren't they?" he said. "Is there some island-wide scavenger hunt nobody warned me about? Is it somebody's birthday party?"

He must have been out walking for ages if he hadn't heard. "No," she said. "It's Hugo McClare. He's gone missing."

Iain continued to watch the search party as it made its way across the crest of the moor. "What do you mean," he said, "'gone missing'?"

"Nobody's seen him since the night of the ritual. That's why everybody's out, everyone's looking for him."

He retrieved a packet of cigarettes from one pocket and a lighter from the other. Leigh watched his hands as he slid a cigarette free, flicked open the lighter, lit up, inhaled. They were elegant, his hands, his way of moving them. He held the packet out towards her, but she shook her head. "He must've gone to the mainland," Iain said, pocketing the cigarettes again. "Or the big island. He's what, seventeen? Just after a bit of adventure."

"There haven't been any boats. Nobody sails on Sundays."

Iain blew a long trail of smoke into the air. It curled and twisted before disappearing into the damp. "It doesn't seem like him," Iain said, "to just disappear."

It didn't, but Leigh was surprised that Iain MacTavish knew that. "Are you two close?" she asked. Stumbling over her words because her mouth had wanted to say "were" instead of "are," a distinction she remained unwilling to make. "I remember you were friends with his brother. Matthew."

(The memory in question: Kate's delight when news came that her brother was on his way back from training, delight Leigh thought misplaced when the next stop was active duty. Matthew McClare riding in to harbour on the last ferry before Christmas with Iain MacTavish standing next to him.)

Iain took a long drag on his cigarette. "No," he said. "I mean—yes, I knew Matthew. But I wouldn't say Hugo and I are especially close, no. He hangs around sometimes, that's all." A flick of his fingers: ash falling to the damp grass. "Are you? Close?"

The search party on the moor was disappearing into the haar. All the many hours they had spent up there as children, Leigh and the McClares. Hugo on Leigh's back when his little legs couldn't keep up anymore, his fist tangled in Leigh's hair. Leigh had always insisted that they let Hugo play with them, over George and Kate's protestations. She knew what it was to be the youngest sibling, always tagging along. She remembered being desperate for a little brother or sister of her own; Sam was fine, but his interest in bridging the eight years between them dwindled daily. "You're barking up the wrong tree, mo ghràdh," Graham laughed once when she was about five, wheedling at his feet. "You and Sam are plenty," Áine agreed.

Then, across the meadow, Hugo arrived. It felt like a long time ago. A sudden sadness crashed into her like a wave, surprising her, because she had thought herself already full up with sadness.

"Before I left, maybe," Leigh said at last. "I've known him his whole life." Iain didn't seem to be listening anymore, he looked like he was many miles away. "I'm going up to change," she continued, "but then I'm going to go help look. You can come, if you want."

Iain took a last drag on his cigarette and tossed it over the cliff. "Thank you," he said mechanically, "but I—I'd better get back to Mrs. Cavanagh. If you'll excuse me."

And he skirted around Leigh and Maisie on the thin dirt track, and disappeared down the hill into the mist.

It was the third of October and night was falling. There was no sign of Hugo McClare. There was no sign of his body. The searchers returned to their homes, to the soft warm glow of oil lamps and candles and, occasionally, a low electric hum. Theories floated about the island on the breeze. Perhaps he fell like Graham Welles and his body would drift to shore with the tide. Perhaps he fell like Graham Welles and his body was swept out to sea. Perhaps the sluagh had gotten him like they got Lucy

McCafferty, only worse. Perhaps there was not enough left of him to find.

Perhaps he had found a way to the mainland without anybody noticing. Leigh had suggested this to Gwen Taylor as they scrambled up the side of the Ben. Gwen gave Leigh a look. "And how?" she said, but Leigh thought what she really meant was, "And why?" and suddenly they weren't talking about Hugo anymore, they were talking about Leigh, and Sam, and Áine, and the persistent question of why the Welleses never seemed satisfied with what they'd got.

Because, with the glaring exceptions of the wars, almost nobody ever left this island. They lived out their little lives on this little stage. Occasionally someone went off to the big island for a year or two, came back with a new wife or husband. Once in a generation perhaps one of the young men, a second son who could not expect to inherit the family show, would go to the big island and stay. (Neill McAllister came to mind, one of the few who survived the war only to be lost to the big island anyways.) There weren't many jobs to be had on this island; there were only so many fish in the sea, only so much land to be farmed. Nobody went to the mainland. Anyone who did never returned.

So nobody much believed that Hugo had found a way to the mainland without anybody noticing. Leigh herself would readily admit that it appeared thoroughly impossible from almost every angle, but until she was shown a body, she would hold out hope.

"Don't you ever want to go?" Leigh asked Gwen as they crested the top of the Ben and the island emerged below them. "Especially these days, with the sluagh the way they are."

The two girls looked down the hill. The wind tore at their clothes and hair ferociously and Leigh could taste salt on the air, whipped up from the sea so far below. A thin haze of mist covered the town, the harbour—model miniatures from this distance, tinier than dolls' houses—and gave one the feeling of standing above the clouds. There had been so many summer nights spent up here, and spring afternoons. Staring down at that little town. "It's like being a Greek goddess on Mount Olympus, isn't it?" Áine had said once. She had been quite the student of mythology. Leigh had been six or seven at the time, and they'd spent the rest of the afternoon concocting their own ridiculous myths featuring all the other islanders.

"This is home," Gwen said, simply.

"Yes," Leigh replied, "I suppose it is."

They wandered around the hilltop for a while, detectives looking for clues. They found none. "Come on," Gwen said to Leigh. "He's not here, anyway."

Nor anywhere else. The town awoke next morning beneath the twin spectres of dread and resignation. Even on the first day nobody had much expected to find Hugo McClare alive, but everyone had assumed that he would turn up one way or another. Slowly the steps of the church filled with candles, until there was one narrow path free to tread. The children returned to school. The minister's long green car could be found from dawn till dusk outside the McClare farm.

Late on the third night since Hugo's disappearance, Iain stood outside the church and stared down at all those little candles, some burning low by now. He had been trying to sleep but he couldn't. Hadn't, not since Leigh Welles had broken the news to him up on the bluff and he had felt his head fill with a familiar hollow buzzing. Hugo McClare, disappeared almost five years to the day that his brother had flown into an eternal violet evening.

He had not joined the search parties. Actually this was the first time he had left his yard since meeting Leigh on the cliff. Now that he had peeled himself out of his dusty room he felt guilty for his failure to help, though he wasn't sure that one more pair of unpractised, unfamiliar eyes would make much difference. "You spotted Mr. Welles," Mrs. Cavanagh said over dinner. She herself had spent the day in a pair of tall galoshes and a long mackintosh buttoned up tight against the weather. "You've better eyes than you think."

Yes, he had spotted Mr. Welles, and how he wished that someone else had borne that particular burden. There were no search parties for Mr. Welles; nobody had known he was missing until Iain stumbled into town with the man's sodden body flung over his shoulder. Iain had found him only because he had woken before dawn, jolted out of a familiar nightmare (a Lancaster aeroplane on fire, a hot slice of sky, a dry garden, the Pyrenees at night), kitted up and stepped into the cool dawn, gone for a long walk along the beach as he often did these sleepless mornings. Saw something strange in the water, drew closer to take a better look, noticed that it was a human hand. Maybe he had better eyes than he thought. He didn't want to use them to spot Hugo McClare.

The worst part about it had been Mr. Welles's face. Iain thought that after the war nothing should shock him anymore, he must be at capacity with horrible images ready to rise to the top of his mind unbidden. Apparently not.

It was the small details he still remembered: A golden September morning, unseasonably warm, everybody else in church. A fly buzzing lazily against the window in the sitting room. The way his collar itched at the back of his neck. His father tapping his fingers nervously against his glass. When he turned to Iain after the broadcast and saw the wildness in his son's eyes, the determined set of his jaw, he sighed. "I should've known you'd be chomping at the bit, lad," he said, switching off the wireless. He had recognised the look; it was the look young men wore when they considered grand adventure. "What's it to be, then? Navy? You'll not be the only island boy, there."

"I'm going to fly," Iain said, and then came all the rest.

A slow march into the machine of war as the island boys were called up one by one. While the others were shipped over to the Continent, Iain sailed the other way, bound for a glorious year at an Initial Training School in Canada. Perhaps "glorious" was the wrong way to describe training for war, but it had been. Without this there would have been his degree, whatever career had already been ordained for him, retirement back on-island like his father. Of course he had a vague awareness of the waste of it all, but thousands of miles across the ocean, soaring above the alternating green and red and gold of Canadian fields, he found it easy to forget about the loss. He woke in the blurry mornings with a sense of such purpose. Always a feeling in those early days of immunity, even when another trainee went down right before one's eyes, even when one heard the stories.

There was nowhere to go but forward. Upward. Initial training passed in a rush and it seemed like he barely had time to blink before he was back on a ship steaming across the Atlantic, steaming towards the war.

"Back to—what do they call it?—the green and pleasant land," Matthew McClare had said, leaning on the railing next to Iain and watching as England loomed into view, looking neither green nor particularly pleasant. Iain wondered how long their wars would follow the same path, their lives. Matthew had signed up a few days after Iain did, and when Iain had asked why the RAF, Matthew shrugged. "I don't know," he said. "Seems more exciting than the army, and I can get on a boat any old time."

Iain was commissioned after attending an interview with one of his father's old friends and, apparently, passing muster. There was no commission for Matthew, but that hardly mattered. Like most of the volunteers, Matthew expected to be a fighter pilot, harboured visions of glory in a Spitfire and continued to even after he'd failed out of his pilot training and ended up a navigator—Iain's navigator—instead. It was as it had always been. Iain and Matthew. As thick as thieves.

Iain stubbed out his cigarette on the railing and tossed it into the waves. It had been a rough trip, and if he hadn't grown up so frequently traversing the sea between island and mainland, likely he would have been sick the whole journey. Despite all his bravado about the sea, Matthew had suffered terribly, and this was perhaps the first he'd set foot above decks. He still looked faintly grey around his edges. "If you really want green and pleasant, you've got to go a good deal farther north, mate,"

Iain said. Matthew nodded appreciatively and said, "I should bloody well think so."

And then came all the rest.

There was a dim glow on the horizon already, morning beginning to approach. Iain turned for home. The feeling of bees buzzing about in his skull was growing, and he paused behind his gate to retrieve a cigarette. The bright flare as it caught light burning into his eyes. He tried to blink the blindness away but it lingered, a yellow ring in his vision.

Something moved in the darkness, right before his face.

Iain leapt backwards, his cigarette falling to the ground in a spray of sparks. His heart pounding against the cage of his ribs in a way it hadn't in four years and never when his feet were planted firmly on the ground.

Another movement, slightly farther away, a tall shadow moving towards the square.

"Who's there?"

The figure stepped into the glow of a street lamp and paused. A man. He turned his head, slightly. "Hey," Iain called to him, "you ought to get out of the dark."

The man didn't respond. Iain's gate made a grating, protesting squeal as Iain slipped through it. There was something about the man's shape that was oddly familiar, something in the set of his shoulders and the way his face was tipped up towards the streetlight.

Matthew McClare. The man looked like Matthew McClare.

Which was impossible. Iain followed him into the street. Missing, presumed dead, five years ago almost to the day.

Not-Matthew stepped out of the lamp's halo and back into the dark, moving quickly down the street. "Hey," Iain called, but the man did not stop. "Hey, wait!"

The man continued, half-invisible in the shadows. Iain could barely make out the shape of him as he trailed behind, like he was being dragged on a string, like a compulsion. Up the street, past the harbour, along the ring road. No matter how quickly Iain moved, he could not seem to catch up to the man.

He did not believe in ghosts. There had been one time—1945, February, almost the end—as he'd stumbled back to his Nissen hut after breakfast, tripped through the mist hanging over the airfield. A feeling he was being watched. He had looked over his shoulder and thought he saw someone standing in the dew. A woman. Caroline. Who had no business being anywhere near the airfield in the morning haze. Who had been dead four months.

He'd blinked the image away and forgotten it. If things had gone differently, perhaps he would have turned to Matthew and asked if he had seen the figure. But Matthew had been dead for months too.

They'd left the village well behind them, Iain and his impossible quarry, and now there was nothing left before him but the empty light stretching over the moors. Iain hesitated. The figure ahead of him stopped, too, as though waiting. "Where are you taking me?" Iain called. His voice was too loud in the quiet.

It struck him all at once. He did not believe in ghosts; it could not be Matthew McClare standing in the mist ahead of him, waiting. But there was someone else it could be, someone who, in the right light, was growing up to be the spitting image of his lost brother.

A chill shivered down Iain's spine. "Hugo?" he called into the mist. The figure turned away onto the moors, and Iain followed.

Though he didn't know it, he wasn't the only one on the moors. In the milky morning light Leigh Welles trooped through the dewed grass, a rucksack on her shoulders, her hair tucked up into her hat.

Everybody else had given up. The previous afternoon she'd gone down to the village, found Tom outside the pub. "When's the search starting?" she had asked him. "I waited to see who would come up the hill, but no one has."

"No more searching," Tom replied. "No one's going to find that boy alive. It'll have been the sluagh, to be sure. With what happened at the ritual? There's no question."

It seemed everyone had come to the same silent agreement. They had spent two days looking and this island, no one could deny, was simply not that large. The fishermen had to return to the sea, the farmers had to return to their flocks. "That's ridiculous," Leigh said. "We've barely covered any ground at all."

Tom glowered at nothing and nobody in particular. "You've not been here for some time," he said, and offered no other explanation. "Don't you go bothering that poor family neither," he ordered, brandishing a charm in her face. "Time for all of us to move on."

Though as she stood in the street with the silent church bells and the propaganda posters, she wondered if anybody knew what that meant at all. She trudged back up from the village alone, considering what Tom had told her. Though thinking more of the time a telegram had arrived, June 1944, declaring

Sam missing, presumed dead. For a week she had wandered through the world in a sort of daze, kept bursting into tears for no reason—until they received another telegram, from the missing soldier himself, saying it had all been a mistake, he had lost his company on a beach in Normandy and attached himself to an American regiment, and they were not to worry at all. Too late, of course.

In the days since Hugo's disappearance she had felt much the same. Found herself crying several times a day for no reason at all, feeling heavy and sluggish and sore. Actually, she thought, guiltily, it was possible that she had felt worse these past days than she had that week when Sam was gone. Perhaps because she had been braced for bad news about Sam, had been expecting it for five long years already. Perhaps because she had always thought of Hugo as her younger, better brother. Another thing she would not admit aloud.

So here she was, out on the moors. She would find Hugo if she had to search every inch of this island herself, with nothing but her own bare hands. She curved round the far side of the Ben and entered the liminal space where there was nothing but her and the earth and the air. A feeling she had never had on the mainland, not once in four years. The Ben protected the southern tip of the island from the worst of the weather, and as she left it behind her, she entered another world. The wide, desolate moor, the thick, unyielding fog. There was something different about this air, about the way that darkness and light hung in it, about how it felt in her lungs and against her face. It made the hair on the back of her neck stand on end, made her think that perhaps she could see shapes moving in the violet mists.

A sound like footsteps behind her. Leigh whipped around but it was only Maisie, rooting around in a dead bit of heather. If Hugo was out here, it seemed possible that he would already have gone mad with it. The silence, the mist, the uncanny feeling. Leigh reminded herself that these moors were in her blood, nobody knew them better than Graham Welles once had. Leigh had tagged along on one of his walks when she was eleven, after Áine and before the war, expecting to meander over the moors, stop to eat the sandwiches she'd packed, toss sticks for Bo, and be home by teatime. Instead it had been a damp day trailing along behind her father as he bounded through the grass and then stopped all at once, crouched down to spend eons sitting before a particularly interesting rock formation, or some symbol carved into a tree, or a part of the coastline he had not yet sketched out.

"You know," he had called to her as she moped by the side of the road, "some sources say that our ancestors used to have these great underground temples where they'd leave sacrifices and commune with the spirit world. Supposedly they're still there, under our feet." Leigh wasn't much interested in any sacrifice other than the sacrifice of her toes to the cold and damp. "I seem to recall that sulking children," Graham continued pointedly, "were often considered the best candidates for those sacrifices." It was growing dark by the time Graham turned them back towards home. Leigh ate both their sandwiches.

Despite her moping Leigh had not begrudged Graham his long days away. Even after Áine was gone, though the year Áine left was also the year Sam went away to the mainland for school and for the first time Leigh was left alone in the house. Graham always returned with some special stone or shell or leaf for her, and he tended the farm faithfully, and when he sold his articles about his latest finds, he would victoriously spend some of the extra income on an especially splendid tea. Later on the mainland she had thought back to those days, after Áine and before the war, when it was Leigh and Graham and a warm summer's afternoon, and thought that Graham must have been trying awfully hard to distract her from how far their once-perfect family had been flung. Now—with the sheep sold, the grass tall like an ocean, the dishes piling up in the sink—she wondered if perhaps she hadn't been the distraction all along.

When day finally broke in earnest, the Ben was far behind her. Where did one begin a search like this? Leigh thought she'd pick up where the others had left off. She cursed the fact that she was here alone, that she would be able to search only as fast as her own two legs could carry her across the island. Time was of the essence. Hugo, if he really was still here, could not survive alone on the moors forever.

Something moved in the haar up ahead and Leigh froze. The fog was thick and deep and possibly she'd imagined it. The shape of a man, or a boy, wandering, pausing, turning about in a slow circle.

"Who's there?" Leigh called into the shifting mists, and the silhouette leapt in surprise, whirling around.

"Sweet Christ," Iain MacTavish said, a hand splayed out on his chest, as he emerged from the fog. "I thought you were—" He shook his head. "Never mind. What are you doing up here by yourself?"

"I could ask you the same thing," Leigh said. Her heart was still beating insistently. It was not a usual place to run into someone, up on the moors, unless both parties were accompanied by some sheep or cows or other grazing creature. "At least I live near here."

Iain pulled a face. "I'm looking for Hugo McClare, actually," he said.

Which Leigh thought was an astonishing thing for him to say. Had Hugo ever mentioned Iain in his letters? She couldn't remember. He wasn't dressed for the moors, Leigh thought, he was wearing good shoes. No hat, the same old flight jacket he always wore. Unless he had deep pockets, he had brought with him no supplies of any kind.

"What a coincidence," she said. "So am I. I suppose you heard too."

"Heard what?"

"Oh," she said. "That everyone in town has stopped looking. They've given him up for dead." She found herself growing choked as she said it, a burning in the back of her throat. I will not cry again, she told herself firmly, and swallowed it.

"No," Iain said. "I hadn't heard. I—well, I couldn't sit around doing nothing anymore."

"Quite right." Leigh watched Maisie roll around in the grass at Iain's feet, flirting. "Well," she said, "if we're both going to be looking, we might as well look together."

Iain paused, and for a moment Leigh thought he might refuse her. He had a way of looking at a person, some unexplained intensity in the set of his jaw and the line of his gaze. What was it that everyone said about him? He had lost his soul somewhere above Germany. Leigh thought, blissfully, of a time when she had no idea where Germany was.

"All right," Iain agreed. "Where shall we start?"

8.

There was a burn that ran across the island from east to west, which, according to Leigh, was where the search for Hugo Mc-Clare had stopped. The bridge had been washed out some years ago by a peculiarly large thaw, and there was little incentive to fix it. There was nothing on the other side but moorland and heather, the small wood in the northwest, the ruins of the old cathedral in the northeast. Nobody had lived beyond the burn since the last of the Bruce women packed up after the first war, leaving their farmhouse to rot away in silence.

So Iain and Leigh started by searching for a place to cross the burn. After nearly an hour of slogging along the muddy bank they found one, a place where the water widened and grew shallower, the stream gentler, and large rocks peered up out of the surface. Maisie leapt joyously into the water, bounded across, emerged on the other side, and shook a thousand diamantine droplets of water into the cold air as Iain and Leigh followed.

"I brought my father's notebooks," Leigh said on the other side. These notebooks, apparently, held evidence of several places an adventurous young boy might have gotten trapped. An outcropping halfway down a cliffside, invisible from the bluff and accessible only by scrambling down a barely there staircase hewn into the rock. A ravine running through the little wood up in the northwest. The old crypts in the ruin of the ancient cathedral. For Graham Welles these places had been oddities, curiosities, things to be studied. For Iain and Leigh they had become a to-do list.

A fruitless one. They spent most of the day clambering along the treacherous ravine and found nothing apart from grass and mud and silence, not even the occasional odd relic of a time when traffic to this part of the island had been heavier. They searched until the light began to fade. There was no sign of whatever figment had led Iain up to the moors in the first place.

"I'll meet you by the Ben in the morning," Leigh said as they parted. They had not made any mention of what they would do tomorrow, or the next day, or the day after that. Perhaps, Iain thought, she felt the same pull he did, up towards the moors, the hills, the heather. Hugo the first thought in the morning and the last before sleep. Though it wasn't just that. A tiny, burning hope, a glimmer of absolution. All the people he hadn't saved, had allowed to quietly sail away into a violet evening, a blackout. It was too foolish to say aloud, but he nurtured the flame carefully. He didn't know what he would do if it went out.

The following morning he tried to leave the house without detection, but Mrs. Cavanagh's inhumanly sharp ears made such a feat impossible, and she found him in the kitchen making a cup of tea, already kitted up. "Where are you off to, then?" she asked, starting to make her porridge, and he told her he was on his way to meet Leigh Welles. She turned, an eyebrow arching. Iain added hurriedly, "It's nothing like that."

"Well," Mrs. Cavanagh said, "you tell that poor lass I was sorry to hear about her father." He watched her for a moment, but she appeared unbothered by it. Probably she was glad that he was leaving the house voluntarily. She'd attempted several reintegration schemes herself (book clubs, card games), though none for several months. Almost immediately upon her arrival she'd gotten him a job at the school, teaching history to the lower years. ("And why shouldn't you teach history? Lord knows you've lived enough of it, and you had your year at Cambridge. Mr. MacDonald was so pleased at the idea.") It hadn't stuck.

The second day of Iain and Leigh's search yielded equally poor results. "Do you think we could train Maisie," Iain said, after slipping on his way across the burn and landing face down in the stream, "to pick up his scent?"

Leigh looked sceptically at Maisie, sitting at her feet and wagging her tail happily. "Doubt it, I'm afraid," she said, and then offered him her sleeve to dry his face. "Unless Hugo smells like dog treats." For the rest of the day Iain's socks squelched in his shoes each time he took a step. Their search took them up to the northernmost tip of the island, past the Bruce farm, all the way to the abandoned cathedral. A place Iain and Matthew and the other lost boys had come sometimes, the rare summer evening that Iain was on the island. As they puttered about the ruins, Iain found an old beer bottle half-buried in the mud and wondered if this was some relic from one of those ancient binges. There was no sign of Hugo anywhere.

"It's a good thing you're doing, dear," Mrs. Cavanagh said when Iain returned in the evening, shoulders slumping, face sagging. Each fruitless step they trudged through the heather made that little flame sputter and flicker.

"Even if nothing comes of it?"

"He'll turn up, one way or another," Mrs. Cavanagh said grimly, handing him a whisky. "People don't disappear without a trace."

Iain said, "Sometimes they do."

Mrs. Cavanagh paused, sighed, brushed a hand across her face. "Sometimes they do," she said.

Mrs. Cavanagh knew something about the disappearance of people. Young men, especially. Thomas, her eldest, was killed in North Africa in March '42, and William fighting through Italy in August '44. Though that news didn't come for weeks, not until after Caroline was already buried. There was no protecting the children who had gone and, as it turned out, no protecting the ones who had stayed, either. Mr. Cavanagh had already died some years before (bad lungs; if it wasn't one thing it was something else), and now her house was empty.

Her friends (the few of them left; it seemed almost everyone had gone one way or another) had expressed their dismay when she announced as winter approached in 1947 that she was leaving Inverness in the new year, moving up to the islands to stay with her son-in-law. ("Shetland?" her friend Isobel had asked. She decided it was close enough.) At Caroline's funeral she had held both of Iain's hands in hers and told him that she expected him to write, at least every few months, let her know how he was doing.

He wore his uniform, of course. She refused to think about the unlikelihood of "every few months," but she treated each letter she received like it might be the last. At first his letters were little more than notes, mostly a report on his whereabouts. December 1944: *At the estate for Christmas, sorry I didn't look in.* September 1945: *Back on the island.* By August 1946—*Relocating to London; you'll find the address on the envelope*—he had begun to add a few extra lines, so she knew all about the disappearance of Alex Brodie and the departure of Angus Gordon. By October 1947—*Back on-island again*—His letters had grown to several pages, chaotic things written in many different pens over, it appeared, many days. Loneliness hung on the paper like perfume. Two weeks after receiving Iain's latest letter she made her announcement to her friends. "The man's almost thirty," Isobel had argued, "surely he can look after himself."

"You'll leave your whole life behind!" Margaret exclaimed. Which was largely the point. What life had she left, anyway? She had not told her friends, or anyone, that on VE Day while the rest of the world celebrated, she had stood in front of her kitchen window and wondered what point there was in carrying on like this. The war won, and for what? She had turned on the range and the pilot light hadn't caught, and she listened to the hiss of deadly gas for a moment before turning the knob off. It had all been terribly indulgent and she wouldn't be so foolish again. She still had something to give.

She raised her teacup. "A fresh start," she said, like a toast.

The days passed. They circled the island once, and then again, in case there was some sign they might have missed. Each morning when they met, Leigh's face was a little more drawn. Iain thought she was probably preparing herself for the worst. Imagining coming upon a torn and twisted carcass in a patch of bloodied grass. Finding a bone, a limb, a clump of hair. Iain had not seen for himself the damage the sluagh could do to a person, but last year the creatures had gotten at one of the Blakes' cows. It had been a bloody affair. The villagers had kept finding pieces of the poor animal scattered about town for nearly a week.

Iain himself was doing his best not to imagine the worst. The days passed, and they circled the island. They picked through the moss-grown ruins of ancient, long-abandoned settlements. They searched the woods in the northwest and little caves that formed in the sides of the hills. They found nothing.

Until. Up ahead Maisie stopped, pawed at something in the grass, tail wagging madly. She emerged from the grass with something in her mouth. "Hey," Iain called back to Leigh, who had fallen a few steps behind. "I think Maisie's trying to eat something."

"Oh, excellent," Leigh said, catching up. "We'll never get her to drop it, she's got jaws of steel. Maisie!" she called, and the dog perked up. Leigh pointed at the ground at her feet, and Maisie trotted over, reluctantly. Whatever was in her mouth caught the light. "Drop it," Leigh said authoritatively, the way one might talk to a small child. Maisie stared up at her with wide, doleful eyes, and then delicately deposited her find in the grass at Leigh's feet.

It was covered in mud and dog spit but it looked, maybe, like an old cigarette lighter. Iain bent to pick it up, wiped it off on his trousers. Burnished brass with delicate engravings along its edges. A familiar weight in his hand.

"This is Hugo's," he said, and Leigh, who had crouched down to praise Maisie for releasing her treasure so easily, looked up at him sharply.

"You're sure?"

"He had it, the last night I saw him," he said. "The night of the ritual, he let me borrow it."

Leigh turned and looked out across the heath, up north, the direction their search was progressing. "So sometime after the ritual," she said, "he came all the way up here."

The wind whistled across the moor, whipping Leigh's hair out of its pins, stinging Iain's eyes. Maisie lay down and pressed her head flat against the ground, looking uncomfortable. Leigh was right: Hugo must have come up here sometime between the first and second of October. The question was why. And what he did after.

A dark shadow passed over their heads, and they turned their eyes skywards. A cloud of crows, cavorting through the air northwards. They had an uncanny ability, the sluagh, to appear out of nowhere, in situations where one should have seen them coming a mile off. Leigh seemed to shrink beneath them, a tightening of her shoulders as she buried her hands in her pockets. Iain felt it, too, a thinning of the air, like there wasn't enough to go around now that the sluagh were here.

"Is it really true?" Leigh asked, her voice low as if the birds might overhear them. "About the sluagh, what they're like now?"

Iain said, "I don't remember what they were like before."

(What he was thinking of mostly was the bomber stream, how from the ground when the searchlights found them it must have looked not unlike the crush of birds in the air above him now.)

"Before," Leigh said, something in her voice turning, "nobody would ever have believed for two seconds that if a boy went missing on a Saturday evening, he'd be dead by Monday. Before, they might have been birds."

Iain thought about the Octobers he had spent here. As a small boy all he remembered was the blur and bustle of the festival as the most tremendous fun. All he had to judge by were the three Octobers since, '45 and '47 and '48. Could they just be birds? Iain had wondered often since he had returned to stay. They didn't seem to do anything that a normal bird couldn't do; they only did things that normal birds wouldn't do. The way that they always alighted in threes, the way that their eyes followed a person walking down the street at dusk. The way that they showed up on the first of October like clockwork—never the thirty-first of September, never the second of October—and disappeared as if atomised into the air at the end of it. The way that they danced in the air, as they danced now: undeniably otherworldly.

And. That first October he had sat in his front room with Angus, diligently working through a bottle of whisky, while outside the sluagh wreaked their havoc, one night nearly pecking right through the boarded windows of the butcher shop. ("Must be all the blood, I bet they like it," Angus had said.) The year Iain returned, in '47, Mr. Lowery was caught unawares, and now where his left eye should have been there was only skin and scar. Just last year a girl was attacked on her way to school, lifted right out of her shoes before she wriggled free and ran to Dr. Delaune's surgery to be stitched up. And none of that was even taking into account the dozens of animals—sheep, goats, ponies, the occasional house cat—that had met their untimely ends.

Were they birds, acting inexplicably, or was there something magical about them? He hadn't noticed the rituals or the sacrifices or the charms doing anything to change the birds' behaviour. It didn't matter much why the crows came and terrorised, as knowing why would not change the fact that they came. Either way, magical or mundane, it didn't seem unbelievable to Iain at all that a boy who went missing on a Saturday evening might be dead by Monday. Actually that wasn't true: it was completely unbelievable—wholly and utterly impossible, a terrible nightmare—but it was real. Which was exactly the problem.

He didn't say any of this. Instead he said, "We should go. Before they get any ideas," and he hurried Leigh off the moor.

The islanders had been right about one thing, at least, in giving up their search for Hugo McClare: this island was simply not that large. There was nowhere new to look. People didn't disappear without a trace, except for when they did.

9.

On a bright afternoon she stood in the garden. The grass pressing against her bare feet. Sunshine. At the end of the field dotted with sheep the Ben crept out of the trees, stretching up towards the sky. In the house behind her she could hear a small boy running barefoot on wooden floors, a man's voice calling out to him in a language she had yet to grasp.

A bright afternoon, summertime. Insects humming in the grass. A large wicker bassinet sat in the shade under the tree by the fence. She walked over to it, stood under the light filtering through the leaves, a green-and-gold patchwork glow on her skin. The baby in the bassinet cooed up at her. All big blue eyes and fluffy golden curls. She reached down and the baby reached up, wrapped a chubby fist around her finger.

A boy called out, *Mama!* and she turned around. (Why did she turn around?) Sam stood in the doorway, Graham in the shadows of the house behind him. It was Sam's birthday, he was eight. Abruptly the day shifted. The sun was too bright, glaring off the windows, blinding. The grass against her feet was sharp like pins. The smile on Sam's face was twisting into a grimace or a jeer. Graham had been behind Sam but now he was next to her and his hand on her shoulder was too heavy, his fingers gripped hard enough to bruise. The baby's hold on her finger was too tight. She looked down at Leigh, three months old, in the bassinet. The wedding ring on her finger felt like it was shrinking, like it would keep getting smaller and tighter and narrower until it took her finger off entirely. The sun beat down, down, down, and her golden hair burned, burned, burned, a molten crown.

Áine pulled her hand out of Leigh's grip, and there was darkness.

Someone said her name, a whisper in the dark.

10.

A gasping breath and Leigh bolted awake. Maisie perked up, her ears pricked, as Leigh pressed her cold hands to her face. "Just a dream," she said—to herself, to the dog, to the room. "Just a dream." The dog licked at Leigh's fingers, her cheeks, until Leigh pushed her away and she leapt off the bed and clattered down the stairs.

The dream lingered at the edges of her vision. There was nothing about it particularly that should have her heart beating so hard, her lungs screaming for air. There was nothing about it that should make her feel so claustrophobic, so trapped. Except, she supposed, for the fact that in the dream she had been Áine, and Áine had made it clear that this house—and the people in it—were things to be escaped.

Somewhere below, Maisie started barking madly, and Leigh peeled herself from bed, retrieved a jumper from the floor, went to the bathroom to wash her face. The cold water returned her to herself, somewhat. She looked up into her face in the mirror. It had been a while since she'd properly looked at herself instead of catching a glimpse of her flyaway hair, and the woman in the glass was almost unrecognisable. There was a smudge on the mirror over her left eye. She reached up to wipe it clean with her cuff. What did she see? A face made small and hard, a sullen sort of anger in the straight line of her eyebrows and the set of her mouth. At the world for changing, at George for being a twat. At her brother for his absence, at her father for dying, at her mother for disappearing so entirely.

At the heart of it, a small, molten ball, held tightly between her lungs: at herself, herself, herself.

Downstairs Maisie was not at the back door as usual but pawing nervously at the front. Her tail tucked between her legs. "What is it?" Leigh asked, and Maisie fled into the belly of the house. "Maisie!" Leigh called, but the dog refused to return. Leigh peered out the small diamond window set into the front door but couldn't see anything through the warped glass. She opened the door.

The smell of blood filled her nose before her eyes understood what they were seeing. A sheep's carcass, torn and mangled, sprawled on her front steps as though someone had begun to drag it towards the threshold and given up halfway. A terrible, irregular slash along its belly, a bit of intestine poking out. Her stomach turned.

Movement in her peripheral vision, a dark shadow. She looked up and stumbled back over the threshold as three crows swept out of the air. They landed on the front steps. One of them stared at her with black, glassy eyes. Leigh's heart leapt into her throat. She reached for the charm Hugo had given her, but she didn't have it; she was only in her pyjamas.

The bird blinked at her once. There was a rust-red smear across its shiny beak. It turned its head unnaturally slowly, seemingly uninterested in Leigh in the doorway. All three of the creatures started to attack the carcass of the McClares' sheep, and then three more birds tumbled down through the air and joined them. Leigh could only watch in horror as the birds tore at the sheep's innards. One of them began to peck at the sheep's eyes and she snapped back into herself. She slammed the door shut.

When she returned, her hands were full of herbs from the bunches that Graham had kept in the kitchen, that were slowly shedding detritus all over the counters and the floor. She could hear his voice in her head. Betony, mint, rue. St. John's wort and thyme. A little bit of sage. "All good things to plant in a garden," he'd told her when she was maybe four or five, crouched next to him in the dirt. He'd leaned in close like he was telling her a secret. "Keep away the fairies."

Leigh didn't know what herbs she'd managed to grab or if they really did keep away fairies, but she had to get the sluagh away from the sheep so she could get the sheep away from her house. She pressed her face against the warped window but she still couldn't see anything, just dark shadows moving across the milky world. She eased the door open a crack. There were now twelve sluagh clamouring for a mouthful of sheep. She was prepared for them to turn on her, but they didn't even seem to notice her presence; they were too busy pulling, tearing, shredding. Leigh opened the door a little wider. Took a step out onto the porch. She held the herbs up to her chest for a moment, breathed in their dry, earthy smell.

She flung the herbs at the sluagh, like rice at a wedding. The birds screeched and screamed and surged into the sky and Leigh dropped to the ground, wrapping her hands around her ears. Their wings beat the air as they took flight, and then they were gone.

Leigh wasn't sure what she was supposed to do with what remained of the McClares' sheep, so she buried it neatly in the yard, wrapped in a bit of old canvas she'd found in the barn. Within moments of fighting the cold ground with an old rusty shovel, she had sweated through her pyjama top, her jumper already discarded, tossed over a rotting fence post. She paused, wiped her hand across her forehead. The McClare house peered out of the morning haar across the field. Perhaps she ought to tell them about the sheep instead of hiding it here next to the barn. But Leigh would not—could not—walk over there and knock on the door and proudly present to them a visual example of what might have become of their youngest son.

She wished she hadn't seen it herself. Last night had been the first that she hadn't stumbled to bed through a mist of tears—for her father, for Hugo, for herself. It was a cigarette lighter but it felt like a sign, it felt like proof that if there were anything of Hugo to find on this island they would have found it, that Hugo must be cleverer than all of them, must have found some way away. She wished she hadn't seen the half-eaten carcass of the sheep, the way the sluagh began to disappear it.

Leigh leaned on her shovel and caught her breath. The Mc-Clare house in the distance was small and quiet, the last of the morning mist spreading out over the field between the two farms like a blanket. A blanket, or an ocean. Leigh had been an excellent navigator of that ocean once. Now the water was rough, and dark, and foreign, and it had been so long since she had gone sailing.

She buried the sheep quietly, and went inside to dress.

During the war Leigh had become good at it. Bereavement. Other people's. Whenever the telegrams came with their terrible news, Leigh would turn up soon after, with a casserole in one hand and some distraction for the remaining children in the other—a game she had invented, a chocolate bar she'd saved up her ration coupons to buy, the small bleached skull of an animal she had found in the grass. Anything to get the children out of the house. When Mr. Taylor was killed, she taught his daughter, Gwen, how to skip stones in the harbour. When David Murray was killed, she taught his little sister Margaret how the engine of Graham's car worked. When Matthew Mc-Clare disappeared, she had sat with Hugo on a little spit of dirt overlooking East Sands, one last outcropping before the island fell away to sea.

This was the same, Leigh thought as she stood outside the McClare farm, only now the war was October. She felt the same dread as she considered the house, the minister's car parked by the fence, and wondered how she would be received, whether they would feel she was drawing out the inevitable. She supposed the McClares had some experience in this regard. Probably,

Leigh thought, they still harboured hope that Matthew would simply step off the ferry one morning. That which was lost now found. It had happened before, a few times. Why not again? "People are coming home all the time," Leigh told George after the war was over, when Matthew had been missing for nearly a year, when she was about to leave herself. "People everyone thought were gone."

George had shaken his head. "It's no good, Leigh," he said. "This is our lot."

It was Mr. McClare who answered the door when she knocked, and everything about him sagged. His shoulders falling in a slow curve towards the floor. It took him some time to focus on her, his eyes clearing only after she said a quiet "Hello."

"Oh," he said. "Hello, Leigh."

What was there to say? Leigh twisted two fistfuls of her skirt in her hands. She said, "I'm so sorry," and it was entirely insufficient.

Mr. McClare's jaw clenched and he nodded. He rolled his shoulders back and pinned them there. Leigh wanted to wrap her arms around him and squeeze as though she could hold him together but she didn't, she couldn't.

"A bad few weeks for this island, isn't it?" Mr. McClare said. "But that's the way of it, I suppose. Seasons."

"I suppose so."

They considered each other, and Leigh tried not to think about how much he had changed since she had seen him last. How deep the lines on his forehead had become, how tired his eyes. She had planned to ask if she could look in Hugo's room, see if she could find any clues, but now that she was standing in front of the house, in front of Hugo's father, she had lost her nerve.

"I'm afraid no one is really at home at present," Mr. McClare said. "I'm about to head back to town. The missus is upstairs with the minister. She couldn't bring herself to go to church today. He was kind enough to come up to see her personally."

"That's good of him."

Mr. McClare nodded. "Kate's gone to the Blakes' to borrow some flour," he said. "And George is—I don't know where George is. He's barely been home since."

Leigh might've had some idea of where George would have gone once, but now she did not let her mind turn to it. "That's all right," Leigh said. "I wanted to—stop by."

"That's kind of you," Mr. McClare said. "I'll tell everyone you called."

He began to close the door, and Leigh turned away. In the few minutes she had spent speaking to Mr. McClare, a host of sluagh had alighted onto the minister's car. Their talons scraped against the paint, high-pitched and grating. For a moment Leigh could smell the iron tang of blood again, could see the gutted sheep on her doorstep. The terrible things these sluagh could do to a living creature if given the opportunity.

"Mr. McClare," Leigh said, spinning around again, throwing her arm out to stop him closing the door. "I don't—you can tell me to get out if you want to, but I couldn't—I don't think we should stop looking for Hugo. I don't think you should give up. If you'd let me, I'd like to see if he left anything in his room, any hints or—anything."

Mr. McClare didn't move, just looked down at her with a vacant sort of expression. "I don't see," he said at last, "what the point would be."

Leigh thought again about how acceptance looked an awful lot like giving up. "My father—" she began, and surprised herself by feeling a lump rise in her throat. "He knew better than anyone that there are more secret places on this island than any of us know. Or maybe he went off-island, some way we haven't thought of."

Mr. McClare said, "Do you really think so?"

There was something in his voice, buried there, that made Leigh lose her breath. Hope. A visitor whose stays on this island had become shorter and shorter, less and less frequent, until Leigh realised she had forgotten what it sounded like altogether. She replied, "I do."

Mr. McClare looked back into the house, like someone had called him, though no one had. There were the faint beginnings of a bald spot on the back of his head. He turned again to face Leigh. "Well, lass," he said. "I suppose you'd better come in."

The last time Leigh had been in the McClare boys' bedroom: 1945, July, she and Kate sitting on George's bed while he hurriedly cleaned up and Hugo trailed behind him "trying to help!" he claimed, but mostly undoing George's work. It was a rare warm day and they were going down to East Sands, but Mrs. McClare had told George he wasn't allowed out of the house until the disaster of the attic room had been rectified. Then George had told Hugo that he couldn't come along unless he helped George clean, so now here they were. George had stood back and surveyed the room that looked no cleaner than when he had started. "Maybe we should jump out the window," he suggested. "Oh, sure," Kate said, plaiting Leigh's hair. "But don't expect me to wheel you around after you've broken every bone in your body."

There was a chance, Leigh thought as she stood in the doorway, that neither McClare boy had cleaned this room since. Clothes and books strewn about, broken pens and single socks littering the floor. An empty cigarette packet, mismatched shoes by the door. Leigh ventured in. It felt archaeological, like she could peel back each layer of ephemera and discover some new secret.

She picked her way across the floor until George's half of the room was behind her. She would prefer to pretend that this wasn't George's room at all, that George himself didn't exist. Hugo's bed sat unmade by the window, the sheets twisted up, the pillow still indented from the weight of his head. A stack of comic books next to his bed, a book left open, upside down, saving his place. As if to taunt her: he was here, he was just here, only a moment ago.

Leigh crouched down next to the comics. Who knew what kind of things teenage boys hid under their beds? Actually she wasn't sure that she wanted to know. She reached an arm under the bed, swiped her hand along the floor. A sharp stinging pain in her finger and she withdrew her hand quickly. A splinter in her finger, one little bead of blood clinging to her skin. Leigh dug the splinter out, wiped the blood away, reached under the bed again. Her hand closed around something smooth and cool. A model aeroplane, a Spitfire she thought, though her recall had grown sluggish since the days of the war when they'd pored over drawings of all the British and German aircraft they thought maybe they'd see overhead one day (an expectation never realised).

It seemed there was nothing else under the bed but dust and more mismatched socks. She turned to the desk in the corner. A mess of papers, mostly Hugo's homework. She thumbed through the papers. Worksheets, essays, notes. A fair share of doodles, too, a few caricatures (quite good ones) of Mr. Mac-Donald. She picked up some of the drawings and a little scrap of paper fell from the pile. A blackened, curled edge. Someone had tried to burn this paper and had not finished the job.

Dear Mr. McClare—

We would be delighted to host you until you have settled in. I've already begun to make some inquiries on your beh

Leigh flipped the paper over, hoping for a return address, any distinguishing features, but there was nothing. Nothing to indicate for which Mr. McClare the letter had been intended, nothing to indicate from where the letter had come. Just those truncated sentences and the gently curling, charcoaled edge.

The floorboards creaked behind her and Leigh spun around, the scrap of letter falling from her hand. George filled up the doorway and Leigh froze, prey caught. "Leigh," he said, and his voice broke the room's stillness, and Leigh remembered herself, pushed past him into the hall. He was not the boy she'd been in love with once; he was a man who thought she was his for the taking. She wasn't, she thought viciously, she was not prey caught. "Leigh, wait, I—"

But she was already clattering down the stairs.

"Of course it isn't much to go on," Iain said to Leigh as they skirted along the cliff at the northwest edge of the island and she told him about Hugo McClare's bedroom, the fragment of a letter she had found there. There was nowhere new to look but neither of them was willing to admit it, especially now, with the old cigarette lighter carefully tucked into Iain's pocket. Perhaps they would keep looping about the island for the rest of their lives. Iain still hadn't told her about the spectre he had seen that early morning. He had tried to convince himself that it had been Leigh, embarking on her search for Hugo—but she was the wrong height, the wrong shape, and he couldn't come up with a good reason why she'd have been down in the village. He had not asked her. How would such a conversation begin? Do you believe in ghosts? A preposterous thing to ask, most places. Maybe not here. Instead he kept it to himself, tried not to jump when he thought he saw something move in the mists ahead and it turned out only to be Maisie, tried to pretend he didn't feel like those mists themselves were watching, tried to convince himself that it had been a trick of the early light.

"I know," Leigh said, trying to prevent the wind from whipping her hair into her mouth. "It could be the mainland, or the big island, or anywhere."

Anywhere indeed. The world, Iain thought, was wide. Just this morning the post had brought a letter from Roger Neilson, the flight engineer on Iain's first aircraft, call sign A for Able.

Roger was in shipping now, and though this letter was post-marked from London, his letters came far more frequently from Australia, America, Japan. It seemed he hadn't had enough travelling during the war, and his letters usually reflected a level of detail worthy of Johnson or Boswell. The food he had eaten and the people he had met, the great art he had seen. The shipping business was going well. Iain looked forward to Roger's letters but found he had little desire of his own to see the world. What he longed for, still, was the sky.

"I think it's a good sign," Leigh said, firmly. "I think it means that he left."

Iain glanced over the edge of the cliff at the water crashing below. Cold and blue. Leigh seemed buoyed up by her discovery, but Iain wasn't so sure; his hope was fading. How much longer could they traipse across the moors? Eventually they would have to start searching the beaches, where nothing good could be found. (He thought again of Mr. Welles's pale, bloated hand.) And as hope faded, it gave way to the first flickers of something deep and dense and devastating. He felt himself teetering on the edge of it, his balance failing a little more with each day that passed. Mrs. Cavanagh had noticed already. "Perhaps it's time," she said, gently, this morning. Iain could not explain to her his inability to come to such a conclusion, not without opening a door to something he wasn't sure he'd be able to close again.

"Don't you think there'd be some clue?" he asked Leigh. "A boat missing, a ferryman who saw him, something?"

"Don't you think we'd have found him if he were still here?"

In the days since Hugo's disappearance this little scrap of paper was the closest anybody had come to finding any evidence that Hugo had ever existed at all. That and the lighter. "Well," he said. "There might be an old pal I can write. Actually I've just gotten a letter from a friend in shipping. He'd know who to ask—you know, at the docks, and everything."

Leigh nodded. "That sounds sensible. It's good to at least feel like we're doing something useful, isn't it?"

Iain agreed that it was. Leigh picked up a stick and tossed it into the heather for Maisie to chase. "Sam's always on at me for not doing anything useful with my life. Well, not compared to him, anyway. But we can't all be decorated war heroes by the time we're twenty-five." She glanced over at him sharply. "Oh," she said, flustered. "I didn't mean—I forgot—"

"It's all right," he said. In two years the only people on this island he'd heard mention the war without turning tongue-tied were himself and Mrs. Cavanagh. For everybody else it appeared entirely off-limits. (*Verboten*, he thought. Caroline had learnt a little German and tried to teach him some too, "in case you get captured," she said. "Know thy enemy.") "Anyway," he continued, "I don't know that I'm much of a war hero."

Leigh shrugged. "You were useful, though." Her voice taking a dark turn. "I wanted to be a WAAF, you know."

"Did you really?" Iain said. He couldn't remember if any of the island girls had joined the WAAF but probably they had. He remembered clearly that Nancy McCafferty had joined the FANY, all rather secretive until word came, several years after the war, that she'd been parachuted into France ahead of the invasion and never heard from again. All the WAAFs at his airfield had been sweet on Matthew. "Nice girls. Women, sorry. Plucky." The word was inadequate for the things the WAAFs had put up with, and seen. A memory, rising to the surface of his mind unbidden—waiting to take off for a sortie one fine evening, and a massive explosion on the runway ahead of them. A Rhodesian crew had not managed take-off and had gone in with their full bomb-load. The WAAFs had been the ones to clean up later.

Leigh shot him a look. "Don't condescend," she said. Iain raised a hand in protest. When the explosion had rung out, he had shimmied out of his seat and gone racing along the runway to see if there was anything to be done. There wasn't. What there had been was this: a single dismembered foot lying on the runway a hundred yards from the tower of flame that had once been a four-engined Avro Lancaster and seven Rhodesian men.

Iain said, "I mean it," and Leigh softened a bit. "What did you do, then," he asked, "during the war, if you didn't join the WAAF?" He'd thought she'd have been too young to join up anyway, but the way she talked about it alluded to some festering shame about it, some reason for Sam to be on at her. Maybe it wasn't shame, he thought, but a misguided disappointment. A feeling that she'd missed something.

Leigh opened her mouth to answer, closed it again. "I didn't do anything," she said. "I didn't do anything at all."

"I'm sorry for making you talk about it," she said later, as they approached his front gate. She'd said she had some errands to run so had come with him all the way into town. "The war, I mean. My brother doesn't like to."

No, Iain thought, most people didn't. Sometimes he felt he couldn't stop talking about it. Or thinking about it, at least.

There were certain things he would never tell anyone (a single dismembered foot), but mostly because he didn't want to trouble anyone else with carrying them. Whether one liked it or not, it was impossible, he thought, to avoid talking about all of it entirely. It had been nearly six years of his life, the formative years, and he didn't know how he could pretend it hadn't happened without denying half or more of who he had become.

"Well," he said, "Sam saw some pretty terrible things."

"Yes," Leigh said, distaste lacing her voice. (For the terrible things? Or for Sam?) "So he's said."

"He liberated Dachau," Iain said, "didn't you know?"

For a moment he wondered if she had heard him at all. She paused, looked back the way they had come. "No," Leigh said at last. "I didn't know."

Before Iain could settle on something to say, Mrs. Cavanagh appeared at his front door and called down the path. "There you are," she said. "I was just putting on tea." She planted her hands on her hips and studied Leigh, standing on the other side of the gate. She said, "You must be Miss Welles."

"Aye," Leigh said, "I'm Leigh."

Mrs. Cavanagh looked her up and down, like she was considering what work ought to be done first. (Iain felt strangely like he was the one being appraised, weighed and measured.) "I was so sorry about your father," she said. "He seemed like a lovely man. I wish I'd known him better."

"Yes," Leigh said. "Me too. I mean, thank you."

"Can I convince you to stay for some tea?"

"Oh," Leigh said, "no. Thank you. I really should be going." She pulled the edges of her coat tight around herself and seemed to shrink with it, as though she drew her ribs inwards too. "I'll see you later," she said to Iain, and then she turned, clicked her tongue at Maisie, and disappeared down the lane.

For a moment Iain and Mrs. Cavanagh stood in the doorway, watching the place where Leigh had been, until at last Iain remembered himself—or, more accurately, his numb, cold fingers—and squeezed by Mrs. Cavanagh to the warmth inside. "Poor thing," said Mrs. Cavanagh, closing the door behind him. "The world doesn't seem to let up on her." It didn't, nor on any-one else particularly. "Try to get her to come for tea, or dinner, or something. It can't be good for her, all alone in that house."

Iain wondered if this meant that he had passed whatever test he thought Mrs. Cavanagh might have been administering. He shrugged out of his coat and fled into the study, which was more a museum than anything else, filled with paraphernalia and dust. A handful of medals in little green boxes. A uniform peeking out from a wardrobe. A stack of photographs on the desk. One of him being forced into playing cricket, one of him and his first crew lounging in garden furniture on the airfield one summer afternoon. One in a simple gold frame. A young man with a girl on his arm outside a register office. This was the only room in the house Mrs. Cavanagh never appeared to enter, and so dust seemed to hang in the air perpetually. On sunny days the light caught on it and danced golden. Today it made him sneeze.

Iain stood at the window and lit a cigarette, gazed out at the muted colours of the world. Rain splattered on the glass. A man was walking down the lane away from the high street, collar flipped up against the rain and hat pulled low. He stopped in front of Iain's gate and turned to face the house.

It was Mr. McClare.

Iain froze, cigarette halfway to ashtray, but Mr. McClare hadn't noticed him behind the warped, rain-streaked glass. For half a second Iain considered ducking out of view entirely but decided that wrapping himself in the drapes like a child playing hide-and-seek was perhaps a bridge too far. He raised his cigarette to his lips again but did not inhale.

Mr. McClare stood and stared at Iain's front door. The man looked insubstantial, like paper slowly dissolving out in the damp. Mr. McClare placed a hand on Iain's gate. Iain braced himself as though for a hard landing. Perhaps—as with a hard landing—it would be better to get it over with, to tap on the window or go to the door, to finally break his silence, to speak to Matthew's father. Hugo's father. He didn't know what he would say.

And then Mr. McClare dropped his hand from the gate and turned away.

Iain released his breath. It wasn't cowardly, he told himself, hiding behind the fogged windowpane. A confrontation would be premature. By the most charitable of reckonings he had allowed the eldest McClare boy to be lost, but he would not let the same fate befall the youngest. He would speak to the McClares. But he'd do it when he had some news, word from Hugo in hand or even Hugo himself. He'd do it when he had something good to tell them.

Iain turned away from the window and went to place a call to Roger Neilson.

11.

It was a mistake to tell him about the WAAF.

As she hurried away down the high street, Leigh felt keenly that she had revealed something to Iain that she hadn't intended to. Something she carried tightly between her ribs like a caged bird.

A miasma of shame hung around the memory. It had been a topic of conversation amongst the girls in her class. "It'd be nice to be useful, wouldn't it?" Leigh had said to Kate as they walked home from school, a few weeks before Leigh's eighteenth birthday.

"Don't be daft," Kate said. "You are useful." And it was true: without Leigh there would have been no home front effort from the island at all. There had been long afternoons spent in the church hall teaching the girls and some of the boys to knit endless scarves and comforters for the soldiers overseas. Weekend contests devised by Leigh and Kate for the children, to see who could procure the most scrap metal and aluminium pans from the neighbours to send to the mainland to be melted down for parts. Letter writing and gardening and morale building. More than anything else Leigh wanted to be useful, but lately "useful" seemed like a moving target.

"I don't know," Leigh said. "I don't think I could bear Sam's self-righteousness if I didn't. I think I'll have to join to shut him up."

A few days later Leigh bounded down the stairs to find her father half-asleep in the sitting room, and she'd leaned against the door and said, "I've decided."

Graham jolted awake. "Decided? Decided what?"

"I'm going to be a WAAF," she said proudly. She'd struck a little pose, a hands-on-hips, chin-raised-defiantly sort of thing, the very picture of a propaganda poster. (We Can Do It!) Graham had looked perplexed and she said, "The Women's Auxiliary Air Force. They do all sorts, codes and radar and such."

Graham peered up at her silently. He looked oddly naked without Bo sitting next to him. The dog had died barely a year before and Graham hadn't yet been able to bring himself to replace him. "You'll do this in May?" he asked. "Once you're eighteen?"

"Yes," Leigh said. "Do my bit, and all that." She wanted to do something that mattered, to put her hands to some proper work, instead of knitting and rolling bandages until her fingers ached. War was no longer confined to the battlefield and she couldn't bear the emptiness of the town, of the people in it. Already she was beginning to feel it, though it would not hit her in full force until the morning after VE Day, a tender, tired morning like a bruise.

"I should have thought you'd have been gung-ho for the ATV," Graham said, "with your cars, and all."

"Yes," Leigh said, "but I already know cars. This way I'll learn aeroplanes."

Graham nodded slowly. "Very admirable," he said, picking up his book again. "But God knows I hope this war doesn't last long enough for it to matter."

As it turned out, it didn't. Leigh's eighteenth birthday came in early May, and three days later Germany surrendered. The celebration in town was like nothing Leigh had ever seen, better than any of the festivals—the May Day bunting still up, strung from window to window, a *ceilidh* in the middle of the street, Tom McAllister drunker than anyone had ever seen him and weaving through the crowd handing out free pints to anyone with a spare hand to take a glass. Leigh danced with George McClare and drank Tom's beer and ended the night (if it could be called a night at all, when in summer the sky never grew dark but simply changed, streaking pink and mauve and gold) at five in the morning at the stone circle with all the others her age, passing around an old bottle of whisky and screaming joyful wordlessness at the open sky.

She had been joyful, truly. She was, she told George, "so desperately glad" that the war was over, that the suffering was finished, that everyone could come home. They lay shoulder to shoulder on the great flat rock in the centre of the standing stones, could hear the others hollering as they gambolled back along the bluff towards the stairs down to the beach. One of the boys bellowed a terrible rendition of "Bewitched, Bothered, and Bewildered" to Brighid MacEwan, presumably, nearly all the boys their age were soft on her. A night that felt like what every day had felt like on the island before this dreadful interlude. Before the news came regularly and seemed to matter, before the telephone box was installed on the corner, before most of the boys and a number of the girls had gone off and not come back.

Leigh would never admit it, but most of the desperation to her gladness was a sprawling, wordless guilt. That while her brother had been off nearly dying, she had been sitting in a warm house knitting. When the summer came, she enrolled in a postal course in shorthand and in September moved to the mainland to begin a job as a secretary. "I'm so excited," she told everybody who asked. "A new adventure!" Which was, of course, barely the half of it.

A cloying smell finally pulled her out of herself as she passed the Gordons' grocery. Sweet and metallic, a smell she felt in the back of her throat. Leigh glanced up to find the source and froze mid-step.

The window of the Gordons' grocery was covered in blood. Strange patterns and spiky, uneven symbols drawn crudely, finger-painted. She turned away and clapped a hand over her mouth. She was not particularly squeamish but this, she thought, would make anybody's stomach turn, because nailed to the door of the post office was something that looked like the entrails of some poor creature. She looked away but found similar sights displayed on at least three other doors.

"It's crude, but it seems to work."

Leigh tore her eyes away from the runic scrawling over the Gordons' door and found Mr. Harrower standing in the gutter behind her. Giving the appearance that nothing had changed at all, dressed as he always had, the same tweed waistcoat under his waxed jacket, the same flat cap on his head. Graham had always hated Mr. Harrower but could never explain why. ("That man," he said on a number of occasions, "sets my teeth on edge.") Leigh thought probably it was because Mr. Harrower had liked to consider himself quite the creature of the modern world. He'd been the head of the town council Leigh's whole life, a title he retained mostly because nobody could be bothered to challenge him for it. It went to his head. There were no sluagh for Mr. Harrower, only superstition and folklore, fancy. The crows were just crows. That they only showed up in force on the first of October? A strange migratory pattern. That they were always spotted in threes? Co-incidence, a pattern spotted where none existed. Even in the war he had remained stalwartly unconvinced. "It'll be all the aero-planes and such," he said, authoritatively, when asked to explain the growing number of birds. "Driving them from their roosts." When Lucy McCafferty was found, he insisted on interviewing each of the islanders in turn, threw around ridiculous words like "alibi" and "suspect." Nobody had spoken to him for weeks.

Graham's ill feeling had rubbed off on Leigh, which she supposed was unfair. Mr. Harrower's son had died in the war and his wife several months later. She wondered if grief might have altered him.

Mr. Harrower put his hands into his pockets and looked up at the bloody symbols as one might appraise a great carving or sculpture. "We've been at it a few years now. Seems to keep them at bay. Of course, it seems we needed something stronger this year. The poor McClare boy, you ken."

Leigh said, "I thought you didn't believe in the sluagh. I thought it was all just stuff and nonsense."

"Well," Mr. Harrower replied. "I suppose things change." He turned and surveyed the street dispassionately. "You should stop round the butcher's," he said. "I'm sure Mrs. Taylor would be able to look something out for you."

Leigh pressed her lips together. If there was one thing she would not do, it was nail rotting offal to her door. There was only so much that one person could endure. And besides, it had been a disembowelled sheep that had attracted the sluagh to her own door in the first place. She said, "Thanks for the tip."

"It's a strange new world we're living in, to be sure," Mr. Harrower said. "But one has to change with the times. Old Mr. Morrison was telling me this morning how it all comes in cycles. Seasons, he called it."

Instinctively Leigh glanced west, up at the Morrison farm sitting on the hillside. The Morrisons had been on this island longer than anybody, maybe since the beginning of it, when rock pushed its way out of sea. At least four generations lived in that mammoth farmhouse. Old Mr. Morrison and his son Young Mr. Morrison and too many other Morrisons to reasonably assign descriptive epithets. Nobody knew more about the island's history than Old Morrison ("Well, he would," Sam had said once, "he was there for all of it"), but she could not remember the last time anyone who was not a Morrison themself had seen him. When they were small, George had told Leigh and Kate that Old

Morrison never left the house because he was so old that when the wind blew, he would drift away into the air like paper. Later Leigh had asked her father how old Old Morrison actually was and Graham paused and said, "You know, I really couldn't say."

"If it's a new season," Leigh said, perhaps too harshly, "maybe we should all stop walking around like it's still the war."

Mr. Harrower stared at her, unblinking, unmoving. She remembered herself, abruptly, remembered what Tom had told her about not bringing up the war. "I just mean maybe things could do with some sprucing up," she said. "Now that, you know, our attention isn't elsewhere."

Still Mr. Harrower didn't respond. Suddenly he unfroze, like a spell being broken. "Yes," he said, loudly. "Old Mr. Morrison has had so many suggestions for the sluagh, he's invaluable. We should get him to write a book so we never have to be without his knowledge, don't you think?"

Like she'd never spoken at all. She wondered what Graham had thought of it, this new make and model of Mr. Harrower. This man who had retreated from the world, gone from scoffing at the fancy to steeping himself in it. Had Graham been satisfied or sad?

Mr. Harrower was waiting for her reply. "I suppose so," Leigh said. "I didn't know Old Mr. Morrison had so many ideas about how we ought to be doing things."

"Well, you know what they say," Mr. Harrower said, stepping off the curb into the street. "Still waters run deep."

There were other changes about the island, things she hadn't noticed at first. Today's search had taken Iain and Leigh past the Blakes' farm. Even from the road she could tell that the barn had not been used in some time. The roof was pockmarked with holes, and the doors hung from their hinges. Birds covered every surface, flew in and out like trains arriving and departing at a station. The place belonged to the sluagh.

What else was different? Less obvious things. Fields that should have been ready for harvest instead wasting and wild, heather and thistles overtaking once-neat rows of crops. The moss overgrowing the memorial to the first war, when before Mr. Murray, the mason, had quietly spent the first Saturday of each month carefully cleaning and polishing it. Potholes ballooning across the ring road, so large a child could comfortably go paddling, when once the campaign against potholes had proved the animating force in Mr. Harrower's life. Nothing in town had been painted and the blackout paper was still up and the street signs still hadn't been replaced. It was home but it wasn't; it was the island but it was another world. A darker one, a shade of what it had been, what both Leigh and her father had once loved to distraction.

The island had changed before, to be sure, but never so suddenly. Even the first war had not wreaked such havoc. When Graham Welles returned from France, it seemed almost that nothing was different, but for the beautiful new wife and beautiful new car he brought with him, a sleek thing that seemed out of place on the Welleses' farm but not at all out of place wrapped around that beautiful new wife. The island still ran on Gaelic and whisky and sea foam. When the sluagh came, Áine Welles liked to watch them. As the year stretched towards ending, Áine would sit in the garden with the sheep dotted in the distant field and turn her face towards the sky. They were more like starlings than crows with the way they danced, and perhaps this was why so much came with them. Sometimes she caught sight of some shape in their movements—a cross, a letter, a boat, a bell—and thought of augury, and of the woman in the village who claimed to be able to read one's fortune in a bit of old mirror, and of Graham's many superstitions. In the early years she thought of these things and smiled at the whimsy of them. Weeks later the dark sky would be pierced with pale green light instead of wings and she would wake her son and they would peer up out the window. The house would close around them with its creaks and murmurs and Graham would tell them his stories and the winter would pass into spring.

Modernity crept in. Electricity, a telegraph machine, wire-lesses, lights. It was the post office first, of course, for the telegraph, and then McAllister's pub: at the end of the twenties a wireless proudly installed in the corner and electric lamps standing against the walls. Some of the houses followed suit and got themselves wired. The MacTavishes, the Lewises, the Beeches. Sometimes the farmers talked of running the wires up the hill, but the expense was so extravagant. The invasion stalled.

Even after the first war, the world felt very distant to them. Doors went unlocked and children unshod. Island ponies roamed the moors, and small white flowers dotted the fields. The birds danced in the autumn, and in the summer the sun shone down. There was still such a sense of timelessness. If you asked anybody what year it was, they would screw up their face and think about it for a moment before saying, "Nineteen thirty-two? Thirty-three?" with no sense of surety at all.

But the whimsy dried up for Áine Welles. It wasn't that Graham had lied about that sweet and simple place, Áine would think later, as she untied Jack Calloway's bright red boat from its mooring, it was that she was no longer sure that life was sweet and simple anywhere. She set off for the mainland and felt something tearing in the fabric of herself. In a lilac sea she floated between two worlds and each one called her home. It wasn't that Graham had lied, it was that she couldn't love this island the way that he did. It was that he couldn't love anything the way he loved this island.

Then, when everybody had finally put the first war behind them, the explosion of the world once again.

It was different this time. There was a ship on every horizon, barely out of sight. A smudge like on the lens of a pair of spectacles, one that could not be wiped away. A constant reminder and a constant worry. Peg Gordon had been to Guernsey once, as a girl, and now the Channel Islands were occupied, and France, and Belgium, and Norway. If one stood on the edge of the bluff and squinted into the east on a clear day, one might think one could see Norway. Mr. Harrower ordered them to take down all the street signs in case they were next. "Much good that'll do," Mr. Blake grumbled. "We've barely got more than three streets."

The ferries stopped running for weeks on end. This island had been self-sufficient once but had traded that self-sufficiency in for a host of modern luxuries. The shelves of the shops in town grew barer, the children grew thinner, the world grew greyer.

The things they heard on the wireless. The news they got through the telegrams. Torpedoes and submarines and

aeroplanes and bombs. Modern technology most of the islanders had not even known existed until now; most of the village
still ran on oil lamps. The full range of horrors one person
could inflict on another. Perhaps it was no surprise that this
island turned inwards, away from the world.

When the boys came back—Iain MacTavish, Angus Gordon,
Alex Brodie—they found the island of their youth a distant mem-
ory. The weight of history hung about its neck like an albatross.
Everybody knew what year it was now.

12.

By week's end the island had given up on ever seeing Hugo McClare again. Word passed quickly that it was over for good, that the McClares were ready to put it behind them. The minister had planned a service. Not a funeral, there was still no body. No trekking down to the sea, just a quiet little thing in the church, Monday night after the boats had been brought in, and then it would be over, and they could all put the boy to rest.

There was other chatter. Unfriendly, uncharitable, unchristian chatter that they kept away from the minister's ears, the McClares'. Is it any wonder that this should happen. After what he did to that creature. He'll have brought them all down on our heads, is what he'll have done.

So here was Leigh, standing before the church in the hazy glow of early evening, trying to remember the last time she had been here. Not on any Sunday in recent memory, to be sure. Graham had made it a point not to force the children into religion, and after a few years Áine had given up trying.

"Can't bring yourself to go in, I suppose?"

Leigh turned away from the church and found Iain striding over to her. "Not quite," she said. They had spent much of the weekend searching the beaches. Iain had been trying to get a hold of his friend in shipping but with no luck so far, and they couldn't put it off forever; Leigh particularly couldn't bear to sit around in the silence of her own house doing nothing. "I can do it alone," Iain had said when they started. No doubt wishing to spare her an image like the one of Graham Welles washing up with the driftwood. He needn't have worried. They scoured the beaches for two days and found nothing more interesting than a few smelly piles of kelp.

Iain stopped beside her. Arms crossed, he peered at the church, at the candles still covering the steps. Leigh's gaze lingered on the old memorial on the opposing corner, which caught the evening light and glowed. Which wasn't the remarkable thing. The remarkable thing was that it was covered with crows, so many crows it looked like they must be sitting on top of each other, crows on the peak of the stone and crows gathered around its base. Each time a bird took flight, another appeared to take its place.

"Feels a bit hypocritical, doesn't it?" Iain said, voice low. "When we're still looking. I didn't want to come at all, but I didn't want it to seem like—you know."

"Like you didn't care."

"Exactly." He shifted his weight between his feet, pulled a cigarette packet out of his pocket, offered it to her, slid a cigarette free when she shook her head. "Probably for the best," he said. "I quit for a while in the war. Caroline didn't like it, said I'd smoke myself to death. Didn't seem like the greatest danger at that point, but it made her happy." He took a drag, looked down at the cigarette between his fingers like it was some archaeological artefact. "Couldn't make it stick after, though."

Leigh buried her hands in her pockets, her fingers brushing against Hugo's iron charm. Iain had a casual way of talking about the war as if he were talking about an errand he had run. She still regretted telling him about the WAAF. Sam had told her a number of times that she couldn't understand what it had been like, the real war, not the far-removed version they'd lived out here, and probably he was right. She hadn't been able to stop thinking about it, since Iain had told her. He liberated Dachau, didn't you know?

"I finally got my friend, by the way," Iain said. "He said he'd send someone round the docks. Seemed pretty confident that if Hugo passed through, someone would remember."

"Oh," Leigh said, relieved at the change of subject, "good, that's wonderful."

"Yes," Iain said. "So I suppose we wait and see." He took a drag on his cigarette, tossed it onto the pavement, and ground it out beneath his heel. "Come on," he said. "We'd better brave it."

The church filled as it always did, everybody in their usual places. The McAllisters. The Llewellyns. The McCaffertys and Calloways and Lowerys. Peppered amongst them, more spaces unfilled. A seat on either side of the Hendrixes: Ross and Leslie.

A spot between the Gordons: Angus. Two spaces between the McCaffertys and the Beeches: Nancy and Lucy.

There was no usual place for Leigh Welles, so she stood near the back. Even she knew well enough that the empty seats scattered about the pews were not really empty. "It's all right," she said to Iain when he paused, glancing between the spot next to Mrs. Cavanagh and Leigh, standing against the wall. "Go on, I'll see you after."

"You know," he said. "I think I'd rather stand."

She was pleased that he would, because her presence was causing a bit of a stir. If it had been challenging for her to re-member the last time she'd been in church, it was impossible for the other islanders. Mary Lewis eyed her sideways as she bustled her family along the aisle. The whispering chatter of the villagers as they settled in spiraling up to the rafters like steam. Tom McAllister turned round in his pew, an arm crooked over his youngest son's shoulder in a way that looked decidedly un-comfortable for the boy. "Leigh," he said. "Your brother rang the phone box earlier, looking for you."

It was, perhaps, the most remarkable thing anybody could have said. "Oh," she said. Stunned like someone had hit her in the stomach and knocked the wind from her lungs. "Did he— did he leave a message?"

"No, said to ring him back when you get a chance," Tom said. The telephone box had been installed just before the war. Everyone had pitched in to pay for it, and the row over where to put it consumed the town for weeks. Eventually they settled on the corner outside McAllister's, as central as it got, and Tom had been pleased until he realised that people could place calls to the island, too, and that the phone would ring and ring and ring until somebody—usually Tom—answered. "He's quite elusive, your brother, isn't he?"

That was one word for it. It had been nearly two weeks since Iain MacTavish fished their father out of the sea, and this was the first word from Sam. She had almost managed to forget him. How he'd looked at her when they last spoke. ("Dressed like that?") Even the thought of it made her feel small and stupid. A feeling he'd become good at drawing from her. She found she couldn't now remember when they'd stopped being friends, when she had given up on him and pinned her brotherly hopes and dreams on Hugo McClare instead.

"Will you?" Iain asked. Leigh blinked, having forgotten him at her shoulder. "Ring him back."

Leigh swallowed the lump that had begun to form in the back of her throat. "Perhaps tomorrow," she lied.

"Well," Iain said, as the minister appeared at the pulpit, and the chattering in the hall quietened, "you can use my telephone if you like."

"Thank you," Leigh whispered back, and then the service began.

It was a nice enough service, Leigh thought, though her mind wandered through it. The minister's voice was soft and lulling as he intoned some prayer ("—when you pass through the waters, I will be with you—"), and the last dregs of the sun came in through the windows at just the right angle so as to light the coloured glass on fire, and soon Leigh wasn't thinking about Hugo McClare at all but a little boat on a little beach, burning weakly.

It didn't feel real, standing here, listening to the minister speak. Nothing had felt real since she stepped off the ferry. Walking along the street or standing in the empty kitchen, roaming the moors with Iain MacTavish, sleeping in her childhood bedroom, cycling through the motions of a life. It felt like her father was about to appear at the door with some rock or leaf or fossil that he had found on his walk. Or that he was round back of the barn chopping wood for the fire. Or down at the telephone box, trying to reach Sam at school. It didn't feel like she was never going to see him again, bury her face in his jumper and let her nose fill with the scent of cigarette smoke and damp sea air and liquorice, listen to him read to her the last paragraph he'd written, fall asleep with her feet in his lap at the end of a long day chasing sheep round the Ben, write him a letter.

A hole was opening in her stomach, her chest. Leigh pressed the heel of her hand to her cheek. Iain glanced down at her and hurriedly away. His fingers brushed the back of hers.

Leigh tucked her hands into her pockets. She could see the McClares, sitting in their usual pew. Mr. and Mrs. McClare, a wide, conspicuous gap—Matthew. George and Kate, and another gap. As Leigh watched, George slid an arm around his sister's shoulders; Kate turned to whisper something in his ear. The other day when Leigh had gone round to the McClares', she had been so relieved that Kate was out at the Blakes' to get some flour, that she wouldn't have to face her yet. How could she apologise for two years' silence, for slipping away slowly with no explanation? Kate had told her once, that summer evening just before Leigh went away, after they'd finished the whisky down at the harbour and as they walked back up through the dry fields towards home, that the thing she feared most with the war over was that everyone would leave her behind. "I don't need a big and interesting life," Kate said, "as long as everyone else isn't having a big and interesting life without me." Leigh had taken Kate's face between her hands and said, "I'm not leaving you behind, I promise."

A promise broken. Leigh didn't think it would be much consolation that her life hadn't turned out to be big and interesting at all.

The service ended with the singing of what the minister claimed was Hugo's favourite hymn. Leigh found it hard to believe that Hugo had a favourite hymn, and she didn't know any of the words anyway, so she stood against the wall and let the music fill her chest. Iain next to her, singing barely loud enough for her to hear but singing nonetheless, in a deep, gentle voice.

And then it was over, chatter rising in the hall again, and Iain turned to her. "Perfectly dreadful, wasn't it?" he said, quietly so that nobody else would hear.

"Perfectly," she agreed, and the corner of Iain's mouth twitched upward. He slipped back into his jacket, turned to the aisle, and froze.

Mr. McClare had stopped in the aisle, and now the two men stared at each other. Iain's jaw set and his face pale, his hands clenched in fists at his sides. Mr. McClare's mouth hanging slightly open, as though he had begun speaking before realising he didn't know what to say.

"Mr. MacTavish," Mr. McClare said at last. "Iain. I wondered if we—"

But before Mr. McClare could finish, Iain had turned on his heel and strode out of the church, took the steps down to the street two at a time, knocking over some of the candles in his haste. Leaving everybody inside stunned into silence for a moment, before Leigh remembered herself and said to Mr. Mc-Clare, "I'm so sorry, he's—he's just upset." Everyone still watching as Leigh chased after Iain, calling his name.

She found him outside, standing before the crow-laden memorial with a slackness to his previously ramrod spine, his arms hanging loosely at his sides. His left hand shaking, though he seemed not to notice.

"Iain," Leigh said. He didn't reply, just continued to stare at the memorial. She stood on her tiptoes before him, put a hand on either side of his face, forced him to look at her. His skin was cold and dry, a day's worth of stubble pricking her palm. "Iain," she said again. "Come along, now. Can't let it eat you up. Not here, at least."

He took a long, broken breath. "Right," he said, and his voice sounded far away. "Right, you're right."

Leigh patted his cold cheek once. "Very good," she said. "Let's go home."

13.

It was nearly morning and she was walking along the bluff. She was closer to the edge than her parents had ever allowed her but she felt no fear, felt as though she were walking along the top of the world. There was the grass and the sky and the wind and the ocean below. She looked up ahead and realised she wasn't alone, there were a man and a woman walking before her, walking through this crisp September dawn. The man was carrying a book and a large pair of bird-watching binoculars, and the woman was wearing a pale green dress. Leigh knew exactly how those binoculars would feel in her hands and where the scratches were on the left lens. She knew exactly how the embroidery on that green dress would feel pressed against her cheek.

Áine paused, turned, reached out towards Leigh. When Leigh reached her, Áine pointed up along the path. Graham had kept walking and Leigh called to him. He turned, and as he turned, his foot slipped perilously close to the edge of the cliff. The loose stones shifted beneath his feet and he was falling, and then Leigh was falling too, tumbling through a dark velvet sky that seemed to go on forever. The air rushed past her face and she felt almost as though she were flying, a bird on the air, her chest peeling open to the world.

A dark velvet sky that seemed to go on forever, until it didn't. All at once she could see the rocks below her. She was nearly there, she was nearly there, she was nearly there. Graham was falling below her. He hit the water, and everything went dark.

And then the dark pulled back like a match igniting. There was a dim light flickering on the wall like a dancer. Someone said her name, a whisper in the dark.

14.

Which was how Leigh woke, all at once, like bursting through her front door. The dream lingered for a moment, the light dancing in her eyes as Maisie, lying at the end of her bed, raised an eyebrow to consider her. Leigh pressed the heels of her hands into her eyes.

She wasn't particularly surprised that she was having these dreams, that Áine was everywhere. One morning Áine had sailed out of their lives and the next the Welleses stopped talking about her. But she lingered. There were parts of her that were too well woven into the fabric of their lives to excise neatly. Every birthday cake was baked from her recipe. Every shirt Graham owned had been her choice. The furniture was arranged the way she liked it.

Other things disintegrated almost instantly. Áine had been quite the disciplinarian, a stationmaster, everything running according to time. Whenever either Leigh or Sam had wanted anything they had always gone to Graham first, hoping to catch him reading or working on his own book, when he was at his most distracted. Usually this strategy resulted in a wave of his hand and an absentminded, "Yes, I don't see why not." Asking him for anything when he was tending to the farm, on the other hand—or when he'd had a bad day with the sheep, or a letter had come from the bank—was sure to result in those dreaded words: "Ask your mother."

And then there was no mother to ask. Without her, any semblance of order fell away. In the last weeks of that summer, Leigh became quite feral. She would bounce out of bed as the sun rose and run off to meet the McClare children and spend the day torpedoing around the island at full speed. Graham hardly noticed she was gone, even when she didn't return till dusk. It was Sam, usually, who would be waiting for her with her dinner and a scowl.

When summer sailed away, so did Sam, off to university. "It's just you, now," he said to her before he stepped onto the ferry. "You've got to keep it together, Lord knows Dad won't." And it was true, there was no longer anyone waiting for her with dinner and a scowl. If she wanted either, she had to find it herself. Graham didn't sing her to sleep or plait her hair as Áine had; mostly he treated her like a miniature adult. No enforced bedtime, no mandatory chores, and Leigh took Sam's words to heart. She was good at fixing things. She was good at keeping things together.

Graham showed his love in other, solid ways. Distractions. Teaching her about the car, presenting her with some artefact he had found on his expedition, asking her what she thought of this or that sentence he couldn't get right. Leigh had always loved him, but now that it was the two of them, her love grew more desperate, searching, straining to make up for whatever inadequacy had pushed her mother not only to go, but to go and never be heard from again, not a Christmas present, not a birthday card, only years and years of silence.

Everyone was already on the beach by the time she arrived, an expensive old fountain pen tucked into her pocket. The Mac-Ewan girls leaned on each other, half-asleep and yawning. Leigh herself didn't feel especially bleary-eyed. She had not been able to fall asleep again after her dream and left the house quietly, Maisie still snoring loudly at the foot of her bed. A few feet away, Kate McClare clung to the elbow of her only remaining sibling, and George stood stoically with his hands in his pockets. The minister lingered in the shadows, almost out of sight. There was no sign of Iain.

The sky was growing lighter, a wash of pale pinks and purples across the horizon, and then it must have been time, because Young Mr. Morrison waded into the waves, carrying a large decorative goblet. The water climbed over his feet, his knees, his hips, until he stopped waist-deep and began to speak in Gaelic.

This was what they did, dawn on the thirteenth. ("Thirteen," Graham had told her once, "is a powerful number.") Offering that cup of ale to the water spirit, Seonadh. A prayer for protection for the fishermen, for seaweed for the farmers to fertilise the fields. For the dead who rested beneath the waves. Leigh remembered the first time she had come to this ritual, as a small, yawning child. An ancient morning and her father had carried her up the stairs again, half-asleep and wrapped up in a blanket that now sat moth-eaten in the back of her closet.

In the water Young Morrison raised the goblet to the sky and then tipped out its amber contents, letting the ale splash into the water. The sun began to peek its head over the horizon.

Young Morrison waded back in from the water and proceeded up the beach, and one by one the islanders peeled off and followed him. Climbed the stairs up the bluff to the standing stones, where the bonfire was already waiting. And the others, in their white robes and the black masks with the long, curving beaks. Leigh paused for a minute until Mrs. Beech behind her gave her a little shove on the shoulder. The masks weren't normally a part of the thirteenth, or at least they hadn't been before. She had lived on this island for eighteen years, she had been gone for only four, and already she was a stranger.

"Hi," Iain said. She turned and found him at her shoulder. Out of breath, a pink flush across his cheeks and nose. "Has it started yet?" Leigh thought involuntarily of how that cheek had felt under her hand. It had been two days since the memorial and she had barely seen him since, some excuse about needing to tend to the farm. She pressed her palm against her thigh.

"It's just about to," she said, and was shushed—loudly—by Mrs. Beech standing next to her.

The second ritual started like the first—a phrase spoken in unison, in one voice made of their many voices:

An doras a 'fosgladh.

(The door opens.)

Before she'd left the island she had sometimes wondered whether, when she came back—if she came back—the bonfires and the rituals and the Gaelic would still hold their magic for her. It was easy to believe the crows might be more than crows when passing a perfect line of three, six, nine on a wall, when the sheep showed up dead with no other explanation. It was easy to believe when they turned their wicked eyes on you and set their talons to your skin. And if she stood and let the Gaelic wash over her like a tide, it was easy to believe this part too: the masks, the fire, the chanting. The terrible magic of this island. In the blinding firelight she felt oddly untethered from her body, as though her mind had been cut loose and she was watching all of this from afar, as though it were all a strange hallucination, a fever dream.

The hum of the chant quieted until there was silence, and then the silence was filled by a single voice ("—*leig seachad na mairbh seachad*—"). Sometimes this part was unbearable. During the war it had taken ages, dozens of islanders stepping forwards clutching various artefacts of their lost sons. Leigh remembered clearly her last October, and George McClare gripping her hand so tightly she thought her fingers might break. None of the McClares had been able to bring themselves to throw anything of Matthew's into that fire; it had been only days since he'd been declared missing, and there was still such hope. Plenty of other offerings were made. The landings at Normandy had not been kind to the island boys.

This year there were only three. Leigh stepped forwards first, drew her father's pen from her pocket. It had been hard to decide what to give away, and she'd fallen asleep last night thinking about what she'd want her artefact to be, when she died. Now she stood almost too close to the fire, felt its heat beat against her face, clutching his best pen in her hands.

Mr. Harrower appeared at her shoulder. "Right then, lass," he said. She looked up at him and blinked the smoke from her eyes. "Your hand," he prompted.

"What?"

Mr. Harrower took her left hand in his. Produced a knife from his pocket and dragged it slowly and deliberately across Leigh's palm, then wrapped her fingers around Graham's pen again. Her blood pulsed out of the wound; she could feel it slick against the pen. "Strength," Mr. Harrower said, his fist clenched around hers still. "To help send him on smoothly."

She was too surprised to think much about the pain. "One of Mr. Morrison's ideas?" she asked. Mr. Harrower did not answer her. He said, "Think of your father, Leigh," and released her hand.

She stared again into the fire, blood dripping between her fingers clenching the pen and into the grass. She tried to think of some sort of prayer for Graham's spirit, something to send him safely on through the veil between this world and the next. All she could think of was sitting in his lap late one October night, after Sam had terrorised her with a horror story about the sluagh. "Will I be a sluagh when I die?" she asked Graham, and he'd rubbed his scratchy beard against her cheek and said, "No, mo ghràdh, because you're going to live a long and happy life, and only die when you're good and ready. All your business finished. That'll make for smooth sailing to the next world, so it will."

Graham had not died when he was good and ready. Graham's business had not been finished. What kind of sailing did that make for?

She threw the pen into the fire. It was time to step back into her place, but she found she couldn't move, she couldn't do anything but stare into the flames. A hand wrapped around her bleeding palm and tugged. She blinked the fire out of her eyes as Iain pulled her back into the circle. He didn't look at her, stared resolutely forwards, but he squeezed her cold fingers in his warm ones. Slowly she returned to herself.

Young Mr. Morrison's son, Freddie, stepped forwards for his grandmother. "She seemed impatient to go," Jenny Morrison had told Hugo at school the day after it happened, in January, and Hugo had written to Leigh. Leigh couldn't make out what it was that Freddie Morrison threw into the fire, but he got it over with quickly and returned to his place.

Then Kate McClare stepped forwards for Hugo. The firelight danced on her face. There was no hope left this year, no hand to cling to in lieu of offering his memory to the fire. Kate took the knife from Mr. Harrower and sliced her own palm open. Stared into the fire long enough for Leigh to catch a glimpse of the offering she held in her hand. It was the model Spitfire, the one Leigh had found beneath Hugo's bed. Kate tossed it in a beautiful high arc through the smoke. For a moment Leigh thought perhaps it would take flight. It seemed to hang in the air, and then the sparks began to catch it, and it twisted and tumbled into the fire.

It ended. The circles broke and the silence broke with it, chatter humming up again as the islanders began to disperse. Filtering through the standing stones back towards the road. Iain turned to Leigh. She had wrapped her arms around herself, looked away, out towards the grey sea. Her breath hitched in her chest and she put a hand to her face. Iain retrieved a handkerchief from one pocket and his cigarettes from the other. He didn't say anything, just offered her the handkerchief and lit up while she fixed her face. Watched Mr. Harrower and Mr. Gordon shovel dirt onto the bonfire.

What an impossible place this was. He had stayed up much of the night reading Graham Welles's book; Leigh had lent him a copy. Iain had been a fast reader once, but ever since the war, his eyes had given him some trouble, probably all that squinting into darkness and sudden flashes of explosion. The book barely mentioned the sluagh at all—perhaps the manuscript had been sanitised for mainland readers who might find it all a little hard to believe—but for a brief chapter near the end, a coda on various persisting legends. *Sacrifices were frequently offered*, Graham Welles had written—

> *to ensure good harvest or to elicit protection from malignant spirits. Offerings were made of food and drink, livestock, and, according to some sources, humans. These sacrifices would be offered at ritual bonfires or else left in underground "mounds" that were considered portals to the otherworld.*

It was largely unsurprising to Iain that, as the sluagh seemed to grow more vicious, the islanders would revert to older and greater superstitions. He thought of how the gunner on his first crew, Jamie Birch, always had to kit up in the right order—left sock before right, left sleeve before right, skip the second-last button on his shirt—or else he'd start all over.

"I didn't think you'd come," Leigh said, suddenly. She put her hand out and he looked at her for a moment before handing her his cigarette. She had told him that she didn't smoke, but he supposed there was a time for everything. She inhaled long and hard. He wondered if it did anything for her other than tickle at the back of her throat, warm her lungs, if it calmed the spinning in her head the way it did his. She handed the cigarette back to Iain. A small intimacy: his lips on the cigarette where hers had been a moment before.

"Fancy some breakfast?" he asked. "Mrs. Cavanagh tells me the MacEacherns do a good one, at their B and B."

"I don't know. I'm not very hungry."

"You'll feel better once you've eaten." He knew it was true. What a magical cure-all a good breakfast could be. No matter how harrowing a night they'd had during the war—a trip to the Big City or the industrial Ruhr, scarecrows exploding all around them, watching their friends go down one by one by one and being sure that the next searchlight would be the one to cone them—they always had returned to a full English. It never seemed as bad after they'd filled up on eggs, bacon, toast, coffee, once there was more sitting in their stomachs than adrenaline and dread.

"Come on," he said, grinding out his cigarette beneath his heel. "My treat."

"I wouldn't have been late," he told her as they meandered back to town, "but my friend called, Roger, the one in shipping."

"This early in the morning?"

Iain waved a hand dismissively. "Who knows where in the world he is right now. Anyway, neither of us sleeps much," he said. "Don't you want to know what he said?"

She did. Most of Roger's calls had turned up nothing at all, Iain told her; none of Roger's employees at the docks at Inverness, Glasgow, Liverpool had seen anyone close to Hugo's description. Which was surprising enough by itself, given that there had to be thousands—millions—of teenage boys with dark hair and dark eyes and thick accents. Though perhaps fewer now than ten years ago.

It had taken a few days, but then Roger received a call from the docks at Aberdeen. "Aye," one of his men had said, "I think I saw a young lad around the beginning of October. Well, they all look like bairns to me these days, but I'd never seen him before, and he didn't seem to know where he was going. Skulking around, he was, like he was up to something."

"Roger's not sure it was him," Iain said quickly, before Leigh could jump down his throat. "He's going to try to figure out which ship this mystery boy was on, see if it came from the big island. But it's a lead." A lead indeed. A mystery boy who didn't belong, skulking around the docks at Aberdeen in early October. The scrap of a letter, half-burnt. It was the best news anybody had had in weeks.

They had reached the MacEacherns' little bed and breakfast. Once upon a time they had done a good business, especially in October, when bird-watchers and folklorists and the like had flocked to the island to watch the sluagh swirl through the air, to dance the ceilidh on festival morning. Nobody came anymore.

When they stepped out of the MacEacherns' tearoom an hour later, Leigh had to admit that Iain was right: she did feel better now that she'd had something to eat. He'd bought her toast and eggs and black pudding and a large coffee, and as she ate her way through it, she felt the bonfire leave her. Mrs. MacEachern had given her a bandage for her hand, and it had just about stopped smarting. "How do you think Hugo managed it?" she asked Iain between bites of toast. "Getting off the island?"

Iain shook his head. "You'd know better than I," he said. "Someone must have forgotten about a boat, mustn't they? Has anyone ever made that crossing in a fishing boat before?"

"Just once," Leigh said. Iain looked at her expectantly for a moment and then it fell onto his face, some bit of gossip he'd heard somewhere settling into place.

"Oh," he said. "Of course. Sorry."

"Don't be," Leigh said, sipping her coffee. "I'm not."

Now Iain held the door for her and she stepped out into the street, into the full-fledged morning. Leigh tugged her coat on and glanced at her watch, a battered old hand-me-down from Sam that was much too big for her thin wrist. "We'd better go," she said, "we'll be way at the back of the line already."

"Go where?" Iain asked, following Leigh as she set off down the street. When she turned the corner, she saw that she was right: a line was already forming down the pavement.

"Mary Lewis," Leigh said. Iain raised an eyebrow at her. "You know, the readings?"

"I haven't the slightest clue what you're talking about."

"I thought that you'd know by now," Leigh said. She settled into line behind Evie Llewellyn and Heather Beech to wait her turn. "After the rituals on the thirteenth, everyone comes down here and gets their fortunes told. Mary's quite good at it, actually."

"I knew about the rituals," he said. "Sometimes I go for walks in the morning, when I can't sleep, so I saw them. I didn't know about the fortunes."

"Yes," Leigh said. "Well. I suppose you're in for a treat, then." They fell to silence. Across the street a host of sluagh were pecking at something in the gutter. A mouse, perhaps, or a rat. There were too many of them for Leigh to tell. Her mind turned to the sheep on her doorstep, and her stomach lurched.

The line moved slowly, one or two islanders coming out and another one or two going in. In the past Leigh had always come to get her fortune read with Kate McClare. The last time they'd sat in Mary's front room together, Mary had looked up at Leigh slyly and said, "Looks like somebody's going to kiss her sweetheart," and Kate, sitting in the chair next to Leigh, had leapt to her feet and shouted, "Who is it! Tell me this moment!" Of course Leigh hadn't told, had flipped her hair over her shoulder and said, "Something must be wrong, I haven't got a sweetheart."

"Well," Mary had said, "not yet, perhaps." Seven months later the war ended, and Leigh lay shoulder to shoulder with George in the middle of the standing stones and watched the sky rise and fall.

The Lewises' front door opened and Evie and Heather bounced out, looking quite pleased with themselves. "Come on," Leigh said, and Iain turned back to her. "Our turn."

It was not a room one would expect of a fortune teller. It wasn't an affair of incense and brightly coloured scarves and costume jewellery, and it would have been less believable if it were. Instead it was this: A small card table in the Lewises' sitting room. A pot of tea if you wanted it, whisky if you asked. Back in time the oil lamps would have been turned low but now the Lewis house had been wired, so instead there were one or two lamps turned on, covered by spare sheets so that they glowed with light instead of buzzed with it. A few large candles on the table that had been lit from the torches kept alight since the bonfire this morning. Mary sitting at one end of the card table, the subject sitting at the other.

Leigh stepped into the sitting room with Iain at her shoulder. Mary was already seated, facing them. Normally there'd be a mirror on the table before her, the mirror that she used to scry, but this year there was instead a large, wide bowl. Filled with something dark like wine.

"Morning, Miss Welles," Mary said. "Mr. MacTavish. A joint reading, then?"

"I don't want my fortune told," Iain said. Leigh glanced back at him but his face was inscrutable. One of her flatmates had gone out with a man from the RAF. A fighter pilot, Leigh thought, though now she couldn't remember. "The most superstitious man I ever met," the flatmate reported, some story about an embarrassing moment at a restaurant with some salt. "And I'm Irish." Leigh supposed that this was not a trait unique to her flatmate's RAF man, that the experience of defying unbearable odds nearly every night must make superstition seem more tenable. Perhaps Iain wasn't sceptical at all.

"Just here for moral support, then," Mary said. It was almost as cold inside as it was out; the window was open to the air. "That's fine, you can have a seat anywhere. Miss Welles?"

She indicated the chair across from her, as if Leigh hadn't done this a dozen times before.

"You don't have to call me 'Miss Welles,'" Leigh said as she sat. "You've known me since I was born."

"Aye," Mary said, primly. "Well, I didn't want to presume, mo ghràdh, not after your grand adventure. That's a lovely coat you're wearing."

It wasn't, actually. She'd bought it in her first winter on the mainland, and its wear was beginning to show. It was just new, compared to most of the clothes on this island. The dress that had so offended Sam the last time Leigh'd seen him ("Dressed like that?") would seem smart here; the fifteen-year-old dresses in Áine's closet barely looked out of date. Leigh could feel Iain's eyes on the side of her face. She pulled the coat tighter around herself and said, "Thank you," even though it had not been a compliment. Iain sat.

"What happened to the mirror?" Leigh asked. Mary placed her hands on either side of the wide bowl in front of her. The liquid inside was thick, viscous, dark. There was a smell in the air like iron and a small red stain on the tablecloth.

"I've found," Mary said, the candlelight throwing her features into relief, "that this makes the visions clearer."

Mary laid her hands palm up on the table and looked at Leigh expectantly. Leigh was still looking at the dark liquid in the bowl. "Where," she said carefully, "did you get that much blood?"

"The butcher's," Mary said. "Obviously." With an exasperated tutting noise she reached across the table and took Leigh's hands out of her lap, laid them on top of her own open palms. "Now hush."

Silence fell into the room like water into a glass, filling up the air slowly.

"What is it?" Leigh asked. More nervously than she thought was reasonable, but it had never taken this long before; normally one placed one's hands in Mary's and within seconds she was rattling off whatever it was she saw—or didn't—in the mirror. But now Mary sat there, her brow furrowed, staring into the bowl.

"It's a strange thing," she said, finally. She tilted the bowl towards her, and the blood sloshed precariously close to the rim. "It's normally much clearer than this. There's darkness around you, lass, like you're in a dark room." Her frown deepened. Balancing the bowl with one hand, she reached out and took Leigh's palm again. "You're standing by the sea—well, that could be anything, couldn't it? There's a choice to be made. And perhaps—you might be taking a fall?"

A strange thing. The fortunes Mary Lewis told were normally much more straightforward, much more mundane. ("Somebody's going to kiss her sweetheart.") When they came true everybody usually attributed it more to her insatiable hunger for gossip than to anything supernatural. Mary knew everything that happened on this island before anybody else did.

But this was different. The back of Leigh's neck prickled and her stomach bottomed out for a moment, like missing a step on the way up. The same feeling as when she woke from her strange dreams. She pulled her hand from Mary's and stood so suddenly that her chair tipped over and she had to lunge to catch it.

"It's just a bit of fun," Mary said. "Don't put too much stock in it." But when Leigh turned to look at Mary again, there was something drawn in her face. She thought of the last dream, the one that had hung on to her all day. The flickering, watery light. Someone's voice in the darkness, saying her name.

"Right," Leigh said. She wrapped her not-lovely coat tightly around herself again. "I know. Just a bit of fun."

Mary carefully rearranged the candles on the table and then looked at Iain, who had gotten to his feet too. "You sure you don't want your reading?"

"Can you read a fortune for a person who's absent?" Iain asked instead of answering. "I mean, do they have to be sitting right in front of you for it to work?"

Mary said, "You're asking me if I can read Hugo McClare's fortune."

"I am."

Mary sighed, folded her arms over her chest. The shadows on the wall jumped and danced. "I've been trying," she said. "But I can't see anything."

"And does that mean—"

"It could mean anything," Mary said. "I've never read a fortune for someone not in the room before."

"Not even during the war?" Iain asked.

The colour seemed to drain from Mary Lewis's face. Leigh remembered like it was yesterday appearing at Mary Lewis's front door, slightly out of breath, the day the telegram came about her oldest son. Leigh had beaten the minister there; she was already ushering the younger Lewis children out the door by the time he appeared round the corner.

Leigh half turned her face to Iain, spoke quietly. "We all thought it was better," she said, "not to know. Seeing as there was nothing we could do either way."

For a moment he didn't say anything, and then he said, "I see."

"It's all a bit of fun," Mary said again. Her voice had changed, tightened.

"Of course," Iain said. "Sorry, Mrs. Lewis."

"Thanks for the reading," Leigh said, and she dragged Iain back into the grey.

There were three reasons why Mary Lewis might not be able to read the fortune of Hugo McClare, Leigh thought on her way home from Iain's house several hours later. She had emerged onto the street after her reading and stepped into a bit of a daze, as if stepping into the haar. By the time she'd collected herself she was already at Iain's front door, and then there was Mrs. Cavanagh emerging with tea and a declaration that she'd heard Leigh was good with mechanics, and she knew it wasn't the same but would she mind looking at the new toaster that had just arrived from the mainland and refused to spring up? It was a brand-new Sunbeam Radiant and it took Leigh some time to realise that all she had to do was tighten a single screw beneath the crumb tray.

Three reasons for the blindness of Mary Lewis. One: it was all fake. Until this year there had never been anything in Mary's fortunes that she couldn't have gotten from gossip. Mary could not tell Hugo's fortune because she couldn't tell any fortunes at all.

Two: it wasn't fake, but the fortune telling worked only for a person who was present. It wasn't as though Mary had tried before to tell an absent person's fortune and succeeded. That Mary could not see Hugo might not indicate anything but the limits of her own ability.

Three: it wasn't fake, and it wasn't a matter of presence. Perhaps there was no fortune left to tell.

Though it had thrilled her at the time, now Leigh almost wished that she had not heard Iain's news of the boy in Aberdeen. She didn't know what she would do if it turned out not to be him, if one day they walked along the beach and saw a pale hand emerging from the waves. How could the island bear another tragedy? How could she? Maybe she couldn't. Maybe that was what her own fortune had been about, maybe the darkness Mary saw was about Hugo. Maybe the fall she saw was something that might happen if Hugo turned up dead. Mary couldn't know that Leigh had stood on the roof of the barn a few weeks ago and thought about what it would be like to tumble over the edge into the deep grass.

A stream of sluagh cut across her path, weaving down the lane like speed racers at Brooklands, somewhere she would have liked to go if the war hadn't put paid to the racing. All at once a shout came from the lane behind the square. A man's voice, surprised and, possibly, pained. Another sound like a great movement of air, the cries of many birds at once.

Leigh thought of the McClares' sheep. Of the Brodies' pig, dragged all the way down from their farm into the village. Of the little island pony in the war, of Lucy McCafferty's torn-up face. She sprinted down the cobbles towards the sound.

And found Tom McAllister, in the lane round back of the pub. A clutch of sluagh circling his head like gnats. Deadlier. Leigh grabbed a broom that was leaning against the wall and swung it through the air like a sword. The risk of hitting Tom in the head with a broom handle seemed insignificant compared to the talons slashing at his face. Tom had flung his hands up over his face but the birds kept coming at him, their talons aiming for his eyes. "Get off!" Leigh shouted.

Impossibly, it appeared to work. One of the crows cried loudly and then, giving up, the birds streamed off towards the sea.

Tom's forehead was bleeding but his eyes had been spared. "Thanks," he said, slightly out of breath, sitting heavily on the back step. He pulled a rag out of his pocket and dabbed his eyebrow gingerly. "Bastards."

"Let me guess," Leigh said. "This is normal, now, too? The birds setting upon a person in broad daylight?"

"It's not unheard of, no." Tom inspected the blood on the rag dispassionately. There were cuts on his hands and arms, too, little specks of blood ballooning up through his shirtsleeves, as if he'd plunged both hands through a barbed-wire fence.

"Of course," Leigh said. "I'll add it to the list of things nobody seems bothered with anymore. Missing teenagers. Murderous crows. Anything I'm forgetting?"

"Don't start."

"I'm not starting anything. I'm trying to understand the breadth of things I'm meant to dismiss as normal."

Tom scowled up at her from beneath his bloody eyebrow. "And there's another thing," he said. "I thought I told you to leave that poor family alone."

"I haven't been bothering them."

He pressed the rag against his forehead again. "Just running around with the MacTavish lad, playing detective."

Leigh crossed her arms over her chest. "Maybe we just both like long walks." Tom raised his bloody eyebrow at her and she threw up her hands in exasperation. "Fine," she said. "We've been looking. We both agreed that two days was hardly enough. Nobody even bothered to search past the burn."

"That's because nobody ever goes past the burn," Tom said, flinging his rag onto the ground and standing up. "You've not been here. Things aren't the same as they were before."

"So everybody keeps telling me," Leigh said. She didn't need to be told at all that things weren't the same; it was obvious. The war still clung to the island with both hands. During those six years they had all gotten used to the helpless feeling of it, being stranded on this little spit of rock way out in the middle of the North Sea, tragedy raining down all around them, and they with no ability to stop it. All Leigh's wartime initiatives—the knitting, the metal collecting, the condolence calls—had been an effort to stave off that helplessness, the surety that an inevitable dread future was marching towards them double-quick.

Then the war ended, but the helplessness didn't end with it. Actually, Leigh thought, it might have gotten worse. Now that it was over, and she had done nothing that really mattered, and there was no longer any opportunity to make her idleness right. Perhaps it wasn't the war clinging on to the island so much as the island clinging on to the war.

"If you have some grand idea of something to be done, by all means, go ahead," Tom said. "Something Old Morrison hasn't thought of. But if you haven't, then maybe you should get on with it, like the rest of us."

"Maybe," she snapped, "we should all stop acting like it's still the war, like there's nothing to be done."

Tom stared down at her from his considerable height. His eyebrow was still bleeding, a bead of blood threatened to drip into his eye, but he didn't seem to notice. The drop fell onto his cheek, streaked down his face. Her words, it seemed, had had the same effect on Tom that they'd had on Mr. Harrower days ago. Like there was some sort of spell cast over this island, like so much as mentioning the war was enough to turn everyone into ghosts.

Leigh looked up at Tom, waiting for him to say something, and then suddenly she wasn't thinking about Tom at all, she was thinking about a tourist in an improbably white coat. She was thinking about Tom's oldest son, Liam, who'd been so eager to tell that tourist about the sluagh. She was thinking about the day that a telegram came with Liam's name on it.

At last Tom spoke. "You should be careful, lass," he said, not unkindly, "the things you go around saying."

And he left Leigh alone in the lane.

She didn't get far before she heard the pub's back door open and close again, and a young voice shouting, "Hey, Leigh, wait up." The youngest McAllister boy, Fraser, swung out of the pub and followed her down the street. He stood before her with his hat in his hands, looking—Leigh couldn't describe how he looked. Penitent, almost. Like she was the minister having caught him with whisky or cigarettes.

"What is it?" Leigh asked, and Fraser twisted his hat in his hands.

"You and Mr. MacTavish are still looking for Hugo."

Leigh couldn't keep herself from rolling her eyes. Honestly, for all Tom's insistence that she keep her nose out of other people's business, he sure enjoyed sticking his in hers. "Your father has already told me off, Fraser, I don't need to hear—"

"No, it's not that," Fraser said. "It's—I have to tell someone, but please don't tell my father, he'll be raging if he finds out."

"I promise I won't tell."

"The night of the ritual," Fraser said. He could not even meet Leigh's eye, he was looking at a place a little over her shoulder, still twisting his hat within an inch of its life. "A few of the lads, we stayed out and—we went up to the old cathedral."

Leigh said, "Who's 'we'?"

Fraser didn't answer, just ploughed on. He sounded close to tears. "We were playing this dumb game, daring each other to go and knock on the door up at the Bruces' old place. You know, because everyone says it's haunted. On the way back he said he'd dropped his lighter, and he was going to go back to find it. We waited, but he didn't turn up again. We thought perhaps he'd passed us, or taken a different route home, and we didn't see him in the dark."

Leigh said again, "Who, Fraser?" although she already knew the answer.

"Hugo," Fraser said. A fat tear plopped onto his cheek. "We left Hugo up on the moor."

15.

The cathedral was a mystery that had lost its allure, mostly. It was easy, when one stood before it, to picture what it would have been like once: terribly grand. The world dropping away on one side, the cliff plummeting to an endless sea. The double spires reaching to the clouds. Now there was little of it left. Those double spires and one wall, set in with small arched windows all along it. The grandness remained, the wonder of it. How any ancient people could have built such an impossible thing.

But now it was a ruin, and when Iain and Leigh returned to it the following morning, it did not take them long to conclude that they had not missed anything on their first visit. "Nothing but some old beer bottles," Iain said when they met again beneath an archway. A few yards away Maisie had happily begun digging a series of impressive holes. On the remaining wall of the cathedral two dozen crows sat perched in a perfect line, spectral shadows. Leigh could feel their eyes on the back of her neck, watching.

She had been in a bit of a state when she had returned to Iain's house, barely an hour after she'd left it, and sent Iain into a flurry of activity because she still had Tom's blood on her face, staining the collar of her dress. "It's not mine," she said, batting away his hands when he reached out to see where the bleeding was coming from. Although the walk from the pub back to Iain's front door had taken her maybe five minutes, it had been more than enough time to work herself into a tizzy, convince herself that they had not searched the island hard enough, that they, too, had left Hugo alone up on the moors. She'd been so upset that she'd had to make several attempts to communicate to Iain what Fraser McAllister had told her. "Don't let's get ahead of ourselves," Iain had said. "We didn't find any evidence of him being anywhere near the cathedral. If the sluagh had gotten him, they'd have left something behind. We'll go up and look again tomorrow."

She had sat up much of the night in the cold, empty house, trying to convince herself that Fraser's revelation didn't change anything. There was still the scrap of a letter on Hugo's desk. There was still the mysterious boy who didn't belong at the Aberdeen docks. Just because Hugo had been up on the moors—because he had dropped his lighter and gone back to look—because nobody had seen him since—it didn't mean that he hadn't somehow slipped off the island.

Iain had wandered away from her, crouched down before the entrance to the crypt and brushed his hand over the words chiselled into the stone. "I'm going to look in here again," he said, already disappearing into the crypt. "Rather stupid of us not to bring a torch or anything," he called, his voice echoing out of the damp earth. Leigh listened to him shuffle around in the crypt for a moment before he appeared once more, shaking his head.

"I suppose you were right," Leigh said, as they stepped over the threshold of the old ruin and headed for home. "About not panicking."

"Hm," Iain said. "Yes. I've found that panic is a generally unhelpful emotion."

It was a long walk back to the village, probably close to an hour. This morning Leigh had stood before her father's car, still hidden under a large piece of canvas, water pooling on the roof, and wondered whether it would be able to ford the burn, in the wide, shallow spot where they normally leapt across. Ultimately she had decided not to risk it but she regretted it now, with the road stretching out before them and rain beginning to fall. She turned to ask Iain if he thought they could make it before the skies opened and found he wasn't beside her anymore.

Leigh turned back. Iain had stopped in the middle of the road; he was looking off at the Bruces' abandoned farm. "What are you waiting for?"

"There's one place," Iain said, "we haven't looked."

"No," Leigh said. "Absolutely not."

"Probably we won't find anything at all but dust," he said, cajolingly, already leaving the road and wading through the tall grass towards the house. "But then we'll know for sure."

"He's not in there," Leigh said. She wasn't sure why she was so adamantly against setting foot inside the Bruce house, if not because of all the stories told about it in her childhood. She distinctly remembered Matthew McClare trying to scare Leigh and Kate with some tale of its haunting when they were small, maybe seven or eight. "If he were in there, don't you think he'd have come out already?"

"Not if something's fallen on him and he was hurt, or the floor caved in, or something," Iain said. Sensibly, though Leigh hated to admit it. "Come on. Don't you like ghost stories?"

"Sure," Leigh said, "when they're just stories."

The Bruce house had stood empty for decades. All the men of the family had left for the first war and never returned. Everyone said that the remaining women, mother and daughter, had both gone mad. It was impossible to say what was true anymore; by the time Leigh was born, the Bruces were already a memory. Now, so many years after the Bruce women had left for a different (better, one hoped) life, their house was little more than the memory of a house, too. The roof had mostly caved in, and heather grew right up to the doorstep. Brown and bare climbers covered the walls. Old farm equipment lay rusting where it had been left. No glass in the windows and bricks missing from the walls. The barn in the neighbouring field not so much a barn anymore as a rotting pile of damp wood.

"It's the only place we haven't looked," Iain said. "I went over your father's notes yesterday after you left and there's nowhere else, unless you think that there's some secret hiding place on this island that he never found."

She admitted that it didn't sound likely. By the time she was old enough to be left alone at home, Graham would sometimes be gone for a day or two at a time, especially in summer when there was no night to speak of to interrupt his expeditions. It did not sound likely at all, that this island might have had a secret he had missed. But it didn't mean she had to like the idea of going into the Bruces' abandoned old farmhouse. "Do you think the floor will hold?" Leigh asked, looking sceptically at the crumbling stairs up to the door.

Iain placed a foot gingerly on the bottom step. It held. "Just be careful where you step," he said. Leigh told Maisie to wait and the dog lay down, disappearing into the grass.

Inside was almost as Leigh expected it to be. Dust hung thick even though the windows were open to the air. Paint hung off the walls in great dry sleavings, slow curves towards the ground. In the front room there were one or two pieces of furniture left behind, an old armchair spilling stuffing through the upholstery's torn seams, a table missing a leg and tilting towards the ground precariously.

"Leigh," Iain said. She returned to the hall, the floor creaking threateningly beneath her feet. Iain stood in the shadows, looking at the ground. He said, "Do you see that?"

She peered down into the dust.

Iain said, "Ours aren't the only footprints in here."

"Fraser said they were knocking on the door," Leigh whispered.

"Well," Iain replied, "someone did more than knock."

A sound came from deep within the house. A sound like a sigh, long and high and airy. A sound like nothing she had heard before, a sound like another world.

Leigh looked up at Iain. "Did you hear that?"

The look on his face was answer enough. "Probably the wind," he said, unconvincingly. There was not even a breath of movement in the house. The day was uncharacteristically still.

"It sounded like it was coming from the cellar," Leigh said, feeling in her chest a kind of compulsion. How reluctant she had been to set foot inside this house, and now here she was, forging ahead of Iain into the kitchen, finding the trapdoor that led to the cellar, clambering down the ladder without so much as a torch, with nothing more to protect her than Hugo's iron charm in her pocket. "Leigh!" Iain hissed from the top of the ladder. Quite a reversal of roles, she thought as her feet touched down in the dust.

It was almost impossible to see in the cellar. The only light came from one tiny murky window at ground level, barely six inches high. "Leigh," Iain said again, following her into the cellar. His voice dropping to a stage whisper. "This is a terrible idea."

She ignored him. She shuffled forwards, dragging her feet along the floor in case of unseen obstacles or unevenness. Her eyes began to adjust to the darkness, to make out vague shapes. It looked like something was piled up against the back wall of the cellar, but there was no sign of anything that could have made such an unearthly sound. "Hugo?" she called. Her voice too loud in the still quiet of the cellar.

She thought she heard something reply. A voice in the dark. The silence ate it up.

"Did you hear that?" she breathed.

"It was probably the house settling."

If this house settled any more than it already had, Leigh thought, it would sink into the ground. She took another step forwards, towards the rough shapes at the back of the cellar, and another, squinting into the shadows until they resolved themselves, until she could tell that those rough shapes were made of a lot of dirt and broken stone. The back wall and much of the floor were crumbling away, revealing a wide hole, a gaping black maw into the ground. "I think that's a cave," Leigh whispered, and stepped forwards again. Iain grabbed her hand and pulled her back.

"No," he said firmly. "You're not going in there right now. It'll be dark in an hour and we haven't got any equipment for—spelunking."

"Spelunking."

"Cave exploration."

"Yes," Leigh said. "I know what 'spelunking' means."

"You've no idea what you might find in there," Iain said. "It could go on for ages. It could be a big hole, you could fall in."

"Hugo could have fallen in too."

"I know," Iain said. "I know. We can come back. We'll come back tomorrow. First thing."

He was right, she supposed, looking back at the mouth of the cave reluctantly. It wouldn't do anybody any good if they ventured into this cave and got lost or trapped. But she felt oddly drawn to it, like there was a hook behind her navel. She felt certain that they would find something in the cave; she didn't know what that something was.

"First thing?"

Iain released her hand and put his over his heart. "I promise we'll be back before the fishermen are out."

A promise Leigh intended to hold him to. She woke naturally before dawn, already preoccupied by the thought of returning to the cave, of whatever had made that otherworldly noise from deep within it, of the possibility that today they would find Hugo, one way or another. She padded across her room to the window, flung open the curtains—

And leapt away with a shout. A bird sat on the little spit of roof beneath her window, its beak nearly touching the glass. The first faint light reflecting off its pitch-black feathers. The sluagh cocked its head at her slowly. Cried once. Beat its beak against the window.

Once or twice before, Leigh had thought she'd seen a sluagh on its own. The first year after Áine left. Again a few years later. When she had written to Sam he had dismissed it, but he'd been dismissing anything about the sluagh for as long as Leigh could remember. Still, she felt silly about it, so she never mentioned it to anybody else. Then came the war, and the sluagh exploded over the island, and she decided it must have been her imagination. In October, the crows came in threes.

As she thought it, the bird took flight. Disappearing into the dark sky as though it had never been there at all. Maybe it hadn't, Leigh thought as she turned around, found her overalls where she'd strewn them on the floor the night before. Maybe she'd imagined it.

On her way downstairs she glanced out the window again, to see if the bird had returned, and stopped. There were no sluagh to be seen but there was a man standing in the lilac morning, out back by the barn, close to where she'd buried the McClare sheep. Just standing there, staring up at the house, arms hanging loosely at his sides. Almost translucent, as if the weak sun shone right through him. Leigh closed her eyes because it couldn't be real; this must be one of her dreams. When she opened her eyes again, the man was still there, was looking right at her.

It was Hugo McClare.

16.

The news of Hugo's miraculous return travelled even faster than had the news of his disappearance. There appeared to be nothing wrong with him. He was a little pale and his skin was cold, but that was to be expected after so many days out alone on the moors. Between gasping sobs of relief, his mother tried to convince him to go see Dr. Delaune down in the village but, "I feel fine," Hugo insisted, "I'm all right."

Which was about as much light as he was able to shed on the situation. "I remember going up to the cathedral with Fraser and the others," he said hours after he had reappeared, squinting as though into the sun, though he sat in his parents' dim sitting room with his family and the minister and Mr. Harrower, and Leigh in the corner. "I remember losing my lighter and going back to look for it. And then—then I woke up in

Leigh's field." A dozen eyes turned on Leigh, but she hardly noticed. She was thinking about a dark cellar, and the mouth of a cave, and a certainty that when she had called out for Hugo, something had replied.

"I'm sorry I can't remember anything else," Hugo said, and everyone looked back at him. But he kept looking at Leigh, right at her, right through her.

It did not take the village long to explain it, Hugo's long disappearance. By end of day everyone had already agreed on the story they would tell themselves for years to come. The boys had been drinking, hadn't they? Well, surely Hugo must have slipped and hit his head, poor thing. Knocked himself out good and proper. Had anybody bothered to ask Dr. Delaune if this was even remotely possible he would have told them something about the improbability of a person hitting his head hard enough to be knocked out for two weeks, but not hard enough to be killed. But nobody did ask, and since the boy was here, before his eyes, Dr. Delaune did not feel the need to point it out.

So this explanation was accepted wholeheartedly. The villagers clapped him on the back when they saw him in town, whispered amongst themselves what a miracle it was, but nobody asked him where he had been, nobody appeared to doubt. It seemed that everyone had made it a policy not to question good news.

Everyone except for Leigh.

"You don't seem glad," Iain said when she stumbled to a halt before him on the ring road two hours after Hugo's reappearance. They had agreed to meet by the place the road curved away from the standing stones and she was desperately late. Of course it didn't matter, he had already heard, the village had been buzzing with it from the moment Kate appeared to fetch the minister and Mr. Harrower. And it wasn't true; she was unbearably glad, her chest spinning with it, her head light. Hugo was home and it was as it should be, mostly. They could bully their way through the rest of the month to winter and return to the normal pace of their normal lives.

"I am," Leigh said. "I am glad."

"You don't seem it," Iain said again.

Well, and gladness, in Leigh's experience, was rarely so simple as gladness. There was the rest of it, all that the village was content to set aside. That Hugo had disappeared for so long, so completely. That in all their searching, Iain and Leigh had found no more than the missing cigarette lighter, anywhere. The islanders were right about one thing, at least, in giving up their search: this island was simply not that large. Where could he have been?

"You heard that sound," she said. "In the cellar, yesterday."

Iain frowned. Slid a hand into a pocket and withdrew it empty. He had a habit, she had noticed, of looking for a cigarette when he was uncomfortable. Which was answer enough to her question, even though what he said was, "It was the wind, Leigh. That house had more holes than walls."

In a choice between believing Iain and believing the hair on the back of her neck, she would believe Iain. The harder choice. But belief, she thought, was mostly a matter of willpower, commitment. "I suppose you're right," she said.

There was no reason for her to stay now that her news was delivered, their goal accomplished. But she lingered by the side of the road. Another layer to the complex feelings that under-pinned her gladness. "Well," she said. "I suppose I should go home."

"All right," he said. "I'll see you later."

She stepped back into the road, and told herself she was not disappointed that he had not given her an excuse to stay.

She was given the opportunity to test her belief in Iain early the next day, as she pushed her bike up the hill out of the village, laden (barely) with the few groceries she could afford, and spotted a figure in amongst the standing stones by the cliff. The boy in question himself, Hugo, standing as still as one of the stones and gazing up at nothing.

She called to him and he turned his head slowly. Now that Hugo had a night's sleep under his belt and was full of what-ever feast Kate had doubtless cooked up for him, the way he had stared right through her in his parents' sitting room would surely be revealed as a passing symptom of being out alone on the moors.

"Oh," Hugo said as she approached, the damp grass brush-ing against the hem of her dress as she waded through it to-wards him. "Hi, Leigh."

"Starting to feel more like your old self?" she asked. She looked up to the sky in the same direction he had been gazing a moment ago, but there was nothing to look at but air.

"I feel fine," he said. There was some quality to his voice, a sense that he was saying lines in a play.

"Everyone's so glad that you're back," she said. "We were worried sick."

"They told me you were looking for me."

Leigh nodded. "Do you really not remember anything?" she asked. "Where you were?" The light glanced off the plane of his cheek. She remembered once thinking that the land between the village and home felt somehow liminal. Now it was Hugo who seemed liminal, insubstantial, like if she breathed on him wrong he would simply blow away.

"I remember the light," he said, gazing up at the stones again. A cluster of sluagh landed atop one of the stones and looked down at Hugo in much the same way he looked up at them. "The way the light moved."

"Where?" Leigh said, insistently.

Hugo turned slowly to look at her, considered her. Opened his mouth a moment before he spoke. He said, flatly, "I don't remember."

"Are you sure—"

"I said, I don't remember!" Hugo snapped, and Leigh drew back as if burnt.

"All right," she said. "I'm sorry. I'll—leave you to your thoughts."

Hugo's outburst passed as quickly as it had come; his face went placid again and he slid his hands into his pockets, turned his face up to the sky. Leigh made to leave, but there was one more thing she had to say, whether he wanted to be alone or not.

"I wanted to say," she began, "that—I'm sorry about all those letters."

Hugo looked at her blankly. "What letters?"

"The ones you wrote me," Leigh said. "While I was away. I felt awful for not writing back, but I didn't know what to say."

Not even a hint of recognition passed across Hugo's face. "Oh," he said. "That's all right."

Leigh frowned. "Well, then," she said, hesitantly. "I suppose I'll see you later."

And she left him standing there, retreated onto the road and tried to ignore the prickling at the back of her neck. When she reached the top of the hill she paused, turned and looked back at him once more. Hugo hadn't moved; he still stood in front of the stones looking up at the sluagh circling in the air above. He raised a hand towards them, as though beckoning to them, then dropped it back to his side.

Suddenly his head turned, sharply. At an angle that surely had to hurt. He caught her watching. His eyes boring into hers, burning.

There were a number of things that Iain had learnt to do during the war, and not least of them was putting on a brave face. How many countless hours he had spent pretending, after a particularly bleak target briefing, an un-fortuitous weather update, that everything was fine, the op ahead would be simple, they'd be back eating breakfast by sunrise. Countless hours with the doubt crushed tightly into a fist in his chest, until the rumble and roar of a Lancaster's four engines shook out everything that made him a person and rendered him mindless but for the task at hand.

Though he had accused Leigh of not being glad at Hugo's return, Iain had suspected, even as they turned in opposite directions down the road, that perhaps he was naming something in himself. And now there was no rattling engine to shake loose the fist for him; he had to find a way to do it himself. Which, he thought, as he went searching for his cigarettes, should not be so hard a task. After all, it was a miracle, the way Hugo McClare had turned up in Leigh's backyard. He ought to feel relieved, but instead he felt like he'd been sitting in damp clothes for too long and now the chill was in his bones.

"I should have thought you'd be pleased," Mrs. Cavanagh commented coolly a few days later, after he snapped at her for no reason, "but I don't think I've ever seen you so irritable."

He had a vague sense of the source of his irritability. It wasn't as Leigh would have it, that there was something left unexplained in the cellar of that abandoned house. Like the rest of this island he had decided some time ago not to question good news, when it came. It came so infrequently. Though he had heard the sound that Leigh now dwelt upon. A sound he was rewriting in his memory so that he could say it was the wind and believe it.

The mystery was not the source of his irritability, he thought as he trudged down the street towards the grocer. Having been banished by Mrs. Cavanagh into the afternoon, punishment for his bad humour. He had told himself that he would speak to the McClares when Hugo was found. Now Hugo was found.

Leigh caught him as he was coming out of the grocery, as though she had been lying in wait. At the sight of her the fist in his chest seemed to uncurl its fingers. And then—

"I think you're wrong about Hugo," she said, without saying hello. The fist clenched up again. "We can't pretend like nothing's happened."

"Hello to you too."

"Hi," Leigh said, trailing half a step behind him down the street, pushing her bicycle. "I think you're wrong about Hugo."

"Yes," he said, "I heard you the first time."

"You didn't say anything."

"That's not true. I said hello."

"Iain—"

"I don't know what you expect me to do about it," he said, rounding on her. "Based on nothing more than your feeling that it's strange."

"It is strange," Leigh insisted. "Two weeks!"

"Stranger things have happened at sea."

"Well, we're not at sea," Leigh said. Which was not a convincing argument, Iain thought, eyeing the cluster of crows that had landed on the fountain down the street. "Have you spoken to him yet? There's something not right about him."

"Of course there is," Iain said. "He was out on the moors for two weeks. You should have seen Matthew and me when we got back from Spain."

Leigh scowled. "I think," she said, "that maybe we should go back to the Bruce house. I think we should explore that tunnel."

How bitterly Iain regretted ever cajoling her into that house in the first place. "We don't even know that he was in there."

"We looked everywhere else," Leigh said. "Twice! Three times! It's the only place he could have been."

"And what do you imagine you'll find?" Iain demanded. Leigh made a scoffing noise. He'd been glad to see her and now he wished she would leave him alone, focus her insistence on somebody else. "I mean it. What do you imagine you'll find?"

"Oh, don't be so condescending," Leigh snapped, and turned on her heel.

She didn't like fighting with him.

What had set her off? It wasn't really about his tone (well, not only), she thought as she pedalled her bike furiously up the hill for home. Possibly she'd already been primed before she'd even set eyes on him. There was too much of it, as she'd stood in the square being stared at by the propaganda in the post office window, as her battered watch ticked off a new hour and the church bells stayed silent, as two dozen sluagh took off from the pub's crumbling roof. As everyone who passed could be heard marvelling at the miracle of Hugo's return, isn't it wonderful, isn't it fine. Leigh could not stop thinking of him standing there in her field, the dew soaking into the hem of his trousers, the morning light shining through him. It wasn't fine. How could nobody else see it?

Though there was a chance, she conceded—only to herself, as she crested the hill—that Iain wasn't entirely wrong. Perhaps the tunnel was an astonishing coincidence, perhaps she ought to consider what she hoped to discover before venturing down. Perhaps she was too inexperienced to venture down at all. She could not help but think that none of this would have stopped Graham from investigating, once he had the mystery between his teeth.

Iain had sounded like Sam. Standing there being patronising, acting like she was a silly child in need of setting straight. She had thought them above this sort of bickering, her and Iain, she had thought them allies. To be fighting with him made her foolishly, inexplicably sad. Not sad enough to turn around and claim the fault for it.

The air cracked with a boy's shout and Leigh whipped around. Maisie began to bark madly and took off across the field towards a group of boys clustered on the cliffside in various states of undress. "Maisie!" Leigh shouted, and the collie stopped, turned back to her, head cocked. Leigh stared at her, hard, until Maisie dropped her no-longer-wagging tail and returned to Leigh's side. One of the boys raised a hand to her in greeting.

It was a cold day for a cliff jump but there was never a good time to fling oneself into the North Sea, and besides, this had become an ongoing dare amongst the boys of the island, passed down through the years. Leigh remembered Sam and his friends careening into the ocean in all manner of weather, and afterwards trooping back across the moor to the Welles house, where Leigh watched shyly from the corner as her father presented the boys with hot chocolate thick enough to stand a spoon in. The colour slowly returned to their cheeks and the sounds of their raucous laughter echoed through the house and it seemed like nothing could ever touch them. Immortal boy-kings of this island, of the sea.

"We're going home," Leigh said to Maisie as the first boy leapt over the edge of the cliff with a shout, and the dog pricked her ears and then tore off down the path towards the house. Leigh followed, but in moments Maisie came tearing back round the corner. "Yes, I know I'm slow," Leigh said. Maisie leapt up against Leigh's bicycle, nearly bowling her to the ground. The dog was frantic, not whining so much as wailing.

Her tail tucked firmly between her legs. "What is it?" Leigh asked. "What's wrong?" Leigh went to round the corner for home, but Maisie wouldn't follow her. The collie wailed louder.

Leigh turned the corner and stopped before the house and felt as though she were plummeting off the cliff herself.

The boards had been torn from the windows, leaving the iron nails still rammed into the frames. The glass smashed and the old slats hanging limply down the side of the house, or else lying in crumpled piles in the mud. The iron charms lying in little piles of red ribbon on the doormats. The house was covered in crows.

17.

Some ancient instinct for flight kicked in and she ran, she ran, she ran, no matter what anybody said about running in October. Where would she go? She didn't know, she knew only that she needed help.

Which appeared out of nowhere, as though she had willed it into being. Hugo McClare, not with the other boys as perhaps he ought to have been but standing in the middle of the road where it curved away from the cliff. Relief coursed through her at the sight of him, for at this moment it didn't matter if he was strange or if he was ordinary, if the cellar was just a cellar or if she had heard some creature sigh. "Hello," Hugo said, sounding almost like his old self. "What's happened to you?"

"It's the house," Leigh gasped. "The house, the sluagh got in, the birds got into the house."

Hugo frowned slightly, his head tilting to the side. "Past the charms?"

"Aye," Leigh said. "They're everywhere. I don't know what to do."

"We should find Kate," Hugo said. "She's good at this. Come on."

Across the pasture Kate McClare pulled a pie from the oven and thought about how tired she was of being left behind. Once she had been glad of it. How many nights had she lain awake reading and rereading her oldest brother's letters, fallen asleep thinking how lucky she was to be a girl, too young and too female to be sent away to fight. Something she never admitted to anyone, certainly not to Leigh Welles, who had been entirely consumed with it. The war. Kate had watched as Leigh threw herself at it. Writing letters and knitting scarves, collecting scrap metal, cooking a casserole each time one of the horrible telegrams came. Eschewing anything even remotely resembling a birthday present for six years in favour of using the ration coupons to send extra tea, chocolate, cigarettes to the island boys strewn across the globe. It was never enough, Leigh was never enough for herself, and her efforts kept getting larger, grander, greater, until the day the war ended. Until the day she sailed away from the island and did not look back once.

Even then Kate was content with her life, her family, this island. She didn't care about doing anything interesting, she told Leigh, she just hated the idea of everyone else doing something interesting without her.

Only later did she start minding being left behind. When Leigh stopped replying to her letters, when she stopped ringing the telephone box in town. "Does she still write to you?" Kate asked George. George only slammed his way out of the house, which was answer enough. They'd been close, once, Kate and George. Before he grew up and started finding Leigh increasingly interesting. Before their father had taken him out for a walk round the fields on his eighteenth birthday and he had returned divested of all his grand plans for joining up, applied for an exemption the next day. What a pair they made, Kate had thought at the time, Leigh and George, neither one of them meeting the desperately high standards they set for themselves. It was, when one stepped back and considered it, an island filled to bursting with dissatisfaction.

Out in the front somebody flung the door open with a loud crack. "Kate?" Hugo called, in a calm voice that did not match the flinging of the door. The tone of his voice didn't matter; every time Kate had heard Hugo speak in the last days, her heart had filled with such heat she had felt she would burn up from the inside. Of course it was only fair, that if one brother should go missing forever, the other should be found. She wiped her hands on her apron and stepped into the hallway, and stopped.

Hugo wasn't alone. He had brought Leigh Welles.

"I didn't know where else to go," Leigh said, wringing her hands together. Her face white. "Hugo said you'd know what to do."

Kate found her voice. "God. What's happened?"

The three of them stood before the crow-infested house, Maisie shut up against her will back in the McClares' kitchen. Kate held an iron shovel in one hand like a spear. Leigh gripped a crowbar in hers. Hugo stood with his hands in his pockets, a picture of teenage indolence. They considered the house with the gaze of surveyors, scientists. Sluagh sitting on the empty windowsills and on the railing of the porch. Sluagh covering nearly every inch of the sagging roof. Sluagh flying out of a smashed upstairs window, the window of Sam's bedroom.

"I suppose you've drawn the short straw," Kate said, and Leigh guessed she was referring to what had once been the Blakes' barn but was now a roost for the birds.

"Should we go get help?"

Kate shrugged. "With the three of us we'll probably be fine, as long as we keep our wits about us."

"Kate is the resident sluagh-clearer," Hugo said, proudly. "She could do it by herself if only we'd let her."

Kate rolled her eyes. "He's exaggerating," she said. "I've just had some practice is all."

Everything about this conversation felt entirely bizarre. "So what do we do?" Leigh asked.

"Hit them as hard as you can," Kate said, "and watch out for your eyes."

They approached the house like soldiers heading into battle, which was exactly what they were. The sluagh saw them coming and instantly sounded a terrible, wailing alarm. Before Leigh could suggest that maybe they ought to call in some backup, Kate let out a sound halfway between a shriek and a war cry and charged towards the house.

It was a swirling mess of iron and feathers. "Watch your eyes!" Kate shouted for the second time as Leigh spun on her heel to see one of the sluagh coming for her face with talons outstretched. Leigh swung her crowbar up to knock the creature from the air, and in the follow-through over her shoulder she managed to catch another one in the head. The bird screamed and shot away into the sky.

Once the fight had begun in earnest, it was simple. Swing, dodge, duck. The sluagh hit by iron let out terrible, unearthly cries and did not come back for seconds. The horde of birds thinned. Kate fought her way up onto the porch and wrenched open the door.

It was harder inside. There were chairs and walls and bookshelves to get in the way. Shoes to trip over, sticks that Maisie had dragged inside and Leigh hadn't bothered to return to the yard. It was harder inside until Leigh yelled, "Don't worry about breaking anything, smash everything if you have to!" She whipped around and her swinging arm collided with Hugo.

Immediately cold burst through her as if she had plunged into a frozen pool, spreading from the place her arm had touched him. She yelped and dropped her crowbar in surprise. It clattered to the floor and the sluagh surged around her and Hugo stared at her, standing in the swarm, black feathers catching in his hair. Leigh scrambled for the crowbar, her fingers tingling and her mind on fire.

"You all right?" Kate called, and Leigh leapt back to her feet in time to watch one of the birds swoop down and grab Kate by the hair, talons digging into her neck, her scalp, its grip strong enough to lift her onto the tips of her toes.

Kate screamed.

There was no way to swing the crowbar without taking Kate's head off with it. Leigh watched helplessly as Kate's shovel fell to the floor and she scrabbled at the bird with both hands. Helplessly, helplessly, uselessly. Hugo appeared at her shoulder, and Leigh could feel the cold radiating off him. He said, in a voice that was not his own, a great and terrible voice, "*Leigeil mu sgaoil i.*"

And with a cry the creature released Kate. It flew for one of the shattered windows, two more sluagh following in its wake. Blood streamed down Kate's face, and she wiped her eyes clear with her sleeve. She looked up again and shouted, "Behind you!" and Leigh wheeled around, crowbar up. The attacking bird smelled the iron and swerved away from her.

Hugo had picked his way into the middle of the room. The birds seemed to part around him like water around a stone. What had happened to him, Leigh thought as she batted three crows off the sofa towards the empty window frame, what had happened to him while he was gone? He stood in the centre of the sitting room with his hands hovering a few inches away from his body like he was about to take flight himself. There was something wrong about him; Leigh could feel it when she looked at him, like the air between them was tearing open. Hugo opened his mouth and a stream of Gaelic began to pour out of him, in a voice that was too deep and too smooth, a voice like heated honey.

The birds began to flee, flying through the windows and the open front door. Across the room Kate paused, caught Leigh's eye. The same alarm on her face that Leigh felt pounding through her blood. And then Kate opened her own mouth and joined in with Hugo's chant. Leigh didn't think she ought to know these words but found them bubbling out of her own throat anyway. A sense memory. Sitting on her father's lap in the big armchair in his study as he taught her words that his own grandmother had taught him years ago. Charms to send bad spirits away. An ancient language screamed past teeth and tongues. Leigh swung her crowbar at the sluagh and screamed the Gaelic and the words reverberated through her bones. Kate caught a particularly big one with her shovel and pounded up the stairs while Leigh shouted her way back into the kitchen.

There was one sluagh here, sitting on the table in the spot that had once been Àine's as though it were waiting for dinner. Leigh wrenched open the back door and turned to the bird, and as she approached it with the crowbar raised it blinked at her, taking in the sight of her.

Hugo stepped into the room behind her. He said, "*Teicheadh.*"

As though obeying him, the sluagh hopped into the air and soared out the back door.

And then, impossibly, the house was quiet.

Leigh listened. She heard the wind rustling in through the shattered windows. She heard Kate's footsteps on the floorboards above her. She heard the goats crying in the barn.

"It's clear upstairs," Kate called down, and a few moments later she appeared in the kitchen doorway. "It's really not as bad as I expected. Well, except for the wall in the hallway. There's a hole in it. That was me. Sorry."

Kate paused. Hugo stood in the middle of the kitchen, staring out through the open back door. Now that the birds were gone he seemed like a normal boy; now that the birds were gone Leigh wondered if perhaps she had imagined the cold that had shocked through her at his touch, the terrible honeyed voice, everything. Of course she had imagined it. She had touched him already since his return—had flung her arms around him in the dew-tipped grass out in the back field the morning he reappeared, and there had been no such sensation then. Of course, she had imagined it.

"Are you going to tell us where you learnt to do that?" Kate asked. Hugo blinked once and turned away from the door.

"To do what?" he said.

"What do you mean, 'to do what'?" Kate said. "To speak Gaelic like that."

Hugo shrugged. "We all speak Gaelic, don't we?"

Not like that. Not in a way that seemed to command the sluagh to listen. If Iain were here, Leigh thought, she would win their argument. He would have to admit it, he would have to see.

"I've got to go," Hugo said, brushing a feather from his hair. "I told George I'd help with the sheep."

He left without a backward glance, and through the open door, Kate and Leigh watched as he waded through the damp grass and vaulted over the wilting fence separating the Welleses' land from the McClares'. "That boy," Kate began, and then stopped. Looked around at the kitchen as though a satisfying explanation for Hugo's strangeness could be found amongst the mess, the dishes piled in the sink or the feathers covering the floor. There was a sweet, rotten smell in the air. After a moment, Kate said, "Do you want help cleaning up? Fixing the windows, relaying the charms?"

Leigh couldn't see the point of relaying the charms, really. The herbs and amulets and charms had done nothing the first time—had everybody else known that they meant nothing, and nobody told her? This seemed different from an infestation of a barn. The protections had meant nothing the first time around. Why would they be any stronger after an encore performance?

But Leigh thought of all the many things she owed to Kate and said, "All right, then."

"Good." Kate propped her bloodied shovel up against the wall and pointed at the herbs hanging above the counters. "Can I use these?" When Leigh shrugged, she reached up on tiptoe and began to pull down the same herbs Leigh had used the other day around the house. Kate glanced out the window. "You might want to check on the goats," she said, and panic fluttered in Leigh's chest; she'd forgotten about the goats entirely. But when she reached the barn the latch was still safely shut, and when she opened the door and peered into the musty dark, she could see two sets of caprine eyes glowing back at her.

She gave them some extra feed as a treat and went back to the house to work on the windows. The boards had been torn from the frames and most of the panes smashed. Leigh tried not to think of what it would cost, replacing the glass. It wouldn't matter for another two weeks, not until October was over and it was time to remove the boards for another year. Maybe by then she'd have worked up the nerve to telephone Sam.

Kate appeared around the side of the house as Leigh moved on to the second window. Watched as Leigh pried a singularly stubborn nail from the frame. Wordlessly Kate scooped a hammer out of the toolbox Leigh had fetched from the shed and began to help. As they moved from one window to the next, Leigh caught Kate looking at her funnily—intentionally—but it wasn't until they were done that Kate finally spoke.

She said, "You stopped writing back."

It wasn't an accusation, or a complaint. Leigh said, "I know."

"Why?"

She didn't think Kate meant to shame her, but she felt shamed nonetheless. She wrapped her fingers more tightly around the handle of the hammer. There was blood caked under her nails and into the lines of her skin. Why had she stopped writing? It was easier to pretend everything had been going fine when she didn't have to put the truth onto paper, and lying was so exhausting. The promise of the mainland had been an illusion. There was nothing more to say. Leigh considered her answer while Kate considered Leigh.

Leigh said, "I was so embarrassed, Kate."

She hadn't looked tense before but still Kate seemed to soften. "Oh," she said, like a sigh. "Leigh, you didn't have to be."

The years of failure wrapped their hands around Leigh's chest. Every time she'd lost her job or not had the money for the bus. Every time she'd skipped dinner or darned another hole in her stockings that were already nothing but darning. Every time Sam had looked her up and down and found her wanting. Why had she not come home sooner? She was still waiting to be made new. She said, "But I was. I had all these big plans."

"I know. We talked about them all the time."

"Exactly," Leigh said. "We talked about them all the time, and none of it happened. I was terrible at all of it. Even if—"

She tried to swallow the thickness in her throat but it was too late, she felt two fat tears squeeze themselves out of the corners of her eyes. She wiped them away angrily. "Sam did everything perfectly," she said, "and I did everything wrong, and it's so, so embarrassing."

Leigh blinked and missed the moment when Kate must have moved because when she opened her eyes Kate was flinging her arms around her. The two of them stumbled back a step before Leigh caught her balance. She dropped her hammer so she could hug Kate back properly. They both smelled of blood and sweat, but the feeling of being heartbeat to heartbeat was unchanged from when they were children.

"I thought you'd gotten too grand for me," Kate said into Leigh's hair. "I thought I must've been so boring to you, with your fabulous new life."

"Fabulous!" Leigh repeated, trying to stop her nose from running onto Kate's shoulder. "I was eating beans on toast for every meal."

Kate laughed and said, "Oh, Christ, I would have given up after a week." She pulled her face out of Leigh's hair and laughed again, said, "What a pair we make!" She wiped her cheeks with the heel of her hand, which did little but smear the blood around, and then wiped Leigh's with the sleeve of her coat.

It'll feel so much better in here once it's done, Kate had said, and though she had meant the house, the herbs, Leigh felt a weight lifting off her shoulders as her oldest friend wiped her face dry. One less thing to stew about, one little bit of relief. Of course other worries lingered. "What did you mean," Leigh said, "before, when you said that I'd drawn the short straw?"

"Oh," Kate said. "Well, it seems to happen every year now, doesn't it? Actually i's lucky we were able to clear them. It's about fifty-fifty these days."

"Fifty-fifty?"

Kate nodded. "First it was the Blakes' barn," she said, counting off on her fingers. "Then it was the McCaffertys and the Lowerys, we got them out but that's how Mr. Lowery lost his eye. Last year it was the Russells, and the Brodies, and I think one of the Morrisons' barns. We only cleared the barn."

"What happens when you can't clear them?"

Kate shrugged. "If you don't get them out the first year, they seem to always come back. Like they claim the house, or something. The Brodies move in with the Gordons for October," she said. "But the Russells left altogether. For the big island, I think. Hadn't you noticed?"

Leigh hadn't. Throughout her whole childhood on this island she could count on her fingers the number of people who had left. An entire family, pack up and decamp? It was unheard of. She had been too focused on Hugo, on her certainty that if Hugo were found, everything would be better. Everything was not better; possibly things were getting worse. "The sluagh are driving people away," Leigh said.

"I suppose so," Kate said. She turned away, placed her hammer back in the toolbox. "My mum said if it keeps going like this then maybe we should go, too, but my dad won't hear of it. It's become quite the fight, actually. Especially now, with Hugo." Leigh rubbed her arm, the spot that had gone cold when her skin collided with his. Kate straightened. "Where did he learn to speak Gaelic like that?" she continued, gazing out towards

190

the barn, the place where Leigh had spotted him in the mist. "He's never spoken Gaelic like that before. All his friends speak English." She turned back to Leigh. "It doesn't make any sense."

"I suppose he hit his head rather hard," Leigh replied wryly, and Kate laughed once without humour.

"George thinks he's lying," Kate said some moments later, as the two of them crunched back down the lane to go fetch Maisie from the McClares' kitchen, where she'd been left for safekeeping. "About not remembering. George thinks he stole some boat everyone forgot about and went off somewhere. The big island, somewhere else."

"Why would he go without telling anybody?" Leigh asked. "Why would he lie about it now?"

"I don't know," Kate said. "But . . ."

"What?"

"I found an application packet in his room," Kate said, reluctantly. "For university." She frowned. "He saw me with it and tore it up. Said it was never going to happen anyways, just a bit of silliness. But I don't know. Maybe he did sneak away. We don't know him at all, really, he's become a whole person while we weren't paying attention."

An island filled to bursting with dissatisfaction. Leigh thought again of all the letters still tucked into the lining of her suitcase. Not one of which had mentioned university, though Hugo had written about school often enough. She collected Maisie from the McClares' kitchen and wondered what might be different if she had not squandered Hugo's confidence with two years of unanswered letters.

18.

"Are we really doing this again?" Mrs. Cavanagh demanded as she flung the curtains open. Iain squinted against the sudden press of light, scrabbled a hand across his bedside table for his watch. "I thought we were past this." She scowled at him like a disappointed schoolteacher, hands planted on hips.

Which seemed at least a little unfair. He had only managed to fall asleep as the first light started to creep across the cobbled street, so it seemed perfectly reasonable, Iain thought, that he should have slept past noon. Besides, it wasn't like he had any appointments to keep.

"Maybe you should go see Leigh," Mrs. Cavanagh continued. By this point quite used to these one-sided conversations. Of course Iain could not go see Leigh. It had taken him some time to realise that what he had started with her outside the

Gordons' grocery was a fight, and even now, several days later, he could not be sure whether her absence was owing to the way he'd dismissed her or to the fact that they had no reason to see each other anymore—they had returned to their separate lives.

Either way he could not go see Leigh; to go see her would be to bend, to admit that there was cause to be suspicious. He was still trying to convince himself of the opposite, in doing so was spending a lot of time thinking of his own miraculous recovery. If the war had taught him anything, it was about the miracle of odds. How quickly they could turn.

"I heard there was an incident up on her farm the other day," Mrs. Cavanagh said.

"What sort of incident?"

She arched an eyebrow at him. "I didn't hear the details. Something about the birds, I think."

Which woke him up well enough. Within a few minutes he was shrugging into his coat and venturing into the late afternoon light, a rare bit of sun.

He rounded a corner and paused. There was a boy crouched down next to the whitewashed wall of the Beeches' little cottage, his hat pulled low and a can of paint at his heel. It was Hugo, painting something onto the wall in thin black strokes. It didn't seem at all like the kind of thing the Beeches would have asked him to do.

"What are you doing?"

Iain expected Hugo to be startled, but the boy just glanced up, sat back on his heels, considered the wall. After a moment he frowned. "I'm not really sure," he said. He blinked once, twice, three times, then said, "It felt right."

An odd thing to say. Iain looked more closely at Hugo's handiwork and realised that it was a series of names. Brodie. McClare. Murray. Taylor. Hendrix. All of the island men and women, boys and girls, who'd gone off to war and not come back.

But not just them. Other names too. Graham Welles up near the top, Mrs. Morrison, Lucy McCafferty. Iain's own father. It wasn't just the war dead, it was everybody. A prickle at the back of Iain's neck. The same sort of feeling he'd had that early morning on the airfield when he had been convinced he'd seen Caroline standing in the dew.

"You said you had something you wanted to tell me," Iain said. Hugo looked up at him. The late light caught on the plane of his cheek and seemed to shine right through him. "That night at the ritual, you told me you had something you wanted to talk to me about."

Hugo stared at him blankly. "Did I?" he said. "Sorry, I don't remember what it was now. *Is dòcha gum bi cuimhne agam.*" He stood, shook his head as though to clear it. "I mean, maybe it'll come to me."

Iain frowned. It had been some time since Gaelic was the dominant language on this little island. Some of the older islanders slipped back and forth between the two languages, even within the same sentence, but he wasn't sure he'd ever heard Hugo speak Gaelic before, save at one of the rituals.

Iain reached into his pocket and his fingers brushed against cold metal. "Here," Iain said. He offered the old lighter to Hugo, the good brass one they'd found up in the grass. "I think this is what you were looking for that night."

195

Hugo considered the lighter for a moment. "You keep it," he said. "I've gone off smoking."

Iain watched Hugo disappear into the afternoon and tried not to feel somewhat unmoored by it. Something about the way that Hugo had looked at him, the way the light passed through. That his memory should be so completely blank. That he seemed to slip into speaking Gaelic without realising it.

Iain returned his gaze to the wall, the list of names that Hugo had copied out from memory. Another strange thing: that Hugo should have held all these names in his mind, written them out—was it in reverse chronological order of the days they died? Iain found Matthew's name, up near the top of the wall. Their wars had followed alarmingly similar paths, until they hadn't. Probably, without Matthew, Iain's would have been over much sooner.

Iain blinked. A series of images behind his eyes like negative slides. A Lancaster on fire, a hot slice of sky, a dry garden, the Pyrenees at night. Two weeks was not such a long time to be missing, he told himself again. Iain supposed he should be glad that he and Matthew got even one miraculous recovery. Most people didn't get that many. He dropped his eyes down the list of names and found his father's again. The paint was dripping down towards the ground like the letters were melting away. He tried to remember the sound of his father's voice but found that somewhere in the intervening years it had slipped away from him.

A Lancaster on fire, a hot slice of sky, the Pyrenees at night. Caroline called them the "lost months" of his war, but they weren't lost. He remembered them in vivid, startling detail. It had begun ordinarily enough. Sitting in the briefing hut as the CO lifted the curtain and revealed the map behind, a thin red ribbon stretching between their base and the target. A rundown from the CO, a weather update from Met, an intelligence briefing from one of the senior WAAFs. At the time it all seemed standard. It usually did. Five-tenths cloud cover on the way in, good visibility over the target. Iain had sat through bleaker briefings. The long wait for evening. As he always did after kitting up he had cracked all the knuckles individually on his left hand, little finger through to thumb, and then his right. He couldn't remember when the habit had started.

Things changed quickly in the air. One moment one was logging another aeroplane being hit, and the next, one was hit oneself. A-Able was coned by a searchlight on the ground below and there was no time for Iain to react before the ack-ack guns took out their port engine in a glorious burst of flame. He didn't panic. With a (rather clever, if he said so himself) bit of flying Iain managed to extinguish the flames billowing from the wing, but the reprieve was short-lived. They'd corkscrewed their way out of the bomber stream and become an easy target for the Messerschmitts circling the city, and soon they lost another engine. More flame began to lick its way towards the Perspex that was the only barrier between Iain and the sky. "Everyone all right?" he called down the intercom.

They weren't. Flak had torn through both the fuselage and Jamie, the mid-upper, who sat slumped in his turret, trapped, as his lifeblood leaked out of him onto the crew below. Iain turned to look for a moment, just long enough for Matthew, face covered in Jamie's blood, to shout at him, "Don't bloody be looking at me, skip!" And Iain turned back to the sky.

But there was not much more sky to be had, no chance of making it back home. By the time Iain gave the order to bale out they were hundreds of miles off course, and as the crew flung themselves one by one into the night, he tried not to think of the odds. Roger Neilson was the last to go. The darkness beneath the aircraft was complete, and there was no way to know what it was they were flinging themselves towards.

There were three of them left now—Matthew, Jamie, Iain. It was nearly impossible to shimmy Jamie out of the turret when the boy was in his full kit and utterly incapable of helping, but Matthew was still trying. The flames licked up the fuselage, but Iain would not bale out until Matthew and Jamie had gone. Something about captains and ships. Finally Jamie slithered free from the turret and collapsed to the floor with Matthew, into a pool of his own blood. "Go!" Iain ordered down the intercom. "Jump!"

"There's only two chutes left, one of them must have gotten tossed," Matthew called.

"Take mine," Jamie croaked. "I'll not make it anyway."

"Don't be stupid," Iain said. "Matt, take Jamie and—"

"He'll be dead in five minutes," Matthew said, and Jamie said, "Come on, skip, take the damn parachute." A rasping sound down the intercom and Jamie added, "Or none of us will ever fucking forgive you."

The flames were licking at the Perspex. They were, Iain thought, trapped in a great metal comet. He tore the oxygen and

intercom from his face and threw himself down the fuselage.
Already Jamie looked like a corpse. His chest oddly sunken, his
face and lips colourless. Iain slipped in the blood covering the
floor and caught himself against the hot fuselage. "Good luck,"
Jamie said as Iain clipped the dying boy's parachute onto his
own harness, the words with which their ground crew had sent
them off hours ago. "See you in the morning."

A hot slice of sky: the French countryside. Iain and Matthew
walked for three weeks. Neither of them was sure what their
plan ought to be; all the capture scenarios for which they'd prepared involved a severe-looking German standing over them
minutes after they crashed down, tangled in their parachutes,
and announcing clearly, "For you, the war is over." No such announcement had come for them. They had drifted back down
to earth unnoticed, like stray flakes of ash.

A dry garden: the days they spent locked in an office in a village
too small to bear a name. They'd been foolish enough to wan-
der into the village in search of some food, thinking mostly of
the single letter their radios sometimes picked up while flying
over Vichy. *V*, for victory. The flustered *maire* didn't seem to
know what to do with them and locked them in his little office
while he tried to decide. There was talk about a fort near Nîmes,
where neither Iain nor Matthew had any intention of going.

They spent nearly a week in the office, Matthew lying on his
back and staring at the ceiling, Iain gazing out a narrow window into the desiccated garden below, before Iain realised that
the little window was loose in its frame.

The Pyrenees at night: a final, harrowing climb, rarely appreciated in the retelling. ("It was that easy?" Caroline said. "You shimmied out a window and waltzed into Spain?" Yes, Iain agreed, they did, although it had not felt particularly easy at the time.) They were back in England less than three months after going down, and they were received with astonishing fuss. No one had seen them bale out, but another pilot had reported seeing them hit, before they stumbled so far off course. When Iain asked, their CO reluctantly confirmed that the rest of the crew were presumed dead except for their flight engineer, Roger Neilson, who, it appeared, had been taken prisoner. When no other capture cards had arrived—because Iain and Matthew had not been captured long enough to fill them out—they had presumed the worst.

But there was more bad news to come, the CO told Iain after sending Matthew off to bed. "It's your old man," the CO said. "I'm afraid he's passed away."

This was how people left: with little fanfare. It had been a heart attack, quick, the CO said, terribly mundane. There was no compassionate leave to be had (*What's the point?* Iain wrote to Caroline. *The funeral was nearly two months ago*) and Iain took solace instead in the task to be done, the ops, the sorties, the tour. Poured all of himself out until he was hollow, filled himself instead with the war.

These were the things Iain thought ought to be remembered. Matthew McClare, Jamie Birch, all those boys. He crouched down and laid his hand against the still-wet paint of his father's name. These were the things that everyone's heads were too full with. There was nowhere else to put them, nowhere safe to lay them down. Just the side of the Beeches' house in thick black paint and the insides of their skulls. When they blinked themselves to sleep for the last time, there would be nothing at all. Paper telegrams atomised into air and the breath of a name on the wind.

By the time he returned to himself he was empty of everything, had entirely forgotten whatever mission had driven him from his house. Iain dropped his hand from the wall, the paint still clinging to his palm.

19.

On a quiet evening Leigh stood on the front porch with her head on her mother's shoulder. *You're getting too big for this*, Áine said. Her hands passing lightly over Leigh's tangled hair. It was already dark out, crickets calling from the tall grass, a twinkle of the bright moon overhead. Áine was right, Leigh was getting too big for this; she was nearly taller than Áine and her neck bent at an uncomfortable angle to rest on Áine's shoulder. Leigh stepped back and looked at her mother. Her mother looked back. She was in the same dress she'd been wearing the last time Leigh had ever seen her, leaning down to tuck her into bed and whispering, I'll see you soon. Pale green and diaphanous.

When are you going? Leigh asked. She reached out to touch Áine's cheek, but her fingers met only air.

Áine said, *I'm already gone.*

Leigh turned around. She was in the house again and it was winter. The lamps unlit and the windows wide open, tiny hard snowflakes blowing in with the wind. The house was empty, everybody was already gone, and the wind blew through, and she was alone.

Leigh turned again to close the door against the wind but now the front steps were covered in crows, on every available surface, and when she jumped to close the door they took flight, pouring inside, a swarm of black talons and feathers, tearing at her skin, tearing at her eyes, screaming, screaming, screaming. She dropped to the cold floor and there was darkness.

Light like a match striking and the darkness pulling back. Dancing on the walls of a round room, watery, flickering. Someone said her name, a whisper in the dark.

Have you come to finish it?

20.

They had become almost routine, these dreams, though they clung to her throughout the day. Sometimes she would turn her head and think she caught sight of someone, a woman, standing on the corner by the post office, lingering in a shadowed spot in the hall. She wished she could ask Iain what he thought of it, if she was going mad. Of course she couldn't. She had been the one to bend so many times. Not with him, but with everyone else. She was tired of bending.

She fled from the dream and the temptation to bend, set out in the early afternoon to begin mending the wilting fence hemming in the Welleses' fields. It seemed unlikely that she'd leave the island again in her lifetime, she thought, not only because of the state of her finances but mostly because of the way she felt rooted here, like she grew out of the green grass. There was no indication that Graham had ever written a will, and in the absence of any word from Sam, she thought probably the farm was hers now. Sam had never wanted it anyway. And if it was hers, then she ought to make it a place worth staying again.

The fence was even more of a job than she'd expected it to be; apparently when Graham had sold off the sheep, he had decided the fence could go, too. Eventually she'd need help to haul new lumber out, but for now she fixed what she could, noted what she couldn't, Maisie bounding ahead of her through the grass.

At the northeastern corner of the land she paused, alongside the ring road before it curved beyond the Ben. The moors were mostly hidden from view, but she could feel the wind whistling down from them. She closed her eyes against the rushing air.

A moment later she was standing in the middle of the road, her hammer dangling from her fist. She didn't remember walking the dozen yards to get here. Something was tugging on her ribs like a string, calling her northwards. A whisper on the breeze. *Come to finish it.*

She blinked and adjusted her grip on the hammer. Iain was right that she shouldn't go gallivanting down that tunnel without so much as a torch. She forced herself to turn back down the road and call for Maisie and head for home. There was more work to be done, but she didn't like how hard it was for her to turn from the Ben, she didn't like the way she felt that maybe she had lost time while standing there.

The house emerged from the trees. A little more distance between her and the moors might be a good thing, while she planned her return journey. Including, Leigh thought, as she approached the back steps, whether to ask Iain one more time to come along.

Her brother appeared at the back door, and Leigh dropped her hammer.

"Hi," Sam said. His shirt was white and his trousers were grey and everything about him was neatly pressed—even the way he'd rolled his shirtsleeves to his elbows had a studied quality to it. His hair was tidily parted and smoothed down. His face sharp and clean.

"Is that all you have to say?" Leigh asked. "Nothing for weeks and weeks, and then you show up and you say 'hi'?"

"There were things to be settled," he said. Even his voice was unrecognisable. His island accent smoothed and sanded into a soft city lull. "It's not easy to disappear without any warning."

"Oh, of course," Leigh said. There was so much inside of her and she could not manage it all anymore. "Well, why don't you go down to East Sands and tell Dad that the next time he's going to die, you'd like more warning?"

A muscle in Sam's jaw clenched, and Leigh felt a guilty spark of victory. "You couldn't possibly understand how much I had to do," Sam said. "I couldn't get up and leave."

He must have noticed her shoulders slump because he stood up a little straighter. When had they stopped being friends? Leigh couldn't remember. They had been, once, when Sam's knees were skinned and his hair was a tangled mop and his cheeks were perpetually flushed. When he would stay up late to peer at the starry sky with his telescope and wake Leigh when he found something exciting, the two of them bouncing at the window until Áine came to shut them up and return them to bed, a ghostly vision in a long white nightdress and moon-bright blonde hair. Years later Leigh sat on his bed as he packed for university, weeks after Áine had left. "I'm sorry for leaving you here all alone," he'd said to her.

"I'm not alone," she said. "There's still Dad."

A look like a storm cloud passed over his face. "Yes," he said. "I suppose there's still Dad."

Leigh didn't know how Sam had turned into this clean-cut, fresh-pressed man. Nothing in this house had ever belonged less.

At last Sam broke the silence. "I haven't come to fight with you," he said. "I've had some letters from the bank, and it turns out our father wasn't exactly balancing his chequebook. Anyway. I'll stay long enough to sort it all out, and decide what to do with you."

"What to do with me!"

"Don't start."

"What to do with me," she repeated. Hot tears pricking at the backs of her eyes but she was determined not to cry. "Like I'm a thing, to be placed on your mantel or shoved away into a closet."

"You know what I mean. You can't keep living here on your own, with no money and no prospects. You're still a child."

"I am not," she said, though she sometimes felt like it, like a girl grown too large for childhood. "I've been doing fine."

"I wouldn't call living off other people's charity 'doing fine.'" His voice dripped with disdain. "And what happened to all the windows?"

"Charity! What was it you were doing at that fancy school with that scholarship, then?"

Sam started towards her as though to throttle her, his composure slipping. Her words had, finally, struck him. "You have no idea how hard I work," he growled at her. "Every goddamned day. And what are you doing? Nothing."

Leigh knew she should apologise but couldn't. She crouched down and collected her hammer from the grass. Sam's eyes followed her as she stalked into the house, walked to the stairs. Kept herself from bolting. "Where are you going?"

She said, "I don't want to fight anymore."

"We're not done talking."

"I am."

"Leigh."

She turned on the stairs. Clenched her fist so tightly that her nails dug painfully into her palm. Sam stood below her and looked up at her and it was the first time they'd both been home in years and her father had died all over again. Áine had left all over again. She'd thought herself angry with Sam for not turning up, but without him it had been so easy to pretend. Dad is out on another expedition and Sam is at school and I am here and these are our lives.

Sam said, "Don't you think I wanted to come sooner?"

There didn't seem any point in lying to him. A tear slipped over her eyelashes, plopped onto her cheek. He wilted. How was this what they had become? She hated it. She hated every minute of it.

Leigh turned and ran up the stairs.

Face down on her bed she realised that she remembered quite clearly the moment that she and Sam had stopped being friends.

A perfect September evening, low slanting light through the windows. The day war was announced. The Welleses had not been churchgoing people since Áine surrendered her battle for the children's immortal souls, and Leigh spent most Sunday mornings alone in McAllister's with the wireless. She'd heard the news, alone, ran home to tell Sam. By the time the king spoke in the evening, everyone was huddled around Tom's wireless. Tom helped Leigh and a few of the other children to sit on the bar. Leigh sat next to Kate, with wee Hugo held tightly in her own lap. Leigh looked around at the pale, drawn faces in the pub. It seemed that everyone she had ever known was here, holding their breath.

The king was speaking but Leigh wasn't really listening, though later she would remember exactly what he had said. ("For the second time in the lives of most of us—") Mostly she was thinking about how they were going to tell Graham when he got home. When the king's speech ended, the pub was quiet for a long time. Leigh could hear everyone breathing, everyone. Outside the sun was slanting and gold, and it poured in through the windows in dusty streams. Dripped over the faces of the people Leigh had known all her life, some of them slack with shock and others already hardened to this new reality like the weather.

Part of the speech she had not been listening to suddenly became clear in her mind like a knock on a door ("War is no longer confined to the battlefield—") and there was a fluttering in her chest like a caged bird, and she found Sam standing against the far wall. He was already looking at her, his eyes locked on hers, but it felt oddly as though he wasn't really seeing her, like he was miles away, thinking about something else entirely. He never looked at her any other way again.

Sam Welles was terrible at keeping promises, except the ones he made to himself.

One morning in 1939 he told his sister, "I'll be back before you know it. Promise." Had he meant it then? Six years later the war was over and Sam's life stretched before him. He stood at the docks one autumn morning, and as he stared at the water reaching interminably into the distance, he felt a great gulf open up in his chest, and then he turned away. He had always been planning to leave, anyway.

When he had stood at those same docks this afternoon, the years had melted away. No matter how hard one tried, this island was not a place for leaving easily. It clung to a person like dew. He was still here, always still here. He sat in the kitchen with his back to the fireplace and surveyed the stage of his childhood. What remained of Graham's herbs hanging above the island. The shells Áine used to collect propped up on the windowsills. After Leigh had stormed away, he had followed her upstairs. Stood outside her bedroom door, could hear her crying inside. He hadn't meant to make her cry, but he didn't know how to talk to her anymore; possibly he never had.

He stepped into his father's study. Exactly as he remembered it. The large armchair in the corner where he or Leigh had once sat with a book while Graham took notes or sorted the bills. A balled-up jumper still sitting on the cushion, flung haphazardly by his father. Sam tried to remember what the last thing he'd said to his father had been but couldn't. They hadn't spoken in nearly a year.

He did not go into his childhood bedroom. He'd already put his suitcase in his parents' old room. He already knew what he had left behind.

It was Leigh who broke the news to him, all those years ago. Years where his world grew so much bigger that he couldn't hold it anymore. A series of moments he lived his life almost solely to forget. Standing hip-deep in murky water at Dunkirk. An airless night in North Africa. A grey morning on a beach in Normandy. After arriving in Germany he spent days wrestling with a letter to his father, eventually settled on a few vague lines. (*The war's as good as won. Do believe we shall all be home soon. Dreaming of a proper meal and bed.*)

Then there was Dachau. The last straw. He hadn't known how he was going to go on living after Dachau, like everything was normal, like he hadn't watched something important about the world crumble away to ash. He was not supposed to have been there; if he hadn't attached himself to that American squadron after D-Day, he would not have been there at all. Eventually he decided that there was only one way to get through it, which was to get through it, and then box it up. Just get through today, he often told himself, and then you never have to think about today again.

But the war was not a thing for leaving easily, either.

Some time later there was a knock at Leigh's door and she found Sam standing in the hallway. His eyes passed over her face (red, puffy) and then slid away. "It's seven," he said. "I saw Tom on my way up and he invited us to dinner. We should go."

"I'm not hungry."

"Leigh," Sam said. He sounded so tired. Some long-beaten-down instinct nearly made her reach out and press her hand to his face. She resisted. "Don't let's fight."

He said it as though it were she who wanted a fight. But she hadn't forced him to come. Upon arriving home she had visited the post office several times a day, in case Sam had called, or written, or telegrammed. After a week of silence and pitying stares from the McGillicuddys behind the desk, she had given up. By saying nothing he had sent his own sort of message. She had not forced him to come. She was not the one who wanted a fight.

She supposed she had to prove it. Reluctantly she brushed past him. By the time he caught up with her downstairs she was already stuffing her feet into her boots, her coat hanging off one arm. His eyes flicked up and down over her and then he retrieved his own coat from the closet. A deep blue wool number, no moth holes, not faded at all. Leigh's own coat, the decidedly not-lovely one, was beginning to split along the back seam. The elbows were wearing thin.

A coat should not affect her so much, but irritation rose in her throat again. But she didn't want to fight, so she said nothing, stepped into the rainy evening. "We can take the car, you know," Sam called after her. He'd turned up the collar of the offending coat, put on a hat. She herself had neither hat nor umbrella, and her hair was already plastered to her head by the rain. She looked at him standing in the yard. This stranger. He said, "I'll drive."

She turned and pulled the canvas off the car without even the tiniest bit of a flourish. It was the first time she'd looked at it since coming home. She had thought it would be rusting under the canvas, rusting and ruined like everything else in the yard, but it wasn't. The paint was glossy and dark and perfect; the chrome accents were polished until they shone, even in the matte black of the stormy night. The car was more beautiful than anything inside the Welles house. Rain began to run down the windshield. How keenly Leigh wished that she had ridden in this car with her father at the wheel. Sam appeared at her elbow, put a hand out for the keys. Leigh said, "Dad told me you were a terrible driver, once."

"I got better," Sam said. "In the war."

Leigh looked up at him. He seemed not to realise the gravity of the thing he had done. It was perhaps the first time that he had ever made reference to the war without somebody else bringing it up. Leigh waited for him to continue but he only brandished his open palm at her. She placed the keys in his hand, wrenched the passenger door open, dropped into the car. It smelled exactly how she had thought it would. Faintly of liquorice and cigarette smoke, damp earth. "I'll never understand why he wasted his money on this thing," Sam said as he slid into the driver's seat.

"Do you have to do that?"

"Do what?"

"He loved this car, and you know it." Leigh remembered the letter Graham had sent her when he bought it, with all the details so she could go find a garage or a dealer and look one over herself. "I don't see why you have to look down your nose at everything because it's on this island. Why you had to look down at Dad."

"I did not look down at Dad."

214

"You did," Leigh said. "You were always fighting with him. You were always so cruel to him. And then you left, and you never came back, and you never wrote or telephoned or anything."

"You left too," Sam snapped. "So stop pretending to be so superior. You left too, just like me, just like Mum."

Leigh opened her mouth to retort but found she had nothing to say. Áine Welles had sailed away one August morning a week after Sam's birthday, and the Welleses had never spoken of her again. She had once asked Sam if he ever looked for Áine after moving away for school. "Of course," he said. "But if she's still in the country, she certainly doesn't want to be found. I tried to find her family, but she never told me anything about them. I don't even know her maiden name." Leigh had spent years thinking about the days before Áine left, whether there were signs that she had missed. A packed suitcase, a coat missing from the closet. But it seemed that she had simply picked up and left with nothing but the clothes on her back. How desperate she must have been to go. How deeply it must have injured Graham, when both his children followed her.

Leigh wished she could tell him how much she wished she hadn't done it, how much she wished she had let herself come home sooner. "You don't sound happy, mo ghràdh," he had told her over her landlady's telephone, about a year after she'd left. She wasn't, not even then, though there was still the buoyant hope that one day it would slip into place like a gear in a clock. But she hadn't gone in search of happiness. Happiness was at home, on the island, in the midnight suns of summer, the winter skies dancing with lights. Tranquil days before she knew the sting of Áine's departure, before the war and all its suffering.

It wasn't happiness or adventure or even Áine that Leigh had gone to the mainland to find. When she'd signed up for her shorthand postal course, she had been thinking of something else entirely, something hard and dense that she carried in her like a stone. Something she felt again, sitting in this car next to her brother. A feeling that had pricked her like a pin each time she sent off a pair of socks or a batch of scrap metal, each time a telegram came. That had filled her lungs like air the moment she heard the war was over.

Sam waited for her to reply. When she didn't, he adjusted the mirrors and slid the keys into the ignition, and pulled away onto the road.

Leigh didn't speak again until Sam was pulling up in front of Tom's pub. Light spilled out of the front window like water, condensation clung to the glass and the shadows of those inside moved across it darkly. Sam turned off the engine. "I'm not pretending to be superior," she said. How could she? When she sat next to him, she felt anything but superior, felt small and useless and inconsequential. "I wish I hadn't gone. I wish it every single day. That's not my point. My point is—you never told me you were at Dachau."

"What?"

"You never told me," she said again. "Iain MacTavish had to tell me."

For a long moment he said nothing. His hands gripped the steering wheel so hard they turned white. The lamplight pressed through the rain-splattered windshield and hugged the contours of his face, turned him skeletal. He said, "I don't want to talk about this."

"You don't want to talk to me about anything," Leigh said. "You wrote Dad letters. From France and North Africa and Germany and—you wrote him letters. You didn't write me a single letter. You won't talk to me about it now even when I know you're thinking about it."

"The things in my head," he said, to his hands, not to her, "things I can't ever unsee, Leigh, and you keep punishing me with it. I don't want to live in the past. I won't do it. Not every time you're mad at me."

"It doesn't have anything to do with being mad at you," she said, feeling dangerously close to tears again. She didn't know how to explain to him what it was, the way it had spun inside her since Iain told her. He liberated Dachau, didn't you know? There was too much of it in her, the war, the war and that wordless guilt, and she didn't know where to put it. "It has to do with— with not knowing what to do with myself now that it's over."

He said, "Stop talking."

She found she couldn't. "You say I couldn't possibly understand, and probably I can't, but you never give me the chance, you won't tell me anything. I want you to talk to—"

"I want to sell the house," Sam said, and Leigh froze as if he had shouted it.

"You want to—what?"

"I think it's right," he said. "Dad was in a great deal of debt, did you know? So we've no choice. Sell the house, sell the car, get on with our lives."

The rain pattered on the windshield. She wasn't sure what she ought to say, or do. Maybe it was shock, though she found she wasn't particularly surprised. It was inevitable, the way things were between them, that it should come to this. It shouldn't feel like he had scooped out her insides with a hot ladle.

She said, "Where am I supposed to go?"

"I don't know. Stay here, if you love it so much."

"I won't be able to stay here without the house, the farm. You know well enough that I'm completely skint."

"So get a job, Leigh," Sam said disparagingly, "like the rest of the world. Come back to Edinburgh, move to Timbuktu. Start over somewhere. I'll give you some money. There's plenty of jobs to be had if you're willing to work hard. Or—"

"Or what?" Leigh asked. Sam said nothing. "Come on, or what? Oh, I know, marry, that's what you were going to say, isn't it? I suppose that's all I'm good for."

Sam removed the keys from the ignition and looked at her calmly. At last, he said, "I won't pretend it wouldn't solve a few problems." As though she hadn't ached for him to say she was being silly, of course that wasn't all she was good for, they'd come up with some plan. As though he hadn't known exactly what she had wanted him to say. "What about George McClare, weren't you soft on him when we were kids?"

She felt dreadfully as though if she opened her mouth, she might scream. "I'd rather set myself on fire," she said, as coolly as she could manage.

"Well," Sam said. "Beggars can't be choosers."

She flung the car door open and herself after it, into the damp night air. "Leigh!" Sam shouted after her, but she was already running down the street.

When she stopped running, where the high street narrowed into little more than a lane, she was gasping for air as if she'd been underwater. Fat raindrops splatted cool against her hot face. She flattened her hand on chest, felt her heart pound.

What was she supposed to do now? The thought of walking through the front door into the house that Sam was going to sell made her stomach turn. The thought of lying in bed and hearing the door open and close as he returned himself, the way he'd no doubt pound up the stairs furious at having been left alone at the pub—of waking up in the morning and finding him in the kitchen taking up too much space, making snide comments about the state of things—she didn't think she could bear it.

She turned away from home.

21.

Iain stood on the bluff in the dark of a night hardly suited for walking. He never had managed to make it up to Leigh's to check that everything was all right. He told himself it wasn't necessary, he'd have heard if everything wasn't all right. Really it was that he was hardly here at all, was trapped somewhere between the war and the light shining straight through Hugo McClare's pale cheek. Down the hill the way he'd come, the glow of one faint, distant street lamp fought against the night and the rain.

Iain turned from the village and was plunged into total darkness. On a clear night it never really grew dark at all on this island, the stars shone down, unhindered by smog and city lights. On a cloudy night there was nothing but the wind on one's face and the ground beneath one's feet and blindness. The last time he'd seen such darkness: London, 1942, a rare week of leave. He had been making his way from the station to his hotel when he'd been stopped at a street corner waiting for the all-clear to cross and somebody unseen tapped him on the shoulder. "Excuse me, but I believe you're standing on my foot."

Iain looked down, though in the blackout there was nothing to see. It was a woman who had spoken, with a soft Scottish accent, a sound unfamiliar in London and especially here at Hyde Park Corner. (He hoped it was Hyde Park Corner; if not, he'd made a catastrophic wrong turn somewhere.) "Terribly sorry," he said, stepping backwards, only to bump into someone else.

"Come here," the Scottish voice said. A hand took his arm. "Where are you heading?"

It turned out that they were both heading to the same hotel in Belgravia ("What are the odds!"), so they linked arms and began the slow journey together. There was something about her voice that was awfully familiar, but blind as he was, he couldn't be sure. It was a cloudy night and there was not even the glow of a distant moon, the pinpricks of stars. Walking about was like being "it" in the games of blind man's buff he and his cousins had played as children. Perfect sightlessness.

"I think we've found it," the woman said some time later, and she was right, it was the hotel looming out of the darkness, and Iain felt a tightly strung bit of anxiousness in his chest start to release. He did not like being here on the ground instead of in the sky. They stepped into the lobby of the hotel, and in the dim light the woman turned to him. Recognition settled into her face like daybreak. "Hang on," she said. "It's Iain, isn't it?"

Iain had recognised her too. A bright face, a lot of auburn hair. An unrestrained rush of memory: a friend of Grace's who always tagged along on their summer adventures. The seventh player at cricket and croquet and conkers. Impish grins on sun-pink faces laying the groundwork for a prank.

"Oh," Iain said. "Hello, Caroline."

This was well in the past but it was all Iain thought about as he began the walk home. All the things that might have been different had he taken his leave a different weekend, had he gotten lost in the blackout, had he not ended up waiting to cross the street at Hyde Park Corner. Mrs. Cavanagh would not be asleep in what had once been his childhood bedroom. Matthew McClare might still be alive. Iain himself might be dead.

He stepped into the square and there was a figure standing in the glow of the street lamp. Turned away from him, head bowed. The same street lamp in which he was sure he had seen Matthew McClare.

The figure turned, and Iain's heart unclenched.

"What are you doing out here?" Iain called to Leigh. Now that she was facing him, it was obvious that it had always been her; she was too short to be the spectre he had seen at the month's start, the set of her shoulders entirely different. She was dripping wet, soaked through. As he approached, her breath caught in her throat, and he realised possibly it wasn't only rain streaking down her cheeks, possibly she was crying.

"It's Sam," she said. Her hair plastered to her head by the rain, water dripping off her nose. "It's Sam, he turned up and—I've been walking about trying to decide what to do. I don't know what to do."

Another breath caught in her throat and she turned away from him. Her thin coat was even less suited to the weather than his, and she was beginning to shiver. "Well," he said. He hadn't liked fighting with her in the first place, and this seemed as good a way as any to put it behind them. "First thing, let's get out of this weather, all right?"

Leigh turned again, looked up at him. "I can't go home."

"Good, because I'm not walking all the way up there in this rain. Come on." And he took her by the arm and led her down the lane. By the time they reached his front gate, she appeared to have stopped crying; at least her shoulders had stopped listing up and down dangerously every few steps. He opened the unlocked door for her and she stepped inside, dripping on the mat. When he put his hand out towards her, she stared at it for a minute before peeling her arms out of her wet coat and handing it over. He draped it carefully over the radiator to dry out and said, "I think a rather large whisky is in order. You?"

Leigh followed him to the sitting room but lingered in the doorway, dripping. "There's a blanket," Iain said, fetching the whisky, "there, on the chair."

"I'm all wet, I'll ruin it."

Iain said, "Don't be silly," and after a moment Leigh scooped the blanket from the chair, wrapped herself in it, sat gingerly on the edge of the sofa. Iain handed her a drink. "Now," he said, "are you going to tell me what's happened, or do I have to guess?"

Leigh extricated her hands from the blanket and took the glass. "Sam," she said. "He turned up today. No note, no telegram, no warning. It's—not going well." She took a large gulp of her drink, blinked against the burn of it. "He wants me to marry," she continued. "He thinks marriage will solve all my problems. Well, all of his problems, or at least his biggest one, which is me."

Iain thought of his own short-lived marriage. He didn't think it had solved any problems, his or anybody else's, and it seemed unlikely that he'd try it again. There had been a girl or two during his brief tenure in London, but they had been, he thought, distractions more than anything else. He had treated them carelessly, and they had treated him carelessly right back. He hadn't wanted anything other than carelessness from them because he still clung doggedly to his loyalty to Caroline. Sometimes he hated her for it, convincing him, dragging him into that register office. Sometimes he hated her so much he could taste it on his tongue, acrid, smoky. Then inevitably he would wake one cold, dull morning and hate himself for hating her.

"What a load of bollocks," he said, and Leigh laughed, bitterly, the end of it turning choked. Iain turned away to fix his own drink, pretended he didn't notice Leigh wiping angrily at her eyes.

"It's not that," she said. "He's going to sell the house. He says there are debts he has to pay and that he refuses to live in the past, that we all have to move on." She drained the rest of her whisky in two gulps. "So I'm to be homeless as soon as he's found a buyer."

For a time there was quiet, only the sound of the rain on the windows. Sam refused to live in the past? Iain himself did nothing but. He didn't know what to say, so he stayed silent. A whole range of cruelties. Her brother, her father, the house. Leigh wiped the back of her hand across her face again. "He's doing it because of me," Leigh said. "Selling the house. Ever since the war he—hates me."

"I don't think that's true."

"He never told me, you know," she said, looking up at him. "About Dachau, that he was there. He won't talk to me about anything, he thinks I'm too stupid to understand."

Nothing about Leigh was stupid. But it was possible that Sam had a point, about understanding. Even Caroline—despite all the nights they'd spent squeezed into her single bed while he told her about his war, a confessional—had not understood it properly. The littlest thing revealed it. Referring to one of his crew in passing as a "friend from the airfield," when "friend" could not possibly begin to describe the way he felt about his men and they about him. Saying, "You just waltzed into Spain?" when he returned from the lost months of his war, as though she was disappointed by the story, wanted something more exciting. Telling him, "Of course it wasn't your fault," in the dark one night when he told her of the terrible guilt he still carried when he thought about Roger Neilson in a POW camp somewhere across the water.

But he didn't say any of that. "Maybe," he said, instead, "he couldn't bear it."

Leigh looked up at him. "I can't bear it either."

He wouldn't dismiss her by telling her that it was different, but of course it was. Surely she had to know. Nothing about Leigh was stupid, but nobody could understand everything.

The clock in the hallway chimed the hour. "Come on," Iain said, "let's find you some dry clothes. You can sleep in the spare room."

Caroline was a secretary in the War Office, which kept her busy. She was cagey about the specifics. (Obviously. She wasn't the only one who'd signed the Official Secrets Act.) She had a lit-tle flat in Clapham, but the week before, the building had been deemed unsafe and torn down. Her flatmate, Maria, was in the midst of a torrid affair with a man high up in the Admiralty. When he'd heard that Maria was to be homeless until they found a new flat, he'd insisted on putting her up in a hotel for the time being, and Maria had insisted that Caroline come with.

"So here we are," she said. She'd allowed Iain to walk her to her room, two floors above his. "I know a girl moving out of a place in Lewisham we might be able to take if nothing else turns up."

There was something about being certain he was in the dog days of his life that made him feel bold. "I know you don't have a chance to do much of anything but work," he said, "but d'you ever get a chance to eat?"

She looked at him slyly. "Occasionally."

"Think you might have a chance to eat tomorrow? Round one o'clock?"

"You know," Caroline said, "I think I might."

22.

Leigh woke in the morning in a strange bed, a strange house, a strange life. She stared at the whitewashed ceiling until a knock broke the silence, and the door swung open. Mrs. Cavanagh appeared with a large cup of tea and Leigh sat up sharply, pulling the sheets up to her armpits. The embarrassment of being found here by Mrs. Cavanagh, wearing a pair of her son-in-law's pyjamas. Her own clothes draped over the radiator in the corner. Mrs. Cavanagh glided into the room and sat on the edge of Leigh's bed, handed her the tea. "I heard about the night you had."

Leigh gripped the cup in both hands. The kindness of these near strangers, these people who owed her less than nothing. She ought to be grateful for it—she was grateful for it—and yet her heart burned inexplicably as Mrs. Cavanagh smoothed out the bedspread at Leigh's feet. A thousand mornings that had been stolen from her.

"I'm so sorry for barging in," Leigh said. "I'm awfully—"

"Not at all," Mrs. Cavanagh said. "You know, I like having you about. I'm used to a full house, what with raising two boys and practically all their friends. All of them dead in the war. And my girl." She reached out and straightened an empty picture frame on the bedside table, caught sight of Leigh's stricken face. "Best not to dwell on it," she said bracingly. And then: "Iain's told me about the house."

There was the quiet of the room and the steam twirling out of Leigh's cup. The tension that had descended with Mrs. Cavanagh's casual invocation of her dead sons. Leigh's embarrassment seeping into that tense air. She did not belong in this bed, in this house. She ought to be at home, alone. How poorly she'd behaved last night, how sorely she regretted it now. "I wish there was something I could say to make it right," Mrs. Cavanagh said. "I wish I'd known your father better so I could tell you that he had a plan for all of this. I wish I knew your brother so I could tell you that he does."

Leigh gripped her mug tightly between her hands. It was almost too hot to hold, but she pressed her palms into the china. She said, "I suppose it was over for me and Sam the moment the war started."

Mrs. Cavanagh was still for a moment. "I suppose a lot of things were." She got to her feet with a huffing breath. "There's porridge on the stove," she said. "And a young man at the door asking for you. I daresay it must be this brother of yours."

When Leigh came down into the kitchen, back in her own clothes, he was already there, standing near the doorway so that she had to push past him to get to the kettle. "Good morning," Sam said. Leigh busied herself making tea even though the pot was still mostly full. "I was worried about you last night." She doubted it immensely. "No clue where you'd gotten to. I ran into George McClare and he said you'd been spending all your time with Iain MacTavish lately so I might check here." He paused. "And here you've been," he continued. "All night. I looked after the dog, by the way. She missed you."

Leigh still couldn't bring herself to look at him, so she ignored the accusation that hung in the air, implicit. There was condensation on the inside of the windows, water running down in rivulets, small stripes of the world outside showing through the steam. "I'm leaving on the eleven o'clock," Sam said. "I'd thought to stay longer, but clearly it'll make us both miserable. I'll telegram when the house has sold. Don't impose on these people too much," he added. "They don't deserve it."

She gripped the counter with both hands. This couldn't be happening. This was not how any of it was supposed to happen.

"Well," Sam said. "Goodbye, then."

"Sam," she said. Finally she turned and looked at him. This fresh-pressed man. His hair combed back, his neat, clean clothes. He was unrecognisable, and it ached like a physical wound. There was so much she wanted to say to him. What happened to you? Where did you go? She wanted to know how he could look at her and not see the aching, worse, how he could not care. She cared for him so desperately. Her voice when it came was little more than a whisper. "What did I do?" she asked him. "How do I fix it?"

He looked at her, his face impassive. She had been so good at knowing what he was thinking, once. "You didn't do anything," he said. "It's me."

"What," she said, breathlessly. "What is it?"

He opened his mouth as though to speak, and then closed it. Looked down, carefully buttoned up his coat, tugged his gloves back onto his hands, looked up at her again. "You know, Leigh," he said at last. "I just can't talk about it."

And then he was gone.

Iain insisted on walking her home, which was both nice and irritating. She didn't have the energy to argue. Mrs. Cavanagh walked with them as far as the post office; she had "some urgent telegrams to send," she said as she left them in the street. "That's unusual for her," Iain said as they continued, conversationally. Leigh didn't respond. It was hard to care about anything as mundane as a telegram.

"What are you going to do?" he asked as they passed the harbour. Abandoning the conversational tone. "You know, about the house."

She hadn't a clue. Of course she wanted to stay, buy some more goats, reseed the fields that Graham had left to grow over. Farming had never been in Sam's future, he had always wanted something clean and crisp and clinical, but Leigh thought she would like to make something grow with little more than her two gentle hands. Enough distractions that she could almost forget the bitterness in the back of her throat, the aching in the pit of her belly—the memory of the happy days of childhood. A quiet, cloudy day.

What else did she want? To be home, but home was a thing that had ended. To sleep for a hundred years and wake up in a new world, in a new life.

"I suppose," she said, "I'll go back to Edinburgh. Or Aberdeen or Glasgow or—anywhere that'll have me."

Iain frowned, buried his hands in his pockets. "You won't stay here?"

"I haven't any money," Leigh said, bluntly. "Know of many people hiring, do you?" Of course he didn't. This was an island where everybody had their place, everybody played their role. Children inherited their parents' trades, and already there were too many children and too few trades. Leigh didn't have a role, her role was being sold away. She wanted to be angry about it but she couldn't clear from her mind the look on Sam's face as he tugged his gloves back onto his hands finger by finger, when he finally faced her and said, "You know, Leigh, I just can't talk about it." It was hard to be angry with a boy wearing that face, and in that moment he had seemed very much like a boy, had seemed small and soft and sad.

Iain must have detected it in her silence because he said, "You know that no one's going to let you be homeless, don't you?"

Which she didn't, not at all. She thought of the way that Mary Lewis had appraised her, the way she'd sneered about Leigh's "grand adventure." She hardly blamed them for not knowing what to do with her, she knew how it looked. The Welles girl, gone off to the mainland like her mother, doesn't even write to her friends anymore, uppity. A betrayal of the blood covenant tying her to this island. Nobody could see these twin agonies that had plagued her, the day she stepped onto the ferry and every day after: that she couldn't bear to stay in the comfortable, careful life that she had not earned, that she couldn't bear to leave it all behind.

They were nearly at the turn for the Welles house when Iain stopped abruptly, peering into the middle distance. "Hang on," he said. "Isn't that Hugo?"

It was. Maybe a quarter mile ahead, continuing up along the ring road past where he ought to turn off to go home. To go anywhere. As they watched, he crested the hill and disappeared.

"If I'd been missing on the moors for two weeks," Leigh said, "I don't think I'd be itching to go back, do you?"

Iain frowned up the road. "Come on, then," he said. "Let's follow him."

They did, at a distance. Hugo led them on a familiar journey. He skirted around the Ben and didn't bother crossing the burn at the easy point Leigh and Iain had found, waded through the water like it was nothing. Carried on and up through the grass towards the cathedral. "Where the hell is he going?" Iain muttered as they walked.

"Maybe he's retracing his steps," Leigh said, her eyes still pinned to Hugo's back. If it were she who had lost great swathes of her memory, she thought it was a thing she might try to do. Not alone. Not alone in October. Hugo had developed an oddly mechanical way of walking, like he was being drawn forwards or else pushed by some invisible hand. The wind whistled across the moor, whipping Leigh's hair around her face, making her eyes water. If there was ever a good day for walking on this island, today was not one of them.

The abandoned Bruce house emerged out of the low-hanging mist, and Hugo turned off the road, cutting a path through the grass towards it. He paused before the front door, and then disappeared inside. Leigh knew where he was going, she knew it like a hand pulling back a curtain. She said, "He's going to the cave."

But inside the Bruce house there was no sign of him. Not so much as a speck of dust out of place from the last time they had been here. Iain called his name from the front hall, but there was no sound in reply. He was in the cave, Leigh knew it, she could feel herself being drawn towards it as though by a magnet. Iain placed a foot on the bottom step of the stairs leading to the second floor, but it crumbled away beneath his weight. There was only one place left to find him.

Iain trailed behind her as she dropped down into the cellar, approached the crumbling opening in the back wall. She thought maybe she could hear that otherworldly sigh again, though possibly it was only in her head, or in her heart pounding in her throat. Just like last time Iain grabbed her by the hand and stopped her from slipping into the dark. "Wait—"

"I know," Leigh snapped, turning on him. "We haven't any equipment. But don't you want to know where he was for two weeks? Why he doesn't remember it?" She felt sure that the answer was down that tunnel.

"I was only going to say," Iain said, "that you should let me go first."

Leigh eyed him in the dark. "What's changed your mind?"

"You were right," he said. "Something's wrong. I spoke to him the other day and he wasn't himself at all." Iain pulled a small object from his pocket. The faint light from the mucky half window in the corner glinted off something gold. Hugo's lighter. "I'll go first," Iain said. "But if I decide we're turning around, I don't want any arguing."

Something in his voice had hardened, leaving no room for equivocation. Leigh supposed this must be the voice he used during the war, a commander of men. He cracked all the knuckles on his left hand, one by one. She said, "All right."

Iain flicked Hugo's lighter open. The flame was small but bright, casting a faint orange glow in a ring around them. They turned together, and ventured into the tunnel.

It was low and narrow, the tunnel, and Iain had to hunch over, both to accommodate his height and to illuminate the ground enough to avoid tripping over anything. The floor sloped gradually downwards, and they shuffled on. After a few slow paces the dirt on the floor cleared, and the light began to flicker off the walls, reflecting. Leigh reached out to the wall. It was smooth and cold against her hand. "It's like glass," she whispered to Iain. Her fingers passed over something rough, a series of grooves in the wall that felt regular, pattern-like. "There's something carved into it."

Iain turned around, came closer to the wall, held up the lighter. Revealing a series of sharp, spiky symbols, much like the ones that had been painted on the Gordons' grocery earlier in the month. "Runes," he said, his voice little more than a breath in her ear. "I recognise them from your father's book."

Runes. What kind of place was this? She thought of a cold, wet day out on the moors, sulking by the side of the road, her father telling her about ancient temples buried under the ground. She'd thought it was one of his stories, just a way to tell her off for her moping. Leigh's stomach twisted, and instinctively she grabbed Iain's hand. The feeling of his palm against hers steadied her. "Come on," he said, and for a moment she thought he was going to tell her it was time to turn around, and for a moment she thought she wouldn't mind if he did. But instead he squeezed her hand and said, "Let's keep going."

There was no sound in the tunnel but the quiet pat of their own footsteps, not even the slightest echo from anywhere farther along to suggest how deep into the earth the tunnel stretched, where along it they might find Hugo.

At last the tunnel began to widen, the wall reaching away from Leigh's outstretched hand. They emerged into a large cavern, almost perfectly circular. The floor sloped down into a black pool of water, moving gently like it had been disturbed, rippling. The walls were dark and glassy and the light from the cigarette lighter danced on them.

Leigh thought she heard a whisper, but when she whipped around there was only air. Her chest filled with the feeling of the place. An impossible familiarity. The light reflected off the round walls, watery, flickering.

"Iain," Leigh whispered to him. "I've been dreaming about this place."

Iain looked down at her sharply, but before he could reply—

Have you come to finish it?

The voice came out of nowhere, maybe out of Leigh's own head. The same voice that called her name at the end of those dreams, those dreams that were somehow about this place, this place she had never been before in her life. Whose voice? Iain's eyes had widened. "Who's there?" he demanded. He had heard it too.

A long, delicate sound, a movement of air, like a sigh.

The thing you're looking for, the voice said. *It's in the pool.*

Neither of them moved, neither of them breathed, but the voice did not come again. The silence pressed in thickly against Leigh's ears, like cotton gauze filling up her head. Iain dropped her hand, passed her the lighter and stepped out of its glow, was swallowed by the darkness. "Iain!" Leigh whispered, but he didn't respond. Rising to the top of her mind—a tourist in a bright white coat with hair the colour of hot chocolate, Liam McAllister telling that tourist about the sluagh. If the sluagh could give a person visions, who was to say they couldn't make one hear things too? She heard the waters part for Iain as he waded into the pool, and then the sound was swallowed by the darkness, and there was only the beating of her own heart in her ears and the faint echo of that voice. *Leigh*, it said, or maybe it was just the water.

A shadow moved in the darkness. Iain, returning. Carrying something large in his arms, stumbling his way out of the pool, emerging into the soft halo of the lighter. It was a boy. His stomach had been torn open, and Leigh thought maybe she could see a loop of intestine through the remnants of his clothing and skin and muscle. Half of his face had been ripped away and the good side was turned from her, cradled against Iain's

238

chest. As Iain took the final step out of the pool, water pouring off him, the boy's head lolled to the side, and his single lifeless, glassy eye turned upon Leigh.

The voice was wrong: the thing they were looking for wasn't in the pool at all. They had been looking for Hugo McClare. This was only his body.

23.

Iain stood outside Dr. Delaune's surgery and stared at his hands. There wasn't any blood to speak of. He thought there ought to be. Smeared deeply into the lines of his palms, a brand, smeared so deeply that it would never come out. But there was only cold, pale skin. He barely remembered clambering out of the pool, he barely remembered the walk back into town, he barely remembered because he was barely here at all. He was thinking about the Pyrenees at night. The great roar of a Lancaster's engines in one's ears as it plummeted towards the ground. He was thinking about the North Sea and the thousands of young men lying beneath its surface, water wearing their eyes away to pearls. He was thinking about how light Hugo's body had been in his arms, as though his bones were hollow, ready for flight. He was thinking about Matthew McClare and the life he was supposed to have had. All of the promises that had come crashing down at the same time.

Crashing down, like a series of dominoes. Perhaps it had started when he bumped into a girl in a blackout at Hyde Park Corner, when he took her to lunch the next day, when she kissed him goodbye outside her office in Westminster. There was something about her that cleared the rough taste of war from Iain's mouth, even though sometimes it was all either of them had to talk about. When he returned to the island for Christmas that year, he had barely been able to contain himself. "Dad," he had said over lunch, "I've met a girl." It was the last time he saw his father.

They were married on a bright afternoon in Kensington, the early spring of 1944, when Caroline took him by the hand and began to drag him down the street in much the same way she had once led him through a blackout. "Oh, do come on," she said. "What point is there in waiting?" As they approached the register office, Iain could think of a few reasons (the odds, his chances, etcetera), but at that moment he wanted terribly to be convinced. Their witnesses were another couple just married, the man in a navy uniform. He and Iain exchanged a look of commiseration, but it was mostly for show. Once it was done, they found a hotel still serving tea, and Caroline ordered cake, which cost a small fortune, and they were happy.

Five months later, September 1944, the crew of E-Easy got lost over Germany. "Can you believe it?" Matthew railed over a pint (not his first). He snatched Iain's cigarette out of his fingers and took a long drag. "A sortie for everyone but me because of a fucking map. I'd like them to try to navigate by rivers and stars with nine-tenths cloud cover and make it out of bloody British airspace. We're supposed to be done. I'm supposed to be done."

They were supposed to be done. Iain had been looking forward to calling Caroline to tell her they could finally go on holiday. Their honeymoon. She'd wanted to go to Dover this weekend but he had told her no, to wait until the tour was done. Last night should have been the end. Iain hadn't even had to bark for silence over the radio as they soared over the Channel; everyone had been afraid to say something wrong and jinx themselves.

Apparently they were jinxed anyway because they ended up hopelessly, desperately lost in the clouds. They had never found the target and eventually their fuel had begun to run low. They had jettisoned their bombs over the North Sea and skulked back home.

McClare's fault, the CO said. McClare's mistake. So the sortie was to count for everybody except him. It seemed unfair, these were things that happened, but the CO was unmoved by any of their pleas.

"We'll all go up," said the flight engineer. Roger Neilson's replacement. "Won't we?"

"Yes," Iain agreed as six pairs of eyes turned to him. He plucked his cigarette back out of Matthew's mouth. "We're a crew. We go up together." It didn't matter whether they were supposed to be done. Matthew had followed Iain into so many messes and it was time, Iain thought, to return the favour. Caroline would be furious, but really it was not so bad. Once he was tour-expired he'd accept a teaching position for a while, relative safety. Just one more.

As it turned out, Caroline would not be furious.

Not twelve hours after the crew of E-Easy had decided they would fly once more, a V-2 rocket exploded in Adelaide Avenue, Lewisham, and shattered the glorious late-summer day.

And for Caroline MacTavish, the war was over.

The news came by telegram, as all news did. Caroline's flatmate, Maria, was gone too. Her affair with the Admiralty man had ended the week before or else she wouldn't have been at home at all. "Don't you think about us for a second," Matthew said to Iain, pressing another pint and a cigarette into his slack hand. "Go. We'll take an odd bod. Don't you think about it for a second."

He didn't. He packed a kit bag and got on a train to Inverness, Caroline's home. He stood next to his mother-in-law, a woman he had not seen since he was a child, at the funeral. When it was over, she'd placed her hand on his cheek and made him promise to write to her.

Down south, the crew of E-Easy took up an odd-bod pilot on their last sortie. It was hard to piece together what happened next. Someone thought he saw them go down over the North Sea on the way home. Someone else thought he saw them shot down over Germany. People didn't disappear without a trace, except for when they did.

The door of Dr. Delaune's surgery opened and Leigh stepped out. Her face was damp, but she wasn't crying anymore. "They're with him now," she said. She had gone inside with the McClares when they arrived, Kate and John. "It'll be a few days before the funeral. Will Llewellyn hasn't got a boat ready." She reached down for his fingers. "Oh, Iain," she said. "Your hands are like ice." She took both his hands and clutched them between her own. Her skin was dry and cold, and he felt her touch only distantly. He was still thinking of the lightness of Hugo's bones.

"What does it mean?" Leigh said, her voice barely more than a breath. Iain closed his eyes. His head was full of bees, spinning and buzzing and vibrating painfully. It didn't mean anything, death never meant anything, it was never more than a stupid, pointless waste.

"I have to go," he said. He glanced down at her. There was a smear of mud on her pale cheek.

"Do you want me to come with you?"

He thought perhaps she wasn't asking for his sake at all but for hers, but, "No," he said. "I think I need to be alone."

Something open in her face snapped shut. "Aye," she said, dropping his hands, "if you're sure."

"All right, then."

"All right," she repeated, and they turned away from each other.

In the morning Leigh sat in the grey light and watched her breath puff in a little cloud before her face. Reminded herself that she had nowhere to go, nothing to do, nobody to look for. She let Maisie out into the yard. The motions of a morning, well rehearsed like a play. The world still turning.

It didn't make any sense, it didn't make any sense. Hugo had been found, he had been alive, walking and talking and breathing. She had stood next to him in her field out by the barn, in his sitting room, at the standing stones. He had been alive, and then he had been gone. She blinked and saw his body again, twisted and mangled. There was no way that his body could have looked like that if he had been killed only moments before, when he disappeared into the Bruce house. Which meant he must not have been killed only moments before, which was equally impossible.

She blinked. When she opened her eyes, the darkness lingered for a moment, like a dark cloud had passed overhead, like all the lamps had suddenly gone out. She reached for the counter but her fingers only swept through the air. Panic rose in her throat because she was blind, she'd gone blind, without any warning—

Light flickered on a distant wall. Dim, watery, dancing. A voice said her name, a whisper in the dark.

Leigh blinked again and the kitchen appeared before her. Maisie scratching at the door to get in. Two dozen crows, at least, lining the peak of the barn roof. Leigh passed a hand across her eyes as though she could clear the vision out of them. What did it mean, stepping into your dreams when you were perfectly awake?

It was as though some invisible hand had pulled a blanket up over the town, a familiar one. Suffering, sadness, helplessness, distrust. This was an island that endured, but it was also an island that believed. And here there was no denying the evidence. Dr. Delaune had looked at the body of Hugo McClare and concluded that the boy had been dead for some time, probably since the night that he went missing. But it was impossible, the islanders whispered to each other, impossible, impossible. I sold him a newspaper on Friday, Mr. McGillicuddy told the

Gordons. I saw him sitting on the curb with Fraser and some of the other boys. I spoke to him after church. They had all seen him, the whole island, they had seen him and spoken with him and rejoiced at his return. Things had not seemed so bad, with Hugo back.

Was it a trick of the sluagh? Mr. Harrower went up to speak to Old Morrison, but when he returned, he reported that the man had simply sat in his chair, fingers steepled beneath his chin, and gently closed his eyes. "This is something new," the old man had said. "I shall have to think on it."

The sluagh seemed to sense it. Their victory. Everywhere one looked there were dark, spectral birds, in nines and eighteens and thirty-sixes. They left detritus behind them, glossy black feathers littering the cobbles like autumn leaves. In the night they screamed across the moors to each other. A mournful sound like wailing children, a sound that urged you to get up from your spot by the fire and go help whatever creature was in such distress. Soon everybody one met wore matching dark circles beneath their eyes.

The creatures attacked at random. It was Evie Llewellyn first. It happened quickly, as she was walking down the high street, awkwardly, because she was carrying a chair her father had repaired back to its home at the McGillicuddys' post office. The birds descended on her without warning. Her screaming echoed down the street as she beat them off with the chair, but it took several moments for anyone to come to her aid. Maybe it wasn't really Evie at all, maybe it was the sluagh wearing her face, maybe it was a trap. Eventually Tom McAllister appeared out of his pub with a long piece of rebar that he kept for this purpose, but by then Evie had already managed to fight her way out of the swarm, abandoning the chair (ruined once again) on the pavement.

Next it was Jack Calloway, as he pulled his boat in from the shore. The fishermen—the only islanders to get some reprieve from it all; everything seemed better out on the sea—were quicker to come to his aid than the others had been for Evie, and Jack got off with little more than some scratches on his hands. After Jack it wasn't an attack but another infestation. The Taylors awoke in the night to find their house full of the creatures, their talons scraping at walls and skin alike. The Taylors fled to the Beeches' next door, and in the morning Mhairi went to the post office and asked for the notices from the big island. "I'll not keep the children here, if this keeps up," she said to Mrs. McGillicuddy. "This island doesn't belong to us anymore, anyway."

They spread like rot. From the Taylors they colonised the shed in the Beeches' yard, and then the bottom floor of the school, though with the enthusiastic help of a lot of bored students Mr. MacDonald managed to drive them out again. And this was not to mention the way they filled the air, always watching, waiting for a person to run or trip or bend to tie their shoelace without someone to watch their back. It seemed not a matter of if somebody else would turn up like Hugo McClare, but when.

"Nothing's working," Mr. Harrower was overheard saying to Tom McAllister in the post office line. "The charms and the talismans. Nothing's working."

"Well," Tom said, grimly. "It's hardly surprising, is it? He killed one of theirs. They killed one of ours. Perhaps that'll have restored some sort of sick balance."

"And if it doesn't?" Mr. Harrower said. "We're running out of options."

There was something about his voice. A tinge of desperation. Mr. Harrower had not been heard so worried since the early days of the war, 1941. "Then what?" Tom asked. Mr. Harrower didn't answer. He bought a newspaper off Mrs. McGillicuddy and left.

In town it was palpable like heavy fog. Neighbours peered out their front windows as familiar faces passed by, doing careful calculations. How long has it been since you last saw Tom, Mhairi, George? Any absence for more than an hour or two was now met with suspicion. It seemed that anybody could be an impostor, could be a ghost. Mr. Gordon stood on the step outside his grocery with his arms crossed tightly over his chest, and his eyes followed Leigh Welles as she passed on her way to Iain MacTavish's. She seemed dazed, not entirely present. The Welles house was so far away from everything. Who knew what she got up to, all alone up there?

Iain's front door was unlocked and Leigh let herself in, away from the villagers' suspicious gazes. Inside it was even quieter than usual. No sign of life in the front hall, just the soft song of the electric lights. "Hello?" she called into the house as she shrugged out of her coat, and Mrs. Cavanagh appeared from the kitchen. "Oh," she said, "Leigh. Do come in, there's tea brewing."

Leigh followed Mrs. Cavanagh back into the kitchen. "Is Iain all right?"

Something in Mrs. Cavanagh's face slipped and she suddenly looked much older than she had before, so exhausted. It lasted only half a moment. "I've been trying to tell him that he can't carry on a war his whole life," she said. "Life's too short to be fouling it up with all that. But I suppose it's not so simple."

"Perhaps I'll try to speak to him," Leigh said, and Mrs. Cavanagh waved a hand vaguely in the air as though to say, "Suit yourself," or perhaps, "Heaven help you." It didn't matter which. Either was permission.

"I have a telephone call to make," Mrs. Cavanagh said, and she disappeared into the pantry.

She found him at the window in his war room. "I came to see how you are," she said.

Iain did not turn from the window. It was an impossible question to answer. How was he? He was feeling like he had made up his entire life in his head. The previous evening he had sat out on the back step chain-smoking, watched the dark shadows of the sluagh silhouetted against the clouds high above him and could not help but think of the bomber stream, the way it started out orderly and choreographed and ended in chaos, fire, destruction. The war, the island, the sluagh, the war. Unreality, all.

"Iain?"

He took a packet of cigarettes from the desk and slid one free. "I've been thinking about the war," he found himself saying. "About the things I did during it."

The only sound was the gentle movement of air. He flicked open his lighter and lit up.

Leigh said, "You did what you were told to do."

Which was true, but a pretty weak excuse. "It's my fault that Matthew McClare's dead," he said. "I was supposed to fly but then Caroline died and I went up to Inverness for the funeral.

They took up an odd bod, totally green, fresh out of training. Nobody knows what happened. It doesn't matter, I suppose."

"Iain," Leigh said, "that wasn't your fault at all."

Wasn't it? He'd been a good pilot, and (generally) a lucky one. Except for when he wasn't. He flicked the ash from his cigarette. He didn't know why he was telling her this, but now that he had started, he found he couldn't stop. "Caroline was my fault too," he said. "She wanted me to ask for leave, for us to go away, the weekend that she died. But I was about to finish my tour, so I said no. Told her to wait. If I hadn't," he said, "she wouldn't have been there when the rocket hit. She'd still be alive. And maybe Matthew too."

There was a long silence. Smoke hung at the window, pressed for escape. Leigh asked, "Is this why you avoid the McClares?"

Iain took another drag. Thought of the last time he had stood at this window smoking, hiding behind the fogged glass from Mr. McClare. And now, the note crumpled into his pocket. It had arrived this morning, slid under the door with the first weak light as Iain sat in the front room next to the wireless, a cup of tea long cold by his left hand, a cigarette smouldering away to ash in his right. He had seen who delivered it. *Mr. MacTavish*, it said in a neat hand. *We hope you are staying safe this October. If you have a spare hour, we would very much like to speak with you, any time that suits.* It was from Mrs. McClare.

Ever since wading into that freezing water, reaching out blindly until his hand brushed against cold, dead skin, ever since carrying Hugo back to town in his arms like a baby—he had been resolved. He would not speak to the McClares, could not. He had missed his chance for reconciliation, absolution, whatever he had hoped to find along with Hugo alive and well, it had slammed shut like a heavy door.

"As it turns out," he said, "I'm quite the coward. I can't bear to think what they might say to me."

"They're good people, Iain, they wouldn't—"

"Don't, Leigh," he said, because if she told him to speak with them, he thought perhaps he'd have to. "Please don't."

"I just think you should—"

"I said, don't!"

Leigh recoiled as though she'd placed her hand on the hot burner of a stove. Iain passed his free hand over his eyes. His temper gone as suddenly as it had come. "I'm sorry," he said. "I'm sorry. Please let's talk about something else. Please."

Silence descended into the room like a curtain falling on a stage. Leigh paused by the wardrobe where the sleeve of his uniform peeked out, reached out as though to touch it, changed her mind. She said, "What are we supposed to do now?"

Which wasn't really about something else, at all, because the only thing she could mean was Hugo. "There isn't anything left to do," he said. "He's already dead."

"Not just that," she said. He hated the way she said it, how quickly Hugo had turned from a person to a thing. "The crows too. And—me, I suppose." This last rather guiltily, and she turned away from him. "I've been trying to make plans for when the house sells. And I find I can hardly think more than a day or two ahead." She reached out again, this time took the sleeve of his uniform between her fingers. "None of this is what I wanted and I can't—I can't fix it." She sighed, her shoulders listing up and down. "I can't bear the thought of leaving again."

"Why did you go in the first place?"

A long pause. "I don't know," she said at last, but it sounded like maybe she did. "I suppose I didn't think I deserved to stay."

Iain took a step towards her, and another one. Leigh turned around and they were inches from each other. She blinked up at him as though clearing dust from her eyes, said, "It must sound rather childish."

"No," Iain said. "I understand completely." He wanted badly to reach up and touch her face, the sharp, flat plane of her cheek, but he wasn't sure what it would mean for him to do so. He could smell the bright scent of her perfume, or shampoo. The thought came into his mind, like the chiming of a church bell, the kind of thought that woke a person up from a deep sleep: this was not a thing of carelessness. There was a smattering of freckles across the neat line of her nose, pale with sunlessness. He opened his mouth to speak, though he was not sure what he planned to say.

The telephone rang.

Leigh jumped and a hand flew to her chest. The silence of the room punctured like a yolk pierced by a needle. Iain released his held breath, rocked back on his heels.

"I forgot you had a telephone," Leigh said. There was something tight in her voice, and she cleared her throat. "Startled me."

"Yes," Iain said. "Me as well."

The door opened and Iain turned away, pressed his fist into the desk. "Your brother is on the telephone," Mrs. Cavanagh said to Leigh. Iain's eyes fell on a photograph in a gold frame. A couple outside the Kensington register office. Heat rose to his face. "He's asking for you."

For a moment he could feel her looking at him, Mrs. Cavanagh, her eyes on the back of his neck. A moment, and then Leigh went to answer the telephone, and Mrs. Cavanagh followed her.

"I tried you at the phone box," Sam said by way of greeting. Leigh pushed the telephone receiver against her ear so hard the cartilage started to ache. "But no one answered. Not even Tom. What's going on?"

Leigh said, "Hugo's dead. Sluagh."

A moment of staticky silence. Sam said, "Jesus."

"Yes. So forgive us for not hopping to it and answering your calls on the first ring."

"I didn't know," Sam said. "How was I to know? You certainly weren't going to tell me."

Leigh leaned her forehead against the wall, considered smashing her head right through the plaster. "What do you want, Sam?"

There was a bit of a commotion on the line, a door opening and a voice calling out, distant and wordless. The line went dull and then there was Sam's muffled voice, and she could picture him cradling the receiver against his chest so she couldn't hear whatever it was he said.

The line jumped to life again. "I've got a buyer for the house," Sam said briskly. "It's almost sorted. There's some trouble with the bank, but it should be straightened out this weekend."

Leigh said, "Oh. That was fast."

"Yes," Sam said. "So you need to sell the car. Have you decided where you're going to go?"

"Do you care?"

"Of course," Sam said. "You're my sister."

As though that had ever made a difference before. "I don't know," she said. "I've got a bit saved, enough for the ferry, but not much more."

"You could sell the goats," Sam said.

It came as a blow, a physical one, like a fist crashing into the side of her head. How could Sam manage to continue surprising her? Of course the goats would have to go. What else would happen to them? Leigh would pack the goats and the dog and her mother's dresses into a suitcase and take them—where? Of course the goats would have to go, and yet.

She said again, "Oh."

"That should keep you for a bit. Can you sell the car by Monday, do you think?"

How her head was spinning. The past ten minutes had tossed her about like a boat on turbulent waters. From that moment in the office with Iain's chest six inches or less from hers, him looking down at her with something that felt like intention, something that was complicated, and complicating—to here, this telephone call, her forehead pressed against the cold wall and Sam taking his latest shots at her.

"It's the festival on Monday," she reminded Sam.

"It's a car and some goats," he replied. "How hard can it be?"

"The goats, not hard," she said, though the words felt like they were choking her. They were not just "the goats," they were Rufus and Matilda, they had been in that barn since Leigh was nine, they had been a birthday present from her parents. "The car—quite hard, and you know it."

Another sound from somewhere in the bowels of Sam's office, someone yelling, "Mr. Welles!" (He wasn't "Mr. Welles," their father was Mr. Welles, Mr. Welles was dead.) Sam said, "Can you just do it, please?"

As though her only goal in life was to make his difficult. There was no point in asking again what it was she had done to make him hate her so. He would not answer. She said, "Is there anything else?"

"No, that's it. But Leigh, about last weekend, I wanted to say—"
She hung up on him.

When Leigh emerged from the pantry, she seemed smaller than she had before. Shrunken, her face drawn tight. Iain felt a sort of spinning in his chest at the sight of her, foolishness left over from that moment in the office. The best thing was to act like it had never happened at all. After taking a minute to let the heat drain from his face, he had followed Mrs. Cavanagh into the kitchen and accepted a cup of tea from her with a perhaps-too-cheery "ta."

"Sam?" Iain asked Leigh.

Leigh nodded once. "I'm to sell the goats and the car," she said. "By Monday." Everything about her bristled, as though if one were to brush against her accidentally, one would get an electric shock, or else send her shattering into a million pieces like china.

Iain did not want to see her shatter. He said, "I'll buy the car."

Both Leigh and Mrs. Cavanagh looked at him sharply. In all honesty he was as surprised by the announcement as they were. Even if he wanted to take it back, it was too late now. The words had been spoken, life breathed into them. "I'll buy the car," he said again. What else was the point of all that money? "The one in your front yard, yes? I'll buy it from you now and you can buy it back whenever you want."

"Don't be ridiculous," Leigh snapped. "You have a car, your dad's old one."

"It's going to break down any minute," Iain said. "He never treated it properly, not like your old man. It's an investment."

Leigh said, "You don't have to do this."

Iain said, "I want to," and meant it.

Leigh twisted her hands in her skirt. She wouldn't look at him, was staring out the window into the garden. "I suppose that leaves the goats, then."

"The Morrisons do goats," Mrs. Cavanagh said. "I'm heading over there now. I'm sure they'll take them, and for a good price, too."

If Leigh had been sucking on a lemon, her mouth could not have been smaller. As though it took a great deal of effort, she said, "Thank you." A pause during which Iain and Mrs. Cavanagh both looked at Leigh, and Leigh looked out into the garden, where Maisie was busy digging a messy hole. Leigh said, "I'd better go stop her," and disappeared outside.

In the silence left by her departure, Mrs. Cavanagh patted Iain's hand gently, a schoolteacher doling out praise. "That was kind of you, lad," she said.

"I'm not sure," Iain said. "She seemed rather put out."

Mrs. Cavanagh said, "I don't think that has anything to do with you."

24.

She stood in the cave and wondered if she was dreaming or awake. The water lapped at her feet, she could feel the cold through her shoes. There was a dim light flickering on the wall like a dancer.

Have you come to finish it?

Áine was standing next to her. She placed a hand on Leigh's shoulder and her touch was cold like the water. *Go ahead*, she said. *It's all right.*

Leigh waded into the pool. The water crept up her legs, her hips, her ribs. The glassy wall of the cave glimmered before her.

Someone said her name, a whisper in the dark.

25.

Twilight was falling, and on the beach the islanders watched Hugo McClare burn.

The sea was calmer than it had been the morning of Graham Welles's funeral, and the boat bearing Hugo's body sailed out into the water easily. Mr. McClare was conspicuously absent. Leigh had not seen him since she left him and Kate in Dr. Delaune's surgery. "He couldn't bear it," Kate had whispered to Leigh as they arrived on the beach. Her face white and tear-streaked. "I don't think I can, either."

Leigh wrapped her arms around her middle and squeezed. Next to her Iain stood in his flight jacket with his hands clasped in front of him, much as he had stood beside her yesterday, in her yard, frowning while the Morrisons took away the goats. Then he had folded himself into her father's car and rolled down the window. "It'll turn out all right," he had said. "With the house." "Don't say things," Leigh replied, "that you know aren't true."

She had told him that she didn't know what she was supposed to do but that was a lie. She did know. They had to return to the cave. Maybe it was in her blood, like father like daughter, but she could not simply pretend that she didn't know of that impossible place beneath their feet. That cave was a place that held secrets, she had felt it in the air. One of those secrets must be the way to put things right again, to return the sluagh to the harmless corps de ballet they'd been before. (A fleeting, selfish thought: if this island did not go back to normal, then she had left it for nothing, had wasted four years on the mainland, for nothing.)

A few yards away Kate let out a single sob and then clapped a hand over her mouth. It didn't matter. The wind whipped the noise away the moment it broke past her teeth. In the distance, the small flame that had once been Hugo McClare quietly slipped beneath the water.

The others had left the beach, but Iain still stared at the sea. He stared at it for a long time, long enough for the tide to shift a few inches, start lapping at his toes. "Shall I wait for you?" Leigh asked as the funeral ended, but he shook his head. He wasn't sure how long it would take for him to tear himself away from the shore. Because of what it meant, because of the life he would be returning to. The empty, quiet house.

Truly empty. The previous morning he had come downstairs to find Mrs. Cavanagh at the door with her suitcase. "Going somewhere?" he had said to her in a flat voice.

She turned round. "I'm afraid," she said, "that I have to go off to Inverness."

Iain blinked at her once in surprise. In the two years since her arrival, Mrs. Cavanagh had not left the island once, had not even mentioned leaving. Once, when he'd felt rather like being alone for a while, Iain had asked her whether she didn't want to visit any of her friends for a few days, a week or two even. As an answer he had received a rather curt "No, thank you," and he hadn't suggested that she go away again.

"Inverness?" Iain repeated.

"Yes," Mrs. Cavanagh said, placing her hat neatly on her head. "My friend Isobel's quite unwell. I've had a telegram from her husband."

"You'll miss Hugo McClare's funeral."

"Yes," Mrs. Cavanagh replied. "I'm afraid I will, but it can't be helped. You'll give my condolences to his parents."

It sounded so clinical, so stiff and formal. "Of course," he said. He hadn't.

So this was what he was returning to. A house empty of everything but reminders of his many failures. He pressed the back of one cold hand to his cheek.

"I'm sorry," he said to the ocean, but the ocean only roared.

What finally pulled him away from the sea? A hard, sharp sound, splitting the air in two. Some long-dormant part of Iain's brain sprung to work—tracer fire, ack-ack guns, scarecrow shell?—as the air was pierced again, and again, and again. A shotgun or a rifle. For the first time in years Iain suddenly felt awake, like he'd swallowed one of the pills they'd always been given before an op. He whipped away from the sea and shot up the stairs inset into the bluff, in search of Leigh.

Instead he found Mr. McClare, standing in the centre of the standing stones with his shotgun, firing round after round after round into the air. His mouth open in a great, lopsided O, his face tear-streaked, his eyes wild. At first it looked like he wasn't firing at anything, but then Iain realised that he was firing at the birds in the air. They frenzied around him, screaming. The gun may as well have been loaded with dust for all the good that it did. Mr. McClare wasn't even trying to aim, and someone was going to get hurt. In the grass the other islanders huddled. Kate and George, clinging to each other. Leigh, over by the stones, half-turned as though petrified. Nobody knew what to do; everybody had been frozen when the first shot rang out.

In fact it seemed that Iain was the only person who wasn't frozen. If he were the type of man to freeze when he heard gunfire, he would have been dead a long time ago. "Hey!" he shouted, striding towards Mr. McClare. This was more important than the burning desire lodged in the pit of his stomach not to speak to the McClares; if no one calmed the man down, then someone was going to get hurt. Mr. McClare swung round, letting off another bullet. Iain dodged but he was slower than he'd been once and the bullet grazed his arm in a flash of hot pain. He clapped his hand over his arm, warm blood already seeping through his shirt. It had been an accident; Mr. McClare wasn't in his right mind, you could see it in his eyes. The sluagh were circling in the air above Mr. McClare's head like a great black whirlpool. One of his stray bullets finally found its target, caught a sluagh in the chest, and something dark and thick splattered down onto Mr. McClare's face. The birds screamed.

"Hey!" Iain shouted at Mr. McClare again, but before he could get any closer, Ben Hendrix appeared, turned back from the cars in the field. He let out a shout and ran at Mr. McClare. It was growing hard to see for all the sluagh swarming in the air. Mr. Hendrix reached Mr. McClare and grabbed the muzzle of the shotgun, tried to wrestle it away. "You've got to calm down, John," Mr. Hendrix was saying, and Mr. McClare was shouting in his face, a wordless stream of grief and agony, and around him the sluagh were falling, the air itself was made of blood and feathers. Someone shouted for everybody to get to the cars, but Iain took a step towards the stones instead, his injured arm pounding out his pulse. He called out for Leigh, but she had disappeared into the dark cloud.

The air was a swarm of beating wings, tearing beaks, screams, as hundreds of sluagh materialised as if out of the air itself. They crashed through car windows and careened around the stones; they tore at hair and skin and clothing. Someone screamed Leigh's name, and as she swung around, a sluagh swooped towards her eyes. She dove out of reach of its talons behind one of the stones, falling hard onto her hands. Peering out from around the edge of the stone, she could barely make out the chaos of the field between the rushing of birds. Brighid and Kirsten MacEwan huddled on the ground with their arms wrapped over their heads. Tom with one of the Morrison children under each arm, shouting for everyone to get to shelter.

What shelter? There was nothing, there was nowhere, there were only the crows in the air. Hundreds, thousands, millions of them. They streamed down the hill towards the village and up towards the Ben, they spilled out over the sea. Somewhere in the distance something shattered, high and musical. Leigh peered out from behind the stone in time to watch as the ancient coloured windows of the church exploded into thousands of glittering pieces, raining to the ground in a spray of glass and feathers, catching the last light of day and burning.

"Stop!" Mr. Hendrix shouted, still trying to wrestle the gun from Mr. McClare's grip. "Can't you see it's only agitating them, man?"

It was impossible to tell who was holding the gun when it went off. When the sluagh cleared, Mr. McClare was on his knees in the grass, his head tilted up towards the sky. "My boys," he wailed, like a baby, "my boys."

And just inches from where Leigh was crouched behind the stone lay Mr. Hendrix. Blood seeping into the dirt from the ragged hole in the centre of his chest.

There were many hazards to this way of life, out in the middle of the sea. An unexpected storm might capsize a fisherman's boat, or a bull might gore a farmer. A child going shoeless in summer might step on something rusted and filthy and get an infection that the cottage doctor could not heal. A person might fall from a cliff. A boy might be taken by the crows.

The islanders had never faced threats from each other before. The sluagh dissipated into the air, returning to their roosts. Mrs. Gordon took Mr. McClare by the shoulders and led him away. Dr. Delaune came, and Will Llewellyn helped him carry Mr. Hendrix back to the surgery. Dr. Delaune had found a pulse; Mr. Hendrix wasn't dead yet, but the look on the doctor's face was grim. The rest of the islanders stood about in the twilight field, stunned. Leigh found Iain and saw his blood-stained sleeve and felt her stomach bottom out. "Oh," she said, and he told her, "It's nothing, a scratch." It wasn't, but it didn't seem to be threatening much more than his shirtsleeve, which was already past help.

Mr. Harrower had wandered back to the stones from wher-ever he hid from the swarm, and now stared at the grass glisten-ing with Mr. Hendrix's blood. His eyes moving very quickly but the rest of him entirely still, vacated. Leigh thought suddenly of the day the telegram came for the Harrowers, around when Sam went missing. The Harrower boy, a bomb aimer, had gone down over Normandy, and all night they could hear Mrs. Har-rower screaming, until sometime just before dawn when the screaming stopped abruptly. A small stroke, the doctor said, and she was never the same again, and barely a year later she, too, slipped away in her sleep.

Mr. Gordon approached Mr. Harrower carefully, the way one might a wild animal. He put a hand on the man's shoulder, and Mr. Harrower started. "Andrew," Mr. Gordon said. "I think it's time."

Mhairi Taylor nodded. She was clutching her daughter to her, Gwen's face crushed against her chest. "We knew it was coming. It's been coming for years."

Mr. Harrower turned in a slow circle, his eyes raised to the air, to the quickly louring sky. "I suppose," he said, in a voice so unlike his usual commanding tone, in a voice soft and dark, "that everything ends eventually."

Leigh clutched Iain's uninjured arm and wished everyone would stop speaking in code. She felt all at once like she was twelve years old again, sitting in McAllister's with Hugo McClare in her lap, waiting for the king to speak while all around the adults murmured unintelligibly about rations, telegrams, Europe, their sons.

"The festival should quieten them some," Mr. Gordon said. "And then we have a year to make the necessary arrangements."

Leigh said, "What arrangements?"

Mr. Harrower replied, "It's time to leave this island."

A month ago at this time Leigh had stood in her landlady's corridor to answer a call from Tom McAllister. ("You need to come home. Your father's been in an accident. We can't get hold of Sam.") It had taken her a minute to understand what he meant. Graham was always getting into accidents—a sprained ankle, a twisted wrist, a bumped head. She was annoyed to be called over something like this. "Iain MacTavish found him this morning," Tom said. "This must be such a shock." She still did not understand, and finally Tom said, "He died, Leigh, he drowned," and it was as though someone had smashed out all the windows in the room and let the cold wind rush through, as though the ground had tilted and shifted, as though the world had ended and in the same moment jerked back to stuttering life.

The ground tilted and shifted again.

Mr. MacEwan said, "We've been here for a hundred years."

Mrs. Beech added, "A thousand."

Mrs. McCafferty said, "This is where I raised my girls."

Mr. Blake said, "We can't afford to abandon everything, and who would buy our farm, the state of it?"

Tom McAllister said, "Are you sure?"

Leigh was still clutching Iain's arm; her fingernails must be digging painful half-moons into his skin, but she found she couldn't move. "We've discussed this before, you remember," Mr. Harrower said. "When the Russells left. We knew it might come to this."

"I can't start over," Mrs. McGillicuddy said, "not at my age."

But already the protests seemed half-hearted. A death knell, not a battle cry. In the twilight, Leigh could see by the islanders' pale faces that they had already accepted it. The way they accepted everything, weather and war and hardship, the way they bore it. Mixed their milk with water to stretch it, turned sheets side to middle and mended socks until they were nothing but mending. Buttoned their collars to the chin and shouldered their burdens and carried on.

"I've already made some inquiries over on the big island," Mhairi Taylor said. "There's some farms in need of hands, and there's always work for more fishermen."

"I have a cousin on the big island," Mary Lewis added. "Biggest house I've ever seen. I'm sure they'd take in lodgers until we get on our feet."

"We can't just leave," Leigh said, and she felt the island's eyes fall on her. What does it matter, she thought they might say, you will be leaving anyway. Which wasn't what she was thinking of at all. She was thinking of her father and trailing after him through the heather, the wind flattening his hair to his head, rain whipping past his waxed jacket. She was thinking of watching the aurora with her mother and running through fields of wildflowers with the McClares; she was thinking of the midnight sun. The years when she and her brother had still been friends. The day she left and all the days she regretted it after.

"No one will be forced to go," Mr. Harrower said. "But I won't stay to watch us picked off, one by one."

"They might all leave tomorrow," Leigh said. "With the festival, they'll be gone."

"Only to come back again in a year, and maybe even worse," Mhairi said.

"Perhaps it's better," Mr. MacEwan said, tentatively, "to cut our losses."

"What if we found a way," Leigh said. Her breath felt shallow and tight, desperation climbing up her throat like acid. "Something that would make them go back to how they were."

Mr. Gordon was looking at her sadly. Like she was a foolish child. "There's no going back, Leigh," he said. "We can't undo what's done."

"But what if we can?" she insisted. Thinking now of a ghostly voice in a cave, a falling sigh in a dream. *Have you come to finish it?* Iain placed his hand over hers and said, "Leigh," a warning. Did he know what she was thinking of? She barely knew herself. She shook her hand free, dropped his arm. "We can't just give up on this place," she said. "It's home."

"It hasn't been home for some time, lass," Mr. Harrower said. And perhaps it hadn't, not since the telegrams and the rationing and the empty places in church, since summer ended with a radio address. (Maybe even earlier, Leigh thought, maybe since Áine left.) But if they left now, what would have been the point of it all? If in fifty, a hundred years, nobody even remembered that this place had existed, that they had. Even if she was going, the idea that this place would quietly cease existing with a ferry pulling into the mist was, somehow, too much to bear.

"Give it another year," Leigh said, imploring. "At least. Just one more year."

"It's been nearly ten years like this, Leigh," Tom McAllister said. (Not Tom, Leigh thought, not him convinced so easily too.) "What's one more year going to do?"

"I don't know," she said. "But we have to try."

"It's no use, Leigh," Mr. Harrower said. "This place is dying, and it'll take us with it if we stay."

Leigh had run out of breath. If she opened her mouth again, she thought, all she would do was cry. No one spoke at all and the sea was very loud, and the wind, the island's resting heartbeat.

"What do we do now?" Gwen Taylor said, little more than a whisper into her mother's chest.

"Tomorrow we have the festival," Mr. Harrower said. "Then we'll start to say our goodbyes."

How quickly the world turned. Once upon a time it seemed that this island would never change. The years passed uneventfully and blurred into one another, the seasons came and went. Only for a single instant to end it. Leigh stood on the cliff and watched the water wearing down the coastline as the field emptied behind her, the islanders fleeing the dark. She watched the water and thought about how one day there would be nothing left to show that they'd been here at all.

Iain took her elbow. "Come on," he said. "It's getting dark."
The sluagh loomed down from atop the stones as he steered
her away towards the road. She didn't feel entirely present as
Iain walked her down the high street, already decorated for the
festival with bunting, tartan, intricately folded paper thistles.
She felt already miles away in some drab corner, spat out into
the wideness of the world, unrooted.

They stepped into the stillness of Iain's front hall. He flicked
a switch and the quiet song of electricity hummed to life.
Iain shrugged out of his coat and revealed his blood-soaked
sleeve, cursed. "I'm going to change my shirt," he said, and he
left Leigh in the hall. When he returned, she was still standing
there, staring out the front window into the evening, watching
the shadows of the birds move across the sky.

Leigh said, "We have to go back to the cave." It was a thing
she had realised quite suddenly, watching the birds fly darkly
overhead. She remembered a wet day out on the moors, moping by the side of the road as her father casually commented
that once upon a time their ancestors had buried their temples
beneath the ground. How many ancient magics could one island possess?

"No," Iain said. He strode into the sitting room and poured
himself a whisky, drained it in two gulps, grimaced a little. "Absolutely not. I'm not going back there."

"Hugo led us there!" Leigh cried. "And you heard the voice,
it asked if we'd come to finish it. This is what it meant! He led
us there."

"To the place he died," Iain said, turning to her. He was so
maddeningly calm, standing there, slipping his hands into his

pockets. She wished he would raise his voice, make her feel less hysterical. "He led us to the place he died, to the place the sluagh killed him. That's why the sluagh can show you things, even I know that much. To lure you to your death."

She glared at him. "So if I go, you won't come with me."

"If you try to go," he said, "I'll do everything I can to stop you."

It was, when she considered it, an irritatingly nice thing for him to say. She felt her cheeks get hot and turned away, as though she were very interested in the ornately carved side table. What else could she say to convince him? He was still watching her, the feeling of his eyes on the back of her neck like a physical touch, his hand against her hair.

"Where's Mrs. Cavanagh?" Leigh said at last. She didn't know what made her say it once she had, only that the house was strangely silent, that she felt his eyes on the back of her neck, that her face was inexplicably hot.

"She went off to Inverness yesterday," Iain said.

"Inverness!"

"Yes. One of her friends is ill, apparently. It was all quite sudden."

She ran her fingers over the cold, smooth grooves of the carvings in the table. How desperately she wished that she, too, could sail away from all of it and not care a bit, how desperately she wished that her heart weren't made of heather and sea spray.

"What will you do?" she said. "If we all leave."

"Oh," Iain said. "I'll be fine. It'll take a while for everyone to go, and the boats won't stop till they have. We'll find some-where. My father left me with more money than I know what to do with."

"Mrs. Cavanagh will go with you?"

"To be sure," Iain said. "Doubt I can get rid of her that easily." She heard him sigh, then the clink of glassware as he topped up his whisky. "I don't know, Leigh," he said. "Maybe it's not so bad, leaving. It's an easier life, elsewhere."

Was it? She didn't think so. She said, "It's different for you." For her part she could not let everybody leave. Too many people had left already, her father and her mother and Sam, all those boys. There had to be some way to convince them to stay, though she didn't have much time to do it. Only until the house was sold for good. If they could be convinced at all, once the season was over. Possibly if the sluagh didn't go properly at midnight tomorrow, the cause would already be lost.

"I don't see what it would matter," she said, "if I were to go back to the cave. There's nobody left to miss me if I didn't come back."

Iain said, "I'd miss you if you didn't come back."

She looked up. He said it like it was the simplest thing in the world. These types of things had not been easily said in the Welles house of Leigh's childhood, not after Áine left. She blinked and for a moment she could see her so clearly, Áine, standing in the corner of the room. She blinked again and the figure evaporated. "Well," Leigh said, in a scoffing sort of voice to hide that she had lost her breath, "I don't think anybody else would."

The corner of his mouth twitched, not a smile, not really.

"I'd miss you too," she said finally. And she would, she thought, when they were all far-flung across the world. She pressed a hand to her forehead, holding at bay the dizziness of

274

the thought. Even with Sam's call, the goats, the car, the fact of her leaving had not felt real until now. Where was she going to go. What was she going to do. How was she going to do it on her own. She looked up and Iain was right in front of her, barely a breath away. He reached up as though to wipe her cheek but then cupped the plane of her face instead. His fingers slipping easily around her ear, his thumb resting on her cheekbone, like his hand had been made to hold her face.

Maybe it was because her heart was already racing from the gunshots, the swarming, the announcement. Maybe it wasn't that at all. He had a few faint freckles across his nose that she'd never noticed before, a little bump on the bridge from a past break. A scar running through his eyebrow. She wanted to envelop him within her, his heart inside her heart, wanted always to be standing here with their breaths mingling. Her fingernails dug hard into the soft wood of the tabletop behind her. She found herself imagining what it would be like to kiss Iain Mac-Tavish. She placed her hand on his hip and he inhaled sharply.

She said, "Can I kiss you?"

His eyes flicked up to hers. He had impossibly long eyelashes. For a moment he looked at her, and then he said, "Yes."

It began slowly, as the thought of a kiss rather than the thing itself. Leigh had not realised how long she had been waiting to kiss Iain MacTavish. He stepped closer to her. Some distant voice in the back of her head told her that this was a terrible idea, they were all leaving and not together, a person was not something she could pack into her suitcase with her mother's old dresses. Complicated, complicating. He kissed her harder, opened his mouth and the tip of his tongue touched her bottom lip. She forgot about the house, she forgot about the swarming, about the gunshots and the dreams and Hugo. Her thumb slipped beneath the corner of his untucked shirt, pressed against his warm, smooth skin.

He said, "Come upstairs."

She said, "All right."

26.

Some hours later she woke in Iain's bed. The room dark except for the moon framed in the window. Large and bright. A surprisingly cloudless night. The pale light fell across Iain's bare shoulder next to her, laced with silvery scars. "Training accident," he had said, his voice vibrating against her collarbone, when her hands had skated across his ribs and paused. "Lot of fire. Lucky to be alive."

Leigh reached out a hand, placed it on the back of his neck, her fingers carding up into his hair. He inhaled sharply and rolled over, lay on his back staring up at the ceiling. Leigh tucked her hand back under her cheek. The light clung to his profile. (A silver lining, she thought, fancifully.) After a moment he rolled over again and got to his feet, collected his trousers from the floor and started to dress. "What time is it?" he asked. He still had not looked at her.

"I don't know. Late."

He pulled on a jumper and all but disappeared into the dark room. He said, "You can sleep in the spare room again."

She had stepped into a trap somewhere; this was the split second as her foot descended towards it, the split second before it snapped shut. "Is everything all right?"

"Yes, of course." He turned away from her, collected a cigarette off the nightstand. He fiddled for a moment with his lighter. A brief, blinding point of light as he lit the cigarette and then a delicate haze of tobacco filling the room. Leigh slipped out of bed, went about the room collecting her clothes. When she finished dressing, Iain was still staring out the window at the dimly lit street, the moon reflecting off the sea beyond. Smoking joylessly.

Leigh said, "What are you thinking about?"

He didn't turn around. He said, "Caroline."

More than anything she would like to pretend that it didn't sting. That her stomach didn't turn, that her chest didn't feel strangely empty. Like she didn't feel exactly the same way she'd felt when Sam had looked her up and down in his office and found her wanting ("Dressed like that?"), when George had grabbed her wrist in the field ("How'd you pay your rent, Leigh?"). She wanted to flee but she couldn't, Iain was perhaps her only friend left—oh, God, she thought, please let him still be her friend—and even though there were these things that she would never be able to unnotice about him (a scar running through an eyebrow, a little bump on the bridge of his nose), it would be better to be friends than to be nothing.

So she swallowed the feeling. "All right," she said. "I'll see you in the morning." She put her hand on the door handle and paused. Clenched her fist and turned around again. "We should go back to the cave," Leigh said. "In the morning. I know you don't want to, but it's—"

"Oh, for Christ's sake," Iain interrupted, flinging the remnants of his cigarette into the ashtray on the nightstand. Finally he turned to her. "Would you give it a rest? It's over, there's nothing more to be done."

Leigh said, "It's not about one person." Actually it hadn't ever been only about Hugo; she just hadn't realised it. It was about Hugo but it was also about the sluagh, it was also about the whole state of things. It was about the voice that she couldn't get out of her head, it was about the dreams, it was about her.

"It's always about one person," Iain said. "You don't understand. It's always about one person, and this one's dead because of us, because I drove you home instead of going after him."

"That's not why he's dead," Leigh said. "He's dead because he went up to the cathedral after, because his friends left him on the moors."

"But if I'd let you walk," Iain said, "if I'd gotten back quicker, I could have stopped him."

She said, "Hugo isn't Matthew."

Iain looked back at her sharply. "I never said he was."

"You think it's your fault that Matthew died," Leigh said, "even though it had nothing to do with you at all, but you think it's your fault and you're ruining your life with it."

"You have no idea what you're talking about."

"Mrs. Cavanagh thinks it too," Leigh said. "She told me that you're fouling up your life with it, carrying on the war. Now you've decided to take the blame for Hugo dying, too, like he wasn't a person, like he couldn't make his own choices."

Iain said, "Stop it."

But she found that she couldn't. "They made their choices and you made yours, and it's no good killing yourself over what might have happened if you'd made a different one. You can't change the fact that you didn't pilot that flight just like you can't change the fact that Hugo—"

"I know I can't," Iain interrupted. "I never said I could."

"And yet you refuse to so much as look the McClares in the eye," Leigh said. "You'd rather turn away from them when they're standing right in front of you than let them talk to you. And now you're so busy making everything about the war that you're perfectly happy to stand there and smoke your god-damned cigarettes instead of doing something about it."

"Oh, I'm the one making it about the war?" he shot back. "When I fucking fought it? When you're the one who has the audacity to go around being disappointed that you missed it?"

"I didn't say—"

"You didn't have to," Iain said, "it's so obvious. Everything has to be about you and your suffering. Christ, I tell you your brother was at Dachau, and all you get from it is indignation that he never told you."

Leigh pressed a hand to her chest, her pounding heart. She didn't know what was happening, she didn't know how she had let this conversation get so far out of her control. "That's not all I got from it," she said, weakly, but Iain shook his head.

"I'm not the one making it about the war, Leigh." He wasn't shouting anymore; his voice had gone dangerously quiet. "I'm

280

not the one ruining my life with it, trying to change things. What about your desperate need to fix everything, things that can't be fixed? What about you, trying to change the fact that during the war you were useless?"

She opened her mouth to defend herself but found that there wasn't anything to say, nothing at all. He was right. She bent to pick up her cardigan from the foot of his bed as he lit another cigarette and took a long drag. "Maybe it's for the best," he said, "that we'll all be going our separate ways."

She slipped out of the room.

But she couldn't bear to stay in the house, in the spare room, and despite everything her father had ever told her she stumbled out the front door, up the high street, waded through the sea of shattered glass and began running on the other side. The look on his face and the words from his mouth following her. Useless, useless, useless.

Something swooped at her out of the darkness and she stumbled and fell, her hands hitting the pavement with a burning scrape, the knee of her stockings tearing open. A pair of sharp talons on her back, her hair, yanking her head up off the pavement, forcing her spine to arch unnaturally. Leigh shrieked and wrenched her hair free, scrambled to her feet. Three more sluagh swooped at her. She wrapped her arms over her head, but their talons found the gaps in her fingers and tore at her scalp. One got a good grip on her neck and lifted her feet a few inches off the pavement and Leigh thought, This is how I'm going to die. The sluagh lost its grip and dropped her back to the pavement. She crumpled to the ground and this time she could not get her hands out in front of her fast enough and the side of her face slammed into the road. There were nine now, circling her, and she pulled her knees to her chest and squeezed her eyes shut. There was nothing but the sluagh's terrible cries ringing out and her own gasping, rasping breath as they ripped at her with their beaks. She felt hot blood trickle into the hollow of her eye.

The sudden roar of an approaching truck, blinding head-lights, and the sluagh receded momentarily, shocked by the light. A man leapt from the cab of the truck, in silhouette. Shouting. The sluagh's cries were still ringing in Leigh's ears, and it took her a moment to realise he was yelling, "Get into the fucking car, girl!" Leigh scrambled to her feet as the sluagh turned on her would-be rescuer and fled towards the car as he swung a large, rusty shovel over his head. Leigh wrenched the door of the truck open and threw herself inside.

The world spun and she thought maybe she was going to be sick. She clutched her forehead with her bloody hands. The cab of this truck smelled like fresh earth and cut grass. It smelled so familiar.

Then the man who came to her aid got into the car and she realised why.

"Wait!" George McClare said, reaching out as though to grab her arm when she started to fumble with the door. "Wait, Leigh, they're still out there."

She wanted to tell him that she'd rather be out with the sluagh trying to tear her apart than in this car with him. She thought she'd be safer out there. She knew what the sluagh would do with her. George was a thing she could not predict. "I'm just going to drive you home, all right?" George said. His hand still extended to her, trying to pacify her the way he might a wild animal. "Just home."

She leaned away from him, her shoulder blades pressing into the cold window. "I don't want you anywhere near my house," she said, her voice a hiss.

George nodded. "I know," he said. "That's fair. But I'm not going to hurt you, I promise. I'm going to drive you home."

A great thud from above them, and George cursed. One of the sluagh had landed on the roof of the truck. George pulled onto the road so quickly that Leigh had to catch herself against the dashboard. The sluagh on the roof cawed loudly and took flight, soaring behind them as they wound their way north until it lost interest and swept into the night.

They were nearly home before George tried to speak to her again. "What are you doing out at this time of night?" he asked. "Coming from Iain MacTavish's?" As though he were allowed to make small talk with her. As though nothing at all had happened. She opened her mouth to tell him it wasn't any of his business, but instead she burst into tears.

"Oh," George said. "Oh, Leigh, no—I'm sorry, all right? Please don't cry."

She tried to tell George to stop the car but couldn't get enough air to her lungs. She wanted him to let her out. George pulled into her driveway and fumbled around in his pockets until he produced a slightly grubby handkerchief. She caught her breath. Blew her nose. Her sobs turned to soft hiccups and she stared through the rain-speckled windshield towards the dark house, the house that was not hers, and George sat next to her with his hands lying uselessly in his lap.

"Leigh," he said after a minute. "You know I am awfully sorry. About—well, you know. At the ritual. I haven't stopped thinking about it since, and—and I'm ashamed of myself, to be sure. I'd say that's not who I am, but I think that's the kind of thing you have to prove, you can't just say it. I don't expect you to forgive me, but I wanted you to know that I'm sorry."

She clenched the handkerchief in her hand. She ought to say something, provide some acknowledgment. All she could think of was the water streaming off Hugo's body, of a fiery boat disappearing beneath a grey wave. At last she managed the breath of a sentence: "I'm so sorry about Hugo."

George inhaled sharply. "Christ," he whispered. Passed a hand over his eyes. "I can't sleep. Haven't, since. I just drive around, and—" His shoulders jerked up and down dangerously, and Leigh thought he might be crying. A thing she thought he'd rather do in private. She slipped out of the car, but George put a hand out to the door before she could shut it again.

"I was looking for a reason to stay," he said. "At the ritual. I'd been thinking about going to the big island. I'd found some friends of my mother's to stay with while I got settled and everything."

A sudden image, standing in the room that Hugo had shared with George, holding the scrap of a burnt letter. (*Dear Mr. McClare, we would be delighted to host you until you have settled in.*) It was never Hugo, planning to leave the island in the dead of night; it was George. It had always been George.

"I was about to tell my parents," George continued, "before you came home. I thought you might be a reason to stay, if things could be the way they were before."

"That's not how they were before," Leigh said.

"I know." The moonlight shone feebly through the window, resting gently on his face and painting him into a younger version of himself. Unhardened. "Now Hugo's dead," he said, "and we're all leaving. I finally get to go."

It was, when one stepped back and considered it, an island filled to bursting with dissatisfaction. "The world isn't better off this island, George," Leigh said. "It's just bigger."

"Sometimes," George replied, "I think bigger might be enough."

27.

Leigh woke late, when the sun was already strong in the sky. The inside of her mouth tasted like a punishment. Her head aching, her hands stinging. Maisie woke with her and licked her chin. The whole night weighing down on her. George, the sluagh, Iain. And today was the day of the festival. The last festival.

Later she wouldn't be sure how she'd made herself get up, how she'd managed to strip out of her dress—another one ruined—and change into thick socks, her father's favourite jumper, her same ripped overalls. Her entire body felt thick, slow, heavy. Bruised and battered. Maisie followed her as she moved through the house, down the stairs, into the kitchen, staying close at her side instead of rushing ahead and scratching at the door to be let out. Perhaps the worst part of it all, Leigh thought, had been the way she had fallen apart. In the sober light of day it all seemed a rather gross overreaction. There were such bigger things to worry about.

The telegram was sitting on the table on top of the other post. Leigh had picked it up yesterday before the funeral, forgotten to open it in the madness that followed. She could already guess what it would say, even as she opened it mechanically.

HOUSE SOLD ALL SETTLED STOP
CLOSING FIFTEENTH NOVEMBER STOP SAM

She folded the telegram up small, in her fingers and in her mind. Outside the sun cut through the fog. What had she left? A suitcase full of letters and her own burning uselessness. She wouldn't be useless this time. She found her boots and her coat, and she slipped out the door.

It was the thirty-first of October, and it was all nearly over. When Iain stepped into the square late in the day, the festival was in full swing, the town alive as it was only once a year. There were paper crows and thistles everywhere. The islanders were clad in a curious mixture of modern clothing and traditional dress; most of the older men had pulled out their kilts for the occasion, and many of the younger ones wore an article or two made up in their family's tartan. The high street was lined with little stalls: Tom McAllister's with hot cider, the MacEacherns' with coffee and tea, the Taylors' with sausage rolls and sandwiches. Iain helped himself to a meat pie from the Taylors as he manoeuvred through the crowd towards the docks. He had seen larger crowds, had been amongst teeming throngs in London, and still this crowd felt bigger, more volatile. It would be the ceilidh first, all down the street, and Mr. Murray was there with his pipes and Kirsten MacEwan with her fiddle, warming up with a reel played so perfectly that one wondered—if this was "warming up," what would a full-throated performance be? Music that made one feel a lifting in one's chest towards the sky, the open air.

The sluagh watched from a distance. So many crows, sitting on mailboxes and chimneys and gutters. They filled the smashed windows of the Taylors' house; they lingered in the piles of shattered stained glass, swept into the gutter. But despite their lurking presence, the street was full. Children chased after each other wearing somewhat less sinister versions of the great beaked masks from the rituals; the street was strung with bunting. An aggressive sort of joy, a happiness that playacted at defiance to hide its own weakness. Take what you want, it said to the sluagh, to the island, and we will do what we must.

There was no sign of Leigh anywhere, but she was all he could think about. When he'd woken this morning from a fitful sleep, the wound in his arm aching, his pillow had smelled fragrant, faintly floral. Shampoo or perfume, an artificial scent one could acquire only on the mainland. He sat up, pressed the heel of a hand into his eye, hard, until he saw stars. On his way downstairs he paused at the closed door of the spare room. She had started it, he told himself, she had started it by standing there and telling him that he was being a coward—if not in so many words—and he had only been defending himself.

Of course it wasn't true. She hadn't started it at all. He tapped on the door quietly and then louder when no one answered.

When the door swung open, it revealed a perfectly made bed. He tried to ignore the misgiving in his belly. She must have slipped out while he was still asleep, made the bed before she went. She must have.

A hand fell onto Iain's shoulder and he jumped in surprise. He had not noticed the ferry coming in but now it was here, and Mrs. Cavanagh standing before him. "I see I've not missed the excitement," Mrs. Cavanagh said as he took the bag from her hand.

"Oh, no," he replied, "there's plenty of excitement to be had still. How's your friend?"

"She'll be fine," Mrs. Cavanagh said. "Rather a false alarm, I think. You look like you've never so much as heard of the concept of sleep."

"Yes," Iain said. "You missed a rather eventful weekend."

"You've not had a falling out with Leigh Welles, have you?" What would make her say such a thing? Could she read it on him so easily? (A flash of memory behind his eyelids: Leigh, in his bed, moonlight painting her translucent skin silver. The topography of her: a delicate wrist, a rib, a hipbone.) He adjusted his grip on Mrs. Cavanagh's bag—what had she packed with her for only two days, the thing weighed a tonne—and tried to keep his face smooth. "You have," she said, "I can tell. You ought to find her and apologise."

"What makes you think it was my fault?" he demanded. A little burst of indignation. Unwarranted. He already knew he ought to find her and apologise. He wasn't sure he knew how.

Mrs. Cavanagh didn't reply immediately, just folded her hands neatly in front of her and considered the lively street. The sky was clear and the sun shining but winter was in the air.

"You know," she said, "if you think I want you to be holed up in your room like a monk for the rest of your days, lad, you really don't know me at all."

Kirsten MacEwan was still playing her painfully perfect music, but Iain could almost not hear it for the feeling of fullness in his head. He wanted one of his goddamned cigarettes, but he'd forgotten his pack at home. "Did you really tell her that I'm ruining my life?" he found himself asking. "Carrying on a war."

Mrs. Cavanagh sighed. "That sounds familiar," she said. "Don't tell me you fell out over something I said."

"No," Iain said. "That wasn't it." He shook his head, but it was too thick and full to clear. "Never mind. Let's go home, all the noise is giving me a headache."

"Mr. MacTavish?"

Iain turned, and found himself face to face with Mrs. McClare.

Instantly the instinct to flee, one he had to push down like grinding out a cigarette beneath his heel. He opened his mouth to speak but found he didn't know what to say, until at last he managed only, "Hi."

Mrs. Cavanagh pried her bag out of his hand. "I'll take this home," she said, and then she left him alone on the pavement with Mrs. McClare.

"Is Mr. McClare all right?" Iain asked.

"He will be, eventually," Mrs. McClare said. She glanced over her shoulder at the chaos of the high street behind her. "He just didn't feel quite up to it this year. He's already been to see Mr. Hendrix this morning. Ben's forgiven him, of course, now he just has to forgive himself." She folded her hands together in front of her, neatly. She was a thin woman, almost flimsy, as though she were made out of newsprint, but she looked so much like Matthew. Something about the shape of the eyes. "But you're a hard one to pin down, aren't you?"

"I got your note," Iain said. "I was—"

"Avoiding me," Mrs. McClare said, but not in a nasty way. Iain took in a breath to deny it, but it was true. He released the breath.

"Well," Iain said. "Yes."

"I don't blame you," Mrs. McClare said. "But I only want to talk about Matthew."

Here it was. Iain closed his eyes. Don't you think about it for a second, Matthew had said the last time Iain had seen him. Don't you think about us. Iain hadn't. Was that what Mrs. McClare wanted to hear? Their wars had shared alarmingly similar paths, until one day they hadn't.

"It's my fault," Iain said. "That Matthew didn't come back, it's my fault. I should have been flying that aeroplane."

Mrs. McClare reached out as though to grab Iain's elbow and then pulled back again. She said instead, "Don't do that to yourself. You were at your wife's funeral."

It had never seemed a good excuse, seemed even weaker now. A funeral wasn't really for the dead, he thought, it was for the living, and when he'd gone off to Inverness, he had thought only of himself. All that was left of the reason he had gone was a dogged loyalty that was disintegrating in his hands, crumbling faster the harder he clung to it.

"Matthew loved you," Mrs. McClare said. "He would have followed you anywhere."

Which was exactly the point. Matthew would have followed him anywhere, and he had. Into the RAF. To Canada. Across the Channel over and over again, down a dirt road in Vichy covered in Jamie the mid-upper's blood, over the Pyrenees into Spain. And yet when it mattered, when it really mattered—the one time that Iain needed to follow Matthew—he had not.

"He left a letter for you, you know," Mrs. McClare continued. Iain blinked at the woman for a moment, uncomprehending.

"For me," Iain repeated dumbly, because it didn't make any sense. But here was Matthew's mother reaching into her pocket and retrieving a crumpled envelope with his name on the front.

Years ago, just back from Spain, he had sat on Caroline's thin mattress and listened quietly while she berated him for the letter he had left her. They hadn't wanted to write them at all, Iain and Matthew, though it was standard fare for an airman. The odds being what they were. Eventually Iain gave in and wrote two letters, one for his father and one for Caroline, to be sent in the (inevitable) event of his demise.

"Here, this is the best part," Caroline said, pacing. "'Go ahead and marry that man from the ministry you're always talking about. I can't remember his name now but he sounds like a stand-up chap.' What's that supposed to mean?"

Iain said, "It was supposed to be a joke."

"A joke!" Caroline cried, flinging her hands into the air. "A joke! When for all anybody knows you've just gone down in a glorified tin can! You thought jokes were appropriate!"

Iain hadn't known what was appropriate. He hadn't known anything at all.

Iain tore the envelope open and barely avoided ripping in half the page enclosed within. At first his eyes refused to focus, sliding over the paper aimlessly. The words swam into view. *Skip*, they began. *I suppose my luck has run out.*

> *You're up in Inverness and the rest of us are going up tonight. I just have a feeling about this one.*
>
> *It's rather odd to write this. I'm sure you understand. Writing yourself out of the world. It's hard to know what to say so I won't say too much, and embarrass us both. Don't fret too much, all right? It'd be a lie to say that I don't mind going, but it matters, what we're fighting for. I know what my part in it is. I believe in it. You're going to blame yourself for not being here, but I'm glad you're not. Don't ruin your life with it. It won't do anyone any good.*
>
> *What a grand adventure we had together.*
>
> *Good luck, brother. See you in the morning.*

He tried to fold the letter back up again, but the paper kept crumpling between his fingers. Mrs. McClare took it back from him, smoothed and folded it, and returned it to its envelope herself. The woman extended the letter for Iain to take but Iain couldn't make his hands move, so Mrs. McClare stepped up to him, opened Iain's jacket, and tucked the letter into his inside pocket.

"He loved you, Iain," Mrs. McClare said, like a secret. "And he was a smart lad. He knew the choices he was making."

This was, for whatever reason, the last straw. Iain MacTavish—who could be seen walking the high street at night speaking to nobody, who had lost his soul somewhere over Germany—burst into tears.

It was as though something tethering him to his body had snapped, and even as Iain struggled to breathe, to calm down, to pull himself together, he felt oddly detached, as though he were watching from above. Mrs. McClare was pulling him into a surprisingly solid embrace, patting Iain on the back as she would a small child. Iain could not catch his breath. "I'm sorry," he said, "I'm sorry." He had been holding so much inside him for so long, but now he could feel it leaving him. Dresden, Braunschweig, Munich, Cologne. A V-2 rocket on the corner of Adelaide Avenue. The Pyrenees at night. Good luck, see you in the morning. Watching the WAAFs scrape the Rhodesian crew off the runway, bumping into a girl in a blackout. He had thought that it was everybody else that was acting so haunted, but it was him. He could feel it leaving him like a tide receding, and it was over.

By the time Leigh reached the Bruce house, the day was already stretching and tilting towards evening. She had never made this walk alone before; she had always had someone next to her, Graham or Iain or Hugo and the other McClares when they were small and adventurous. Today there was not even the dog for company. Possibly Maisie would be useful in the tunnel, if this journey was as dangerous as Iain apparently thought it was—clearly there was a reason that Graham had taken the dog along on all his expeditions. Though as far as Leigh knew, all his expeditions had been above ground, skirting through familiar heather, boots and paws sinking into familiar mud. As far as Leigh knew, none of his expeditions had taken him into a dreamworld, a place where the walls seemed to hum and the air shifted like voices. There might be nobody to miss her if she didn't come back, but she would not take Graham's poor dog along with her. She left Maisie at home.

She was almost there now, the light falling and the Bruce house sitting there on the horizon. When she blinked, she thought she saw a woman wandering through the grass ahead of her. The same woman she'd been seeing everywhere, blurred and out of focus as if Leigh were looking at her through a dark glass. Leigh blinked again, and she disappeared.

The house was as they had left it when they climbed out of the cellar with Hugo's body. The floor creaked ominously when she stepped inside, loud and long like a groan, threatening to collapse under her. She reached out to the wall as though that would save her if the house decided to crumble.

Down the hall, into the cellar, deep into the shadows. She had found a small mechanical power torch in the shed on her way out the door, something Graham must have picked up at some point, and she pulled it from her pocket. Shook it hard and it sprung to life. Her heart was pounding so hard in her chest that she thought if anyone else were with her they probably could have heard it, danced a ceilidh to it. Leigh stepped into the tunnel and a spray of dust fell onto her head. She aimed her torch up at the ceiling. There was a long, narrow crack in the rock that might have been there years or minutes. She reached up and laid her hand against the cold, dark stone. No more dust fell from the crack.

She ventured into the earth. The tunnel felt shorter today, with the benefit of the torchlight forcing back the dark. She trailed her hand against the wall and felt the deep grooves of the runes carved into the rock. Was the stone buzzing beneath her hand, or was it the energy zipping along her own nerves? A feeling that something was beginning, or changing, or ending, a feeling that she walked into more than dirt and rock. The tunnel widened and she was there, the wall falling away from her hand and her torchlight beaming out across the water.

Leigh paused. The air felt thick, pregnant, somehow hard to breathe. "Hello?" she called out, but there was nothing but the dark. She took a step forwards, and another, until the water lapped against her toes.

Something moved in the dark. A blurred shape like a silhouette. "Who's there?" she called, but no one replied. The light from her torch bounced off the water, flickered on the walls like a dancer, silvery. Leigh took another step into the pool and the water began to seep into her socks. The water was the only sound, dripping from the ceiling, lapping quietly at the shore.

A voice said, *Have you come to finish it?*

Or maybe she only imagined it. She flattened a palm over her ear to muffle out the drip drip drip of the water, the whispering of it against the rock. The air smelled of earth and sea and it clung to her throat, her nose. There was silence for a long time, silence like a curse.

The voice came again, passing through the water, the air, Leigh's fingers: *Have you come to finish it?*

Another silhouette in the dark. Leigh swung the beam of her torch around the cave, but still there was no one else with her. Someone whispered her name and she whipped around. There were shapes against the back wall of the cave. Or perhaps behind it. Like it wasn't a wall at all but a window. One voice whispered her name and another repeated it until the cave was filled with the sound, like gently rustling leaves. At first all the voices sounded the same, but then they began to clarify and separate. A man, a woman, a boy. Some sounded close, others far away. Some clear and some muffled.

"Who are you?" Leigh asked, although the voice that had spoken sounded rather familiar. It was stronger than the others, nearer, as though whispering in her ear. A boy's.

Leigh, the boy said. *Have you come to finish it?*

She squinted in the half-light towards the back wall. If she looked very closely, she thought she could see human figures moving slowly, crowding into frame like a family posing for a photograph. Reaching towards her as a drowning man reaches for a lifeboat. When she blinked they disappeared, her fresh eyes erasing them. Just before she blinked again they reappeared. She could not be entirely sure that she was seeing anything at all. They were still saying her name, over and over, and their voices grew louder, more desperate, as though begging her to do—what?

The boy's voice whispered, as though right in her ear, *Have you come to finish it?* All at once Leigh recognised the voice, like waking up from a long sleep.

It was Hugo.

28.

He had to find Leigh.

The ceilidh had begun in the street, a breathless, whirling thing. Leigh had told Iain once that she loved the ceilidh, but now amongst the whipping kilts and hair and laughter he couldn't find her. The hours ticked by and Leigh did not appear. The sun began to dip towards the horizon and the ceilidh ended, and Leigh did not appear. Tom McAllister started handing out mulled cider like it was water and Iain sipped carefully, eyeing the sluagh that watched from the rooftops, the shadowy lanes. The birds still seemed to be growing in number; each time one trio took flight into the evening, at least six birds took its place. It had all been forgotten during the ceilidh, but now that night was near, it came rushing back. What was still to come, if the birds refused to leave. Maybe Leigh was right about that too. Iain turned away from the street to go look for her, and collided with George McClare. The rest of Iain's cider sloshed onto the man's jumper. "Watch it!" George snapped, wiping his hand down his front.

"Sorry," Iain said. He didn't want to make up with Mrs. Mc-Clare only to get into a scrap with her son in the street. "I was looking for Leigh."

George glared at him. "What do you want with her?" he demanded.

Iain shrugged, trying to seem casual. "Just haven't seen her—"

"Since last night?"

It was impossible to ignore the accusation in George's voice. Iain paused. He didn't know how it could have gotten around so fast, the gossip. "Yes," Iain said. "Since last night. Have you seen her?"

"Aye," George said. "I've seen her. I found her in the wee hours, at the side of the road, set upon by sluagh. In a bad way, and not just because of the birds. She said she'd been with you."

Panic flooded into his stomach. Set upon by sluagh, found by George. It felt like much longer than a month ago that he strode into the dark and found Leigh Welles gasping for breath in a field where George had left her. He demanded, "What did you do to her?"

"You know what, pal," George said, with a withering look as he turned away, "you can fuck right off, all right?"

Iain grabbed the collar of George's jacket, swung him round to face him again. "What did you do to her?"

George shoved Iain hard with both hands and Iain stumbled backwards a step. "I took her home!" George shouted. "All right? Just took her home."

The Welles house was still and silent when Iain reached it, as the last light disappeared behind the edge of the sea. Boards firmly nailed over the westward windows, charms dutifully hanging from the front door. He knocked and inside Maisie started barking. After a moment paws scrabbled at the door. He knocked again. Nothing. He tried the handle and the door swung open. Maisie leapt at him and he forced her down. Her heart raced against his hands as he tried to calm her. "Where's Leigh?" he asked, and the dog whined. Inside there was no sign of her. He called her name, but nothing in the house answered. He went upstairs, an imposition. There was a suitcase in the smallest bedroom, clothing spilling out of it like kelp on the beach. A thick layer of dust covered everything in the other rooms. Downstairs in the sitting room there was a half-finished cup of tea long gone cold. Lying open on the kitchen counter there was a telegram from Sam Welles. Iain looked out the back window, at the mist rolling down from the Ben in the dark, and knew that he had arrived too late.

The water in the pool was punishingly cold. As Leigh waded deeper, closer to the glassy veil of rock, the water crept higher, past her hips and waist and ribs. It was impossible to tell how deep the water might get. She had left her clothes in a neat pile at the water's edge, only her flimsy step-ins between her skin and the water.

It was Hugo's voice whispering in her ear, Hugo's lanky silhouette moving darkly behind the rock, and she had to get closer, had to press her hands against that shadowed glass and feel it for herself. It could not be real; it must be happening in her head, she must have finally gone crazy. A person could talk to the dead all she wanted, but the dead couldn't talk back.

She reached the other side of the pool. The anaemic light from her torch was fading fast, and she stood shivering in near-total darkness. She reached up and laid her trembling hand against the glassy rock, the veil. It felt like rock should feel, cold and smooth and solid, and from this close the human silhouettes had all but disappeared. *You shouldn't be here,* Hugo's voice said, from somewhere between Leigh's own ears. *It's not a place for living things.*

There was no need to ask what he meant, she could feel it. The cold seeping into her bones and a feeling that the air was too thick to make it into her lungs, a feeling like she was wearing a heavy coat.

Who led you here? Hugo asked. *It was Matthew's voice, he called me here. Who called you?*

"I don't know," Leigh said. Which wasn't true; for her, too, there was a voice that filled her dreams, that she thought she had heard echoing in the Bruces' cellar the first time she ventured into the dark with Iain. There was the vision of the woman lingering out of sight, disappearing every time Leigh tried to look at her properly. "No one. I came here to find out how to fix it. The sluagh. All of it."

The silhouette she thought was Hugo's seemed to push closer to the rock. *Yes,* he said. *Fix it. It's cold here. We want to leave.*

"Where are you?" Leigh said. "How do I fix it?"

I don't know, Hugo said. *I'm only a ghost.*

The flickering torch back on the shore finally sputtered and died. Leigh thought perhaps there was a faint glow somewhere far beyond the rock before her, but maybe it was only the torch-light hanging in her eyes. "Was it your ghost that came back?" she asked. "Was it the sluagh, trying to trick us?"

The sluagh aren't like that, Hugo said. *Not really.*

Leigh pressed a freezing hand against her chest and felt her heart fluttering like a bird. "How can you say that," she said, "when they killed you?"

I don't think they meant to. I think I just got in the way. They're like us. They just want to go.

"Go where?"

On.

The air hummed with a long sigh, high and clear. A sigh like Leigh had heard before, up in the Bruces' cellar. A new voice. *You don't know how any of this works at all,* this voice said. *Do you?* It was the voice from her dreams. (Who called you? Hugo had asked, and she supposed it must be this voice, this faintly familiar voice.) Leigh found the source of the voice, barely more than a dark outline. *How can you fix something you don't understand?*

"I want to understand," Leigh said. "Tell me."

Dying is a sea, the voice said. *Death is another world. Some of us find it harder to leave. We are not good sailors, or we are unfinished. We linger here. The sluagh are creatures of the sea, the liminal. They are there to help the crossing.*

"Who are you?" Leigh asked. "How do you know all this?"

Another sigh. *I've been lingering for a long time,* the voice said, and nothing more.

"Because you weren't finished." A memory floating to the surface, one she'd recalled before: sitting in Graham's lap late one October evening, some talk about unfinished business. "Does everyone who dies suddenly get trapped here?"

Not necessarily, the voice said. It was so familiar. Why was it so familiar? *People live their lives differently.*

Leigh had begun to shiver. She wrapped her arms around herself, pressed skin on skin. Her body felt smooth and cold like glass. "So you'd have me believe," she said, "that the sluagh are just—just ferrymen? Doing some job. Carrying you across."

It's not so simple, the voice said. *We are them. They are us. We're tied together. It's not so easy to separate. Even harder now than it used to be.*

"Why?" Leigh asked. She sounded, she thought, rather like a petulant child. "Why is everything different?"

Can't you feel it? the voice asked. It sounded so tired. Leigh didn't think spirits should be tired. *Can't you feel their suffering?*

"Whose?"

Theirs. Ours.

"The sluagh don't suffer," Leigh said. "The sluagh are just the sluagh."

They don't exist without us, the voice said. *And do we not suffer?* Leigh was so close to recognising the voice, it was just beyond her grasp. *They aren't evil, but they are dark. Creatures of the in-between. And there's been so much sadness, senselessness. They carry that, too. There's supposed to be a balance. We're supposed to balance them. But there's too much grief, too much sadness, too much violence. We can't compete with that. We can't drown it out.*

"And that's why they're—the way they are. Vicious and cruel."

Carrying the weight of the world's suffering. Wouldn't you be?

It happened suddenly, like the ringing of a bell. The voice resolved. Leigh recognised it. It was Áine Welles.

Leigh's breath left her in a great rush. "Stop doing that," she said. Áine Welles's voice had no business being in this cave, Áine Welles was somewhere on the mainland, somewhere far away, voyaging. "You can't have her voice."

There's something you need to understand, Áine's voice said. *I can show it to you. If you lie back in the water.*

"How could I trust anything that you would show me?" Leigh gasped. "This is just the sluagh, isn't it? Wearing Hugo's face, wearing her voice. It's all just a trick."

I will show you only true things.

"You won't show me anything," Leigh said. She found that she was crying, but she did not know why. It was just a trick of the sluagh, all of it. Iain was right, it wasn't real. "You don't know anything. I shouldn't have come." She turned away from the wall and began to push back through the water. Her breath was rough and shallow, and she wiped her wet hands against her face angrily. Another step and her foot slipped out from underneath her. She plummeted under the surface and kept plummeting, deeper than she thought was possible. Down through the water and into another world.

Some hundred feet above, Iain stepped into the Bruce house.

There was no sign of Leigh. He hadn't brought a torch and already it was deep night; he could barely see his hand before his face. Maisie snuffled through the dust ahead of him—she had refused to be left behind and besides, he thought having

305

a dog about might not be such a bad thing. "Leigh?" he called into the house, but nobody answered.

He took a step forwards. The house gave a loud, danger-ous groan and a burst of dust and decaying plaster fell onto his head. Possibly he felt the floor tilt, barely. Another step for-wards and his foot plunged through the rotting floorboards, all the way up to his hip. Only a week since they'd last been here and already the house was crumbling. Iain pried himself free, collapsed near the wall. "Leigh!" he shouted again, but again there was no reply.

The cellar was worse; it looked like some of the kitchen above had already caved in. Dust fell from the ceiling almost constantly, like snow or ash. Iain shuffled forwards, regretting his failure to bring a lamp. At the tunnel's entrance he paused. It seemed that if the wind but blew, the entire house might come down upon his head. He didn't much care for the underground, he was an air-man. What if the house should fall, the earth cave in, while he and Leigh were still within it? A sudden memory of a week of leave in London, 1941. He'd seen the wardens and the fire watchers and the people, ordinary people, trying to dig their neighbours out of what had once been a street but now was simply a mound of smouldering rubble. ("Buried alive," Caroline had said once, shuddering, telling him about the Blitz. "I should much prefer to be taken out by the blast." A wish that had gone unheeded.)

But Leigh was already within. Trying to do this impossible thing, in the place that had killed Hugo McClare. If the house should fall, if the earth caved in, it would take her with it.

Iain delved into the dark, one hand outstretched before him and the other to the wall. He could hear Maisie following him, whining lowly. Iain knew how to navigate blind. He didn't much care for the underground, but the dark had no power over him; he had lived a thousand lifetimes in the night.

Time passed strangely in this cave, he had learnt the last time. It might have taken hours to shuffle down the tunnel, his heart in his mouth, or it might have taken only minutes. When the wall finally fell away from his hand, he was winded, as if he'd sprinted the whole way.

The cave was just as they had left it. The only sound was the faint lapping of the water at the shore. Maisie disappeared into the dark towards the water. Iain didn't know what he had expected, but he had not expected the silence. He had expected to come upon Leigh, to find her instantly. There was no sign of her.

He thought he saw a light flicker against the mirror-smooth back wall of the cavern, like the glimmer of a silver fish, like the arc of a distant searchlight. Maisie growled and barked, once. It reverberated through the cave. "Hello?" Iain called, but there was no reply. He shuffled closer to the pool. Perhaps he'd miscalculated and Leigh was not here at all. Perhaps he had missed her on the way up to her house, ships in the night, and she was already down at the festival.

His foot connected with something hard. He crouched down and found a mechanical torch, a small pile of women's clothing. When the torch flickered to life, he swung it in a wide, slow arc. He saw a girl, pale and diaphanous, floating in the pool like something by Millais, blonde hair spread out around her head like a halo. Leigh.

29.

The darkness cracked open. Leigh was out on the sea in a small red fishing boat, and the sun was rising, glimmering in the water, orange and pink and red. Beneath the waves she could see the movement of hundreds of tiny silver fish. The green and black cliffs of the island were receding, slowly, behind her. The cathedral spires reaching into the morning sky. Where had she been before this? She could not remember getting into this boat, could not remember where she was going.

There was a woman in the boat with her, back turned. Her blonde hair was piled on top of her head and her pale green skirt clung damp to her legs. Possibly just a moment ago this woman had told Leigh that there was something she had to understand. She rowed, and rowed, and rowed. Leigh felt the salt spray on her face, stinging her eyes. It was not a quiet sea this morning. The waves grew taller and the woman struggled against the oars. Leigh called into the wind, *Let me help you*, but the woman didn't turn. The boat rocked perilously and seawater sloshed over the side. *Hey*, Leigh called to the woman again. *Let me help you!*

The woman turned her head and Leigh recognised her mouth, her eyes, the upwards turn of her nose.

Mum, she said, and a black wave crashed over Áine's head.

The boat was gone and it was just Leigh and the water, tumbling through the dark again. No up or down or in or out, just her lungs burning for air, just the sea pulling her down. She fought it, she fought it, she fought it, until her head burst back above the surface and she gasped for breath. She shook the salt from her eyes, treading water madly, trying to catch enough breath before another wave came.

She looked about for Áine and found her, a small blonde head bobbing in the ocean a hundred yards away, struggling against the water. Áine was a good swimmer, strong. She had taught Sam and Leigh in a little sheltered cove nestled on West Sands. *Mum!* Leigh cried, but the wind ripped her voice out of her chest and buried it in the sea. She started to swim towards her mother, a haphazard breaststroke. Áine's head dipped beneath the surface for a moment, before she emerged again, spluttering. Leigh had to swim faster. She could not let Áine submerge, could not let her disappear. If Áine disappeared, all of this would happen the same way it had happened. Sam would leave. Her father would fall to his death. She would be left with nothing.

Áine disappeared beneath the surface again, took a little longer to reappear. The distance between Leigh and her mother seemed to be growing rather than shrinking. Áine's voice came to her through the water, from inside her own head. *Choose.* Choose what? She could feel the call of something deep and singular, something far beneath the waves, a doorway opening. Things could still be different, she thought desperately as she swam. If Áine stayed, everything could be different. Leigh could be. Maybe the war could not be stopped, but maybe Sam wouldn't go, and Leigh wouldn't go either, and Graham wouldn't tumble from the edge of a cliff, and everyone's lives might not unravel. Things could still be different.

Áine slipped beneath the water. A wave crashed over Leigh's head, buffeting her downwards. Everything couldn't be different, everything had already happened. This was only a vision, it was only the past. When she fought her way back to the sunlight, she was alone in a vast lilac sea.

30.

Leigh surged out of the pool, gasping for breath. Water streamed off her hair, over her eyes. She was temporarily blinded by the brightness of the vision as it left her, and the darkness of the cave bore down on her, squeezed.

We're already gone, all of us, Áine Welles's ghost told her. *It's time for you to choose.*

"Leigh!"

She pushed through the water towards the glassy rock. Laid her hand against it but barely felt anything; all the sensation had gone from her fingers. "Why did you show me that?" she said, breathlessly.

You need to understand, Áine said.

"You said you would only show me true things," Leigh said. "I just wanted to know how to send the sluagh away."

Don't you know? Áine said. Her voice was fading away again, back into the ethereal whisper that had haunted Leigh for weeks, years. *It's life*, she said. *It's always been life.*

"Leigh!" Heavy hands fell onto her shoulders and Leigh re-alised that the sound came from outside of herself, it wasn't one of the spirits at all. She spun around and found Iain there, in the water with her. Maisie barking at them from the shore. Iain had come after her. His voice seemed to come from another country, a place that hardly meant anything at all. "What the hell are you doing?" he shouted at her, shaking her by her shoulders. "We have to—"

There was a low groan, from somewhere deep within the world. Maybe so deep it was the next one. *You've been here too long*, Hugo's voice said, sharply. The spirits were receding from the rock, growing fainter. *This is how it happened*, Hugo said, *this is how it happened to me. You've been here too long.*

"You haven't told me how to fix it!" Leigh cried.

But there was no reply. "Leigh," Iain said. "There's nobody else here. It's just us, we have to go."

"No," Leigh said. "They were just here. They were going to tell me what to do."

Everything was quiet and thick, as though Leigh had plunged back beneath the water, and then Hugo's voice came, somehow all at once a whisper and clear like the ringing of a bell.

He said, *Run.*

The silence split, and the cave flooded with sluagh.

It was like a dam bursting, birds suddenly pouring into the air. It was impossible to tell if they'd appeared through the tunnel or from the air itself; it was impossible to tell if they'd started the cave to collapsing or if the crumbling rock had released them. Maisie sprang into the pool as the tunnel back into the Bruces' cellar disappeared into earth. She leapt through the water and disappeared into the dark. She barked, and sounded very distant, almost as if—

"A second tunnel," Iain said. "There must be a second tunnel. Go!" He splashed across the pool, snatched Leigh's clothes and shoes from the shore, followed her as they ran, blind, into the dark after Maisie. The air filled with birds and talons and feathers and dust and rock. The ground was sloping downwards, but Leigh didn't think about how they were racing deeper and deeper into the earth, how she was hastening her own burial.

The ground became softer, covered in dust or dirt. The incline gentler. All at once Leigh and Iain burst into the world, tumbled onto black sand, wrapping their arms over their heads as the birds spilled into the sky above them, keening into the night.

She was shivering violently, her wet hair slowly turning to ice. For a moment she could barely move, could only curl herself into a ball on the rough sand and press her freezing hands to her face. "Are you all right?" Iain was saying, and his hands were on her arms, and Maisie was licking her feet, and Iain was trying to pry her fingers away from her face. "What happened back there? You need to get dressed, you'll freeze to death."

She came back to herself quite suddenly. Lying on the beach half-naked, Iain crouched over her. She snatched her clothes out of his hands, shoved her wet body back into them. He had the decency to drop his eyes.

Possibly nothing that had passed in the cave was to be believed at all. Certainly not whatever had happened underneath the water, that thing Leigh still resisted understanding. It was not a true thing, she told herself, a brand-new, bright red boat overturning on a rough morning sea. Overturning long before its captain had a chance to reach the mainland, disappear into some dark city, start a new life. It was not a true thing, though it sat in her chest like truth—heavy and solid; it didn't spin and whirl around her ribs the way a lie did.

The birds cried through the night as they careened down towards the village, more birds than Leigh had ever seen before in her life, like a seam had ripped open and released the full force of them into the world. She asked, "What time is it?"

"I don't know," Iain said. She couldn't bring herself to look at him. "Late."

How late? Time had passed strangely in the cave. It had felt like she was there only for minutes, but clearly it had been some hours. Was it midnight yet? The sluagh were still here. She could hear them in the air high above her, crying discordantly. The sluagh still here, sluagh that Leigh had released into the world from that cave, and now none of it could be stopped. A year-long march away, the end of everything, no hope of return. How many more people could she allow to leave her?

She crouched down and wrapped her arms around Maisie. Carded her fingers in the dog's wet fur. "Good girl," she muttered to the dog. Iain was still trying to talk to her, about stupid, worldly things, about things that didn't matter. "Leigh," he said. "About last night—"

"We have to go," Leigh said, more to Maisie than to Iain. She stood up, off-balance.

"What are you planning to do?" Iain called after her as she began to stagger away, southwards.

She didn't know. "Right now," she said, "I'm planning to find a way off this beach. There has to be somewhere, where the cliff's not so high."

"I walk along here in the mornings," Iain said, appearing at her shoulder and peering up at the cliff. "If we are where I think we are, I might know a spot."

It was nearly November and the sluagh were thick in the air as the islanders processed up from the high street back to the standing stones. The torchlight seemed to be the only thing keeping them at bay; while climbing the hill up to the bonfire that roared at the cliffside one could see the creatures' small hard bodies darting around just out of sight like bats in summer. Kate McClare tripped and the birds set upon her in seconds, pulling at her hair, ripping at her skin, before George beat them away from her. There were more birds than anybody had ever seen before. They whistled down the high street and shattered through the windows as though neither board nor glass were there at all. Mrs. McCafferty stumbled out of the procession towards them like a clockwork doll, until her husband pulled her back, while she cried, "It's Lucy, I can hear her, she's calling me, let me go." There were voices on the air, whispers and cries, coaxing the islanders away from the safety of the torchlight, coaxing them into the black storm.

Iain and Leigh scrambled up the cliffside from the beach, up a roughly hewn staircase so long forgotten that time had rendered it nearly vertical, Maisie speeding up the rocks ahead of them. The birds were everywhere, Leigh could feel them spinning through the air, but she dared not turn to look. Every so often she felt their talons scrape against her neck, tangle into her hair. If one of the creatures got it into its mind to tear either of them from the cliff, there would be little to stop it.

She shifted her foot and let out a cry as the rock beneath it tumbled away. Her foot dangled in the air helplessly as she clung to the cliff. "Don't worry," Iain called up to her, "I've got you," and he took her foot in his hand and guided it to a sturdier rock.

At last they clambered over the edge of the cliff, collapsed into the soft mud. Leigh's hands had gone numb and she hardly noticed her bloody, torn palms. Even without the cold she would have had no room in her mind for the pain. A great bonfire roared into the sky on the horizon, bigger than the one on the first, bigger than she had ever seen, so big it seemed to consume her. Iain reached a hand to her arm. "We should get you some dry clothes."

"No," she said, yanking herself away from him. "I want to go to the festival." The cave had held no answers, and she had wasted her time, time she could never get back, the last October festival. She had missed all of it to stand in a frigid pool and imagine herself hearing her mother's voice in the dripping water. She had missed all of it, and now it was ending without her.

She started to run.

Finally the bonfire loomed in front of her, the smoke curling down her throat and choking her. It was almost just like it had been thirty days ago, on the first of October when the world felt so different. There were the islanders in wide rings around the fire, there were the elders in their white robes. Their hands joined in rings around the fire, one final communion. There was the Gaelic thrumming in the air. The sluagh circled in the column of sparks and smoke above, a flock of bombers.

As Leigh approached, a woman in the outer circle turned her head. Kate. "Where have you been?" she hissed, a stage whisper. Leigh opened her mouth to speak but found she couldn't. Smoke and sweat had mixed on Kate's cheeks and turned her skin ashy grey. "Never mind," she said. "You're just in time for the end."

"What end?" Leigh asked, but Kate didn't answer. She dropped the hand of the man standing next to her—George— and took Leigh's instead. George seemed about to take Leigh's other hand when Iain finally caught up, stepped between them. Maisie circled their legs anxiously until Leigh nudged her with her foot and the dog lay down in the grass. The circle closed again, and here they were. The last generation of islanders. The McClares and McAllisters, MacEwans and Beeches, Gordons and Taylors and Harrowers. A handful of Morrisons and one surviving Welles. Leigh stared through the fire at the faces she had known all her life and tried to commit every bit of it to memory, something solid and smooth like a piece of beach glass that she could hold in her palm and examine some day in the future. The Gaelic hummed through the air, rich and deep, and she thought about Hugo standing in the middle of her sitting room, commanding the crows to leave. Her breath spun and buzzed in her chest, shallow. She thought about all the things that had changed already, all the things that would change again in the coming weeks. She thought about stepping onto a ferry and watching the cliffs disappear into the mist for the last time; she thought about sitting in some dark and musty flat alone.

One by one the white-robed islanders removed their masks, placed them carefully in the grass around the bonfire, retreated into the outer circle so they were one. The last of the Gaelic. One unison voice.

An doras a 'dùnadh.

(The door closes.)

Here was how it ended in past years: Seven men would douse the fire, and the smoke would roll out like water, bathing the islanders gathered around. Burrowing into clothes and skin and hair, painting them in ashes. They would stand there in the silence and let it roll over them, November, and then they would wipe their faces and return to the village and drink Tom's cider and dance to Kirsten's music and it would be a celebration, they would welcome the winter.

Here was how it ended tonight: It didn't. The fire burned on. Mhairi Taylor stepped towards it. Across the fire a man stepped forward, too, something in tow.

It was Young Mr. Morrison. The thing in tow was a white goat. A white goat named Matilda, named by a Leigh just turned nine.

"What's going on?" Leigh asked, in a voice that was louder than she meant it to be, high and clear and cutting through the air. She turned to Kate, whose face was unreadable. She turned to Iain, who simply shook his head that he didn't know.

"It's how it has to be, Leigh," Mr. Harrower said. Calling to her from across the circle. "Don't you see? This is all out of balance. Hugo McClare killed one of them. His father killed more. It's only fair. An eye for an eye."

"An eye for an eye," Leigh repeated, dumbly, and then she understood. They were going to sacrifice Leigh's goat. They were going to sacrifice Matilda.

Leigh lunged towards the fire. Tom McAllister appeared out of nowhere, a brick wall in her way. He grabbed her arms. "Lass," he said, and Leigh looked up at him, desperately. Surely Tom, of all people—Tom would be on her side. It was one thing, slicing one's palm and throwing some bloodied relic into the fire. This was another thing entirely. Tom had to see it too. But he just said, "You have to stop." Leigh looked around again, but the islanders all wore matching expressions, like they would do whatever it was that Mr. Harrower said, like this wasn't unthinkable, like it didn't matter what it took as long as it would be over.

Leigh shook herself out of Tom's grip. "You're not killing one of my goats for some stupid sacrifice," she said. Across the fire Matilda wailed plaintively. Maisie began to bark again and Leigh ran to Matilda, flung her arms around the goat's neck before Young Morrison had a chance to pull her away. She buried her face in Matilda's neck and breathed in her musty, goaty scent. A gift from her parents, her parents at the bottom of the sea. "Find something else," she said, her voice muffled. "It's not right. Find something else."

"It's already been decided," Young Morrison said. He pried Matilda from Leigh's grip and there was Tom again, grabbing her arms and trying to stop her struggling. "Just let's get it over with, aye? And it'll be done for another year. Let's not drag it out."

"No!" Leigh cried, as Tom pulled her back to her spot in the circle. She struggled against him but he was much stronger than she was, she didn't stand a chance. "Wait! Please, wait!" Tom deposited her at the edge of the circle, and when Leigh lunged towards the fire again, Kate McClare grabbed her by the hand once more, dragged her farther away. "Hey," Iain said. "Get away from the edge."

No one listened to him. "They don't even milk anymore, Leigh," Kate said, putting her hands on Leigh's shoulders. Her face was white, her eyes wild, like she was in the throes of some nightmare. They were all in the throes of some nightmare, they had been for years. "It won't do any good!" Leigh cried. She had come into understanding suddenly, like a swimmer emerging from the sea. It wasn't about her, or Hugo, or anyone; it was about everything else, all the ways the island had been battered and bruised and forced to change since the simple hazy days of childhood, the days when they still had summertime in them. This island had survived centuries off the land and ancient magic. Charms and sacrifices, the great machinery of superstition. So many sacrifices, through the years. Youth, innocence, sons, daughters, timelessness. Nothing would ever be the same but she felt—she knew, the way one knew how to breathe or blink or walk—that if she let them do this thing it would mean something, that the world had cracked open like an egg. That something in them had broken that could not be put together again.

"It won't do any good," she said again. "Killing an innocent thing won't put it right. There's been so much violence and death and suffering already and we're just making it worse. We have to stop making it worse."

Leigh wrenched her arm out of Kate's grip. Iain shouted her name and she turned her head, saw him lunging for her as the stones beneath her boot shifted and her foot slipped out into negative space. She flung her hand towards Iain, but she had already taken flight.

31.

She fell like a flaming star. Air and salt and feathers streaming behind her. The sluagh swarmed around her, she was the eye of their storm. Dark and thick like a cloud so that she couldn't see anything, just darkness, darkness and the fall and the winter pulsing through her heart.

She fell like a star and the sluagh came with her. She felt it in her chest, like sucking the poison out of a snakebite. They wrapped their feathers around her, astonishingly soft, no trace of talon, and Leigh could see how it might be quite nice, to be carried by these birds across the ocean. In threes the birds began to leave her, peeling off into the morning air. She could see the water below her now, fast approaching. From that height, hitting the water was like hitting pavement, Dr. Delaune had told her once, a September morning on a cold curbside, her father's body under a crisp white sheet. Leigh thought of all the people consigned to the bottom of this frigid sea. Her father and her mother, a thousand years of islanders, a generation of young airmen, Hugo. She would never leave this island, she would be here forever, her heart in the salt and spray, her heart crashing against the rocks with the waves.

Dying is a sea. The water rushed up to meet her.

32.

It was the first of November, and the sluagh were gone.

Iain ran past the bonfire and the stones and the cars in the field. He ran past the boats tied up at the pier and the fishing nets piled high next to them. He ran and he could hear the islanders following behind him, a great rush of bodies. He ran onto the damp sand and down the beach, through the morning haar to the spot she must have disappeared, and ignored the voices shouting his name, calling him back from the sea. He ran into the water and felt the shock of it in his bones.

(She sank fast and far, down towards something deep and dark and blue. There was no pain or cold or feeling of any kind and it was quiet, it was unreality, all.)

The waves were already returning her body to shore. Floating face down, her hair clouding around her like seaweed. Iain lifted her out of the water and stumbled with her back onto the sand. Her skin was colourless, icy, as he dragged her awkwardly into his lap, tried to push her hair back from her face with his cold, wet hands. Maisie caught up to them and started licking at Leigh's cheeks, whining desperately. "Come on, Leigh," Iain said, but she didn't answer. "You're not dead. You're not dead." He tried to feel for a pulse, but his hands were shaking too hard. The islanders had begun to join him on the beach, but no one would come near; they all just stood around him and stared as though they were watching the final act of some terrible play. "Somebody help me!" Iain shouted. Nobody moved. Leigh's lips were blue.

(The darkness began to recede, or perhaps she only got used to it. She was bodiless, consciousness floating in space. The island spread out beneath her like a quilt on a bed. The harbour and the high street, the church and the old memorial. The abandoned Bruce farm, and the Ben, and the standing stones. Here were all the people on it, the dramas of their little lives played out on this little stage. Hundreds of undisturbed years and then war descending like a storm. Here were the McAllisters and the McClares and the Brodies and the Gordons, McCaffertys, Murrays, Blakes, Morrisons. Amongst them great dark blossoms of rot, grief and horror and loss, following the lines of the coast and the peak of the church spire. Leigh could feel the years ticking by like seconds and the rot only grew, creeping, festering. There were certain places where it was thickest. The McClare farm. The Gordons' grocery. The Hendrixes' cottage. The Welles house. She considered the shape of it, all the many ways this island had been forced to change since her childhood, all the people who had left and all the sadness that had replaced them.)

Someone shoved through the crowd, lumbered over to Iain. Tom McAllister, pulling Leigh out of Iain's lap and laying her on the sand. "Fraser!" he barked. "Go find Dr. Delaune!" The boy took off running down the beach to find the doctor, presumably tending to Mr. Hendrix back in town. Too far, Iain thought, it was too far to run. Tom leaned down over Leigh and blew air into her lungs, started pressing rhythmically on her chest and stomach as though to force the ocean out of her. "Come on, lass," Tom said. "Breathe for me, come on."

(There was a light on the waves above her, pale violet and growing, and deep below her life appeared before her like a film, racing forwards in vivid Technicolor, so bright and sharp it hurt her eyes. Barely old enough to run, Leigh reached out for her mother's affection. Áine leaned over to tuck her into bed after a long summer's day, a diaphanous green dress. I'll see you soon, Áine said, and then she was gone. Leigh sat on the front step all day until darkness fell, waiting to hear the crunch of gravel, a mother returning. Graham retreated into his office or off onto the moors for days. Leigh rifled through the post for a letter or a postcard or a telegram and pretended she didn't notice the way the McGillicuddys behind the post office counter looked at her. Sam went away to school without a backward glance. Leigh bought a newspaper and flipped to the obituaries—and again a little older, and again a little older, and again a little older. The silence filled her ears like water. Leigh crept into Áine's closet after Graham was already asleep and curled up amongst the dresses and the delicate, dissipating scent of perfume. Leigh crossed the ocean and chased a woman down Princes Street, sure she had finally found her, only to discover just another stranger. Leigh started a hundred letters she would never send. Where did you go, why did you leave, what did I do.

It's hard, but it's good, Áine's voice said. Already the vision was fading, Leigh was returning to the world or the world was returning to her. *You have to let us go.*

Leigh said, *I can't.*

We're already gone, Áine replied. *Choose.*

Leigh chose.)

On the damp ground of East Sands with the water lapping at her feet and the island all around, Leigh Welles gasped back to life.

33.

The day dawned blue and blurry. A light frost on the grass, a pale, clear morning. It was the first of November, and the sluagh were gone. The light trickled over the island slowly. It brushed against the ruined church spire and dripped down to the memorial, reaching into the crevices of the names writ therein. It poked through curtains and shutters to creep along countertops and kiss sleeping foreheads. It ran along the high street, knocked on the door, danced over the boats in the harbour, and made a sprint up the hill away from the village. It ricocheted through the fields and through the trees, paused reverently at the standing stones, rocketed up to the ancient cathedral where the seagulls swooped, keening.

It found Leigh Welles back down in the village, lying on a narrow cot in Dr. Delaune's surgery. It laid a gentle hand on her forehead, a touch like a mother's. It rested on Iain MacTavish's shoulders as he dozed on the floor, propped up against Leigh's bed frame.

It whispered peace.

Leigh woke with her cheeks damp and cold, but she didn't remember crying. She felt lighter, as though she had taken off a heavy overcoat.

It was miraculous, Dr. Delaune had said, that she was alive at all. From that height, hitting the water was like hitting pavement, and yet here she was, with a dislocated shoulder and several broken ribs and great purple bruises blossoming across her skin but otherwise, it seemed, unharmed. How was it possible? The only explanation was the birds, the birds that had swarmed around her in the air, that had slowed her fall with their wings. It seemed ironic, Leigh had thought last night as Dr. Delaune bandaged her ribs, that it should be the sluagh that had saved her. She could hear the sounds of celebration outside, celebration that would continue all night. Kirsten MacEwan playing her beautiful fiddle, children shrieking and laughing, and Mr. Gordon calling out the steps for a ceilidh. Kirsten's music was lively and bright, but it hardly moved Leigh at all. As she had fallen she had felt so keenly. Now she didn't feel much of anything at all, not even when Dr. Delaune said, "All right, Leigh, this is going to hurt," and slipped her shoulder back into its socket. After he gave her something for the pain, he told her that there were people waiting to speak with her, Mr. Harrower and Mhairi Taylor and "your young man, Mr. MacTavish." Leigh pretended it didn't make her chest ache the way he said it, "your young man."

"I don't want to see anyone," she said to Dr. Delaune. Whatever he had given her was working quickly and she had felt somehow like she wasn't here at all, like maybe she was still in the sea, passing through on her way to some other place just out of sight.

Now the November light crept in. She felt, in spite of herself, like perhaps she had woken different, in a different world. Iain sat against the bed, slumped over on the mattress, Maisie curled up tight next to him, pressed against his thigh. Iain was asleep but he had a hold of Leigh's hand. She wondered who had let him in. She could feel his heart beating against her skin, his pulse in her palm. The strangeness of bodies. It couldn't have been a comfortable place to sleep all night. There was a chair in the corner, though that would not have been a comfortable place to stay all night either.

She looked up into the cobwebbed ceiling. Miracles. Maybe it wasn't ironic at all, that the sluagh had saved her. She was thinking about the many arguments Sam and Graham had tried to hide from her, those early days of the war when Graham was determined to stop Sam from going. "I've been to war, I've seen it," Graham had told Sam, in the low and level way he had. "It strips you of your humanity, and it's hard to get it back. Violence begets violence." Sam had replied, "The violence is already here." It stayed for a long time, it still hadn't left. Violence begets violence but maybe compassion begets something else. Maybe saving her gave the sluagh something else to do, a reason to put down their suffering.

She freed her hand from Iain's and he stirred, blinked sleep-sticky eyes open. "Hello, you," he said.

"You look younger when you sleep."

"I should hope so." He reached up towards her face, placed his cold fingers against her bruised cheek. Behind him Maisie lifted her head, considered them for a moment, tucked her nose back underneath her tail. "Who was with you," Iain said, "in the cave? You were talking to somebody, but no one was there."

"But they were," she said, thinking of bodies crowding into a window frame. "They were all there."

He didn't ask her what she meant. He said, "Do you know how you did it?"

"Did what?"

"Made them go."

The way he was looking at her made her feel desperately exposed. She took his hand from her face, placed it back on the mattress, sat up gingerly. "I don't know," she said. "I think maybe I—broke some cycle, I don't know. When I tried to stop them killing my goat." She looked down at her knees. "It sounds quite silly, when I say it out loud."

"I don't think it does," Iain said. "I think it's a remarkable act of selflessness. Standing up for something that can't stand up for itself. I can see that having some sort of power."

He was still looking at her, she could feel it. "Well," she said. "It probably doesn't even matter. Everyone is still going to leave, anyways."

"Oh, I don't know," Iain said. "Mr. Harrower went and spoke to Mr. Morrison, after you were asleep. When he came back, he asked me if I would meet him by the old war memorial tomorrow. I think he's going to agree to put up a new one. Another one."

Leigh closed her eyes for a moment. It was too good to be true, that everything might not end, so she would not believe it until it was sure. It didn't matter much either way for her, she supposed. All of the things that were gone. Her mother, her father, her brother, Hugo. The goats, the car, the house. Leaving only the blank page of her life, spreading out before her. She didn't know how to say any of this to Iain, so instead she just said, "The house sold."

He said, "Where are you going to go?"

"I don't know."

A pause. "You could stay with me."

Leigh looked at him. The freckles across his once-broken nose. The scar running through his eyebrow. Things she could not unnotice. Even if she could, even if none of the past days had happened, still she would not do it. Refused to do it.

She said, "That's not the point, at all."

He looked away from her, stood abruptly, and walked to the back of the room, where above a desk laden with papers, books, an articulated model of the bones of the hand, a small window looked out to the sea. The morning sunlight on his face painted him in gold, and she dropped her head so she didn't have to look at him.

"Do you remember the day the war started?" he asked. "One of the most beautiful days I can remember. And then everything that came after, all the bombs and the death and the waste, and this stupid, beautiful island is still here." She wasn't sure what point he was trying to make. Something about carrying on, she supposed. "When it ended, I asked to stay in the air force, you know," he continued. "Flying was the only thing that had kept me going, and then it was over. But there were too many of us who wanted to stay. So there was just the rest of my life, stretching out in front of me, and the thought of it being over, of coming back and starting new—it was just unbearable. Still is, sometimes."

It was not hard for her to understand how he must have felt. Being told to go up to an island as far north as one could get before there was nothing but sea. His father dead, his wife dead, his purpose stripped away. Poor, heartbroken boy. She asked, "Why did you come back?"

"Angus Gordon made me."

Poor, heartbroken boy. The floor creaked as he turned from the window and sat gingerly on the edge of her bed. She wanted to envelop him within her, his heart inside her heart. She wanted to smooth away his suffering and make him fresh and clean and new again.

"I was trying to be brave," she said. Her voice small and quiet. "Before. Going to the cave by myself. I was trying to be brave."

"You don't have to try," he said. "You are."

Leigh said, "Not always."

He sighed, hard, his smoker's exhale. "Was it because of what I said?" he asked. "Because it was all nonsense. I just said those things. I didn't mean it. I'm sorry."

"I don't know," she said. "You were right about some of it. I wasn't disappointed about missing it, though. I was relieved. I hated how relieved I was."

Iain looked down into his hands, seeming to consider carefully what to say. "I think you think we all went out of some great moral calling," he said at last. "I don't know, maybe some of us did. But I didn't. I just went. Because I thought I was supposed to, because I thought it'd be some grand adventure. But it was just war." He looked up at her. "You were only a child, Leigh," he said. "Sitting around here was what you were supposed to do. I'm glad of that." After a moment, he added, "So's Sam, even if he can't say it."

How long ago it was, that she'd sat next to Sam in their father's car and felt so small and useless, inferior. "He said I was punishing him," Leigh said. "Asking him about it."

"Were you?"

"I wasn't trying to." She thought of everywhere Sam had been. Dunkirk and North Africa and Normandy and Dachau. The things he couldn't unsee. Punishment enough, not that he deserved it. "I might have been punishing myself."

Iain picked at a hole in the blanket covering Leigh's knees, the thread unravelling between his fingers. He said, "I think probably we should all stop punishing ourselves for the things we did or didn't do."

Leigh closed her eyes and for a moment she was back in the cave, though this time only in her mind. She could still hear her mother's voice, like a dream. She could still see a black wave crashing above her head. When she opened her eyes, Iain was watching her. He had a way of looking at a person, of looking at her. He said, "Then there's the other thing."

He didn't need to tell her what he was talking about, she already knew. Her chest ached with it. "Oh," she said. "It's all right."

"I was going to ask that we just forget it ever happened."

This was not what she had expected him to say, but it hardly mattered. What difference would it make if it were remembered?

A person was not a thing she could pack in her suitcase and take with her when she left. Leigh shrugged her uninjured shoulder and said, "If that's what you want."

"That's just it," he said. "I'm not sure it is."

A breathless, quiet moment. At last she said, "I'm not sure either."

Iain leaned forwards and kissed her. Just once, just barely. It felt neither complicated nor complicating, it felt terribly simple. When he pulled away, Leigh dragged the heel of her hand across her cheek. "Were you kissing me," she asked, "or somebody else?"

He said, "You."

34.

In the afternoon Dr. Delaune announced that Leigh could go home, and she stepped out into the street on Iain's arm. Maisie following steadily beside instead of snuffling along in the gutter ahead. As Leigh limped her way along the high street, leaning heavily on Iain's shoulder, the other islanders emerged from their houses or peered out their freshly opened windows and watched her pass. "You're quite the celebrity," Iain said, leaning his head down so his lips brushed against her hair when he said it. Leigh wished she weren't.

It took ages, at their pace, to reach Iain's house, where the car was parked messily, two wheels banked up on the pavement. Leigh paused, trailed her hand along the cool roof like the car was an old and faithful pet, and then let Iain take her inside.

He left her in the sitting room and went to find Mrs. Cavanagh. He had told her to sit, but for a moment she just stood there, on the old, threadbare carpet, and the sun streamed in through the window, pressed against her bruised face. Leigh could hear them talking in the kitchen in quick, hushed voices, and then the voices stopped and they appeared in the doorway, Mrs. Cavanagh carrying a large tray. "I told you to sit," Iain said as Mrs. Cavanagh looked Leigh up and down. Leigh imagined how she must look. Hair a tangled mess and brined with seawater, face covered in bruises. She could feel her shoulders slumping towards the floor.

"Oh, darling," Mrs. Cavanagh said. She looked like she wanted to march over to Leigh and embrace her but stopped herself. All Leigh wanted was to return to bed, sleep for the next week. She opened her mouth to speak, but it took a moment for any sound to come out.

"The house sold," she said at last. "I don't know where I'm going to go."

"Ah," Mrs. Cavanagh said. "Yes. Well, this isn't how I'd planned this, to be sure." She placed the tray on the side table and turned to Leigh. "I bought the house, dear. Now, you'd better sit down."

Leigh sat in Iain MacTavish's sitting room with a cup of tea at her left hand and a dram at her right, feeling rather dazed, as Mrs. Cavanagh explained how it was she came to buy the Welles house from Sam. There'd been a bit of money left to her by her late husband, she said, and it all just sitting there in the bank accruing dust. She had mentioned her plan to Tom

McAllister, who had insisted on pitching in. A few days later Mrs. McCafferty slipped Mrs. Cavanagh an envelope in church and whispered, "That sweet girl sat with me all night after my Lucy was killed. Time to repay the favour, to be sure."

In the following days Mrs. Cavanagh had been stopped on street corners and coming out of shops by all manner of islanders bearing small envelopes and stories. Margaret Murray had delivered a donation on behalf of her parents and said, "She taught me how engines worked, the day we heard my brother died." Heather Beech's mother, Eleanor, handed over a cheque and a memory of the slumber party Leigh had hosted for the younger girls on the island during the long stretch when the ships weren't running and everyone was starving and there was no news to allay the growing fears of invasion. Mhairi Taylor could spare only a few banknotes but she hoped it would help. "She taught Gwen to skip stones the day we heard my husband had gone," she said. "That girl got us through the war, so she did."

It was repeated by every islander as they handed over banknotes and cheques, spare coins and goodwill. The Hendrixes, Gordons, and Brodies. That girl got us through the war, so she did.

"So when you went to the mainland—" Iain began.

"I was going to see my lawyer," Mrs. Cavanagh said, nodding. "You'll be shocked, I'm sure, to hear that a run-down sheep farm with no sheep is not considered a particularly good investment for an old city woman like me. I'd have told you sooner, lass," she said, "but I didn't want to get your hopes up in case it went away."

Leigh felt oddly like she was about to overflow. Up on the cliff she had felt that there was nothing left in her, that she had poured all of it out and was left hollow. Now things were being poured back into her, and she was afraid she didn't have room for them all anymore. "Did you know?" she asked Iain, and he shook his head.

"Like I said, I didn't want you finding out and getting your hopes up," Mrs. Cavanagh said. "And I wasn't convinced that Iain wouldn't accidentally say something."

"But what if everyone leaves?" Leigh said. "I can't take their money, they'll need it to start over."

"Let's cross that bridge when we come to it, why don't we," Mrs. Cavanagh said. "If we come to it. I was talking to Mrs. Taylor this morning, and I'm not entirely sure that we will."

Leigh dared not believe it. "I can't take their money," she said again.

"Well, try to give it back, then," Mrs. Cavanagh said blithely. "I think you'll find you have rather a hard time convincing anyone to accept. Everybody on this island is awfully fond of you, dear."

Leigh said, "So I can stay?" and her voice was thin and weak and tired. Iain placed a hand on her knee.

"Yes, lass," Mrs. Cavanagh said. "You can stay." She reached a hand out, placed it on top of Leigh's. "Oh," she said, "I almost forgot. The Morrisons are returning the goats today."

Leigh burst into tears.

This was an island of many seasons; each time it woke, it was a little different than it was before. Summer lasted many years and then shattered, on a warm and bright morning, butterflies

fluttering through the tall golden fields and crickets humming
in their hiding places. Leigh Welles lay on her back on the bar
of McAllister's, listening to the wireless while the town was all
in church. The lazy sunshine seeping in through the windows.

Already a new season was approaching, though Leigh didn't
know it yet. Autumn. Iain MacTavish listened with his father as
the world was brought abruptly into war, and then he stepped
into the street, still morning-quiet. He walked out of town and
snaked up the hill, left the road and cut across an uncultivated
field thick and wild with nettles and pale flowers. A feeling that
he'd been sleepwalking and now suddenly had awoken. Jolted
out of timelessness and back into time, from one world into
another. He felt an opening of his heart, of his life.

Winter. The years when the sluagh were all that mattered,
when they took Lucy McCafferty and filled the sky, legion. Sam
went to France, and North Africa, and France again, liberated
Dachau atop an American tank and was forever changed. Iain
walked into Spain and then into a register office. A V-2 rocket
crashed into the corner of Adelaide Avenue and Eastern Road.
E-Easy disappeared into the night. Leigh's sacrifice was perhaps
smaller and softer and easier to overlook, but she got this island
through the war. And then it was won, but it did not really end,
it was not really over.

But on this beautiful September day, this was all safely in the future. For now there was just this moment. The careful quiet of a
Sunday morning, Leigh's shoulder blades pressing into smooth,
oiled wood. Iain's father tapping his fingers against the side of
his glass. The summer sunshine golden and hazy in their eyes.

Leigh stood in the half-light of Iain's pantry with the cold press of the telephone against her cheek. After the operator put her through, the phone rang three times, before: "Hello?"

She had not expected to hear Sam. Not until she fought her way past his secretary and waited ages for him to answer. "Hello?" he said again, because Leigh found she had lost her voice. "Is anybody there?"

"Hi," she said. "It's me."

"Oh," he said. "Is something wrong?"

"No," she said, gripping the phone so hard her fingers were beginning to go numb. "Yes. No. Everything's fine."

"Leigh," Sam said, "what's wrong?"

She stared at a smudge of dirt or flour on the wall of Iain's pantry. Her throat thick and her eyes stinging. She did not want to cry again. She said, "I think Mum's dead."

The line hummed and suddenly Edinburgh felt very far away, farther than ever before. At last, Sam said, "I think so too."

"It's just us now."

Another long, staticky pause. "I suppose it is."

"Were we ever happy?" Leigh asked, twisting the telephone cord around her fingers. "Before she left, were we happy?"

"Yes," Sam said. As though he was convincing himself as much as he was convincing her. "We were. I was."

"But she still left," Leigh said. "So she mustn't have been. I should have tried harder, I should have been better—"

"You were ten, Leigh," Sam said. "It wasn't your fault."

It didn't feel like it. It felt like her mother had only just left this morning, it felt like Leigh had killed her with twelve years of bitterness and rage. Twelve years of feeling so keenly the weight of some unknowable inadequacy. Twelve years of trying to make up for it and never quite succeeding. What had changed, from yesterday to today? Nothing, nothing, nothing but a vision in a pool which might have been true or false. And yet today the bitterness felt different. Pulling away from her skin like a spent scab. A wound that might eventually fade away to nothing.

"I don't want to fight anymore," she said. She had said it before, but this time she meant it—this time she was playing for keeps. A sound that was either static or a sharp and choked inhale. Sam said, "I never wanted to fight with you."

"I know I hurt you with it," she said. "Talking about the war. And I'm sorry. I won't try to make you anymore." He didn't say anything; the static rose. Of course he didn't have to say anything, that was the whole point. If anybody deserved to pretend like the war had never happened, maybe it was Sam.

When he finally spoke again, there was something funny about his voice. Like he was trying not to cry, like maybe he already was. "I'm sorry," he said. "That I am how I am with you. I didn't want to hurt you either. When I came the other weekend."

"I know."

"I should have talked to you about the house."

Leigh hesitated. Once she had thought she could predict Sam's moods, the things to which he would and would not react. This conversation had already gone differently than she'd expected in so many ways that she wasn't sure she could anymore. "Mrs. Cavanagh's the one who bought the house," she said. "Iain MacTavish's mother-in-law. She's going to let me stay." She braced herself for his anger, embarrassment ("Living off other people's charity"), but it didn't come. He just sighed, a long, hard exhale, relief.

"I don't know what to say," he said. "That's wonderful." A sound on the other end of the line, a door opening, a faint female voice. "Leigh," Sam said, "I have to go. I have a client coming in. Can I call you later?"

"Aye," Leigh said. "I'll be here. At Iain's."

"All right," Sam said. "I'll talk to you later. Maybe around seven."

"All right."

"Leigh?" he said, quickly, before she could hang up. "I'm sorry I left you there, all alone."

Out in the kitchen the kettle began to wail. Iain shouted to Mrs. Cavanagh that he'd get it, and then his footsteps fell softly along the hall. Maisie's feet skittered along after him. Leigh said, "You didn't."

35.

Leigh Welles and Iain MacTavish crouched by the water's edge. Wind brushed the sand in mists across the shore, but the sea was calm, the sky reflecting pink off its mirror waves.

It wasn't much of a funeral. There was no body and no minister, no petrol, no ornately carved boat that Will Llewellyn had laboured over for hours. There was just Leigh and Iain and a small model boat, glossy red. Iain handed Leigh the cigarette lighter that had once belonged to Hugo McClare, and Leigh flicked it open. Ashes to ashes, she thought. Dust to dust. In the sure and certain hope of resurrection.

She set the little boat alight and pushed it into the sea. She stood to watch it go. Its tiny sail caught flame first, like the wick of a candle. Iain slipped his hand into Leigh's, and the sky slowly darkened. The boat made its way determinedly towards a horizon it would never reach. Already another world was opening for it, another world just out of sight. It was an accident, Leigh thought, Áine had never meant to leave her forever. An accident, and now Áine's business was finished, and she was voyaging.

Leigh dropped Iain's hand and stepped towards the surf, the lacy edges of the waves lapping at the toes of her boots. The boat disappeared beneath the water and it was night, the deep blue sky wrapping the world in its arms. The winter wind tugged at Leigh's hair as she stared into the soft dark, at the place where the boat had been and where a phantom light still hung in her eyes.

A sharp inhale of the salty air. Leigh turned away from the November sea.

With Thanks

To my wonderful agents, Claire Friedman and Catherine Drayton, for their patience, guidance, and passion, and to their colleagues at InkWell Management;

To my inimitable editor, Masie Cochran, for so often knowing what I was trying to say better than I did myself;

To the incredible Tin House team: Craig Popelars, Nanci McCloskey, Diane Chonette, Jakob Vala, Alyssa Ogi, Elizabeth DeMeo, Becky Kraemer, Alex Gonzales, Sangi Lama, Anne Horowitz, and Allison Dubinsky;

To Ann Hood, for being perhaps the earliest believer in this novel;

To Katie Brennan, for reading every one of my (probably quite bad) drafts with unwavering enthusiasm and support;

To my other early readers, Taryn O'Connor, Megan Shaefer, and Jenny Elwin, for their exceptionally helpful comments and questions;

And, always, to my family, for everything.

EMMA SECKEL is an award-winning writer and photographer living in Vancouver, Canada.